DIAMOND
OF
WAR

Forbidden Conflicts
~~ Book Three ~~

ANN M PRATLEY

BY ANN M PRATLEY

Forbidden Conflicts Series
Amethyst of Youth
Ruby of Law
Diamond of War
Sapphire of Prejudice
Emerald of Wisdom

Power Moore Investigation Tales
Resolution of Happiness
Home by the Sea
Tiger in our House
Catch a Catfish Killer
DJ of Incapacity
Hoonigan

Freedom of Flight Series
Christian
Brandon
Trinity

Painful Deliverance Series
Painful Deliverance
Darkness of Heart
Friendship of Desire

Chisholm Manor Series
Alessandra
Elizabeth

CHAPTER 1

The countdown to the next job was on. Six weeks. In six weeks, a hoard of gems was coming to the city, and not one but two groups had their crews assembling and planning. There were gems for the taking, and both sides intended to take them. Neither group knew of the other. Each assumed they'd be the only ones making a play to earn a great score.

On one side were the Stonewardens. They were well experienced in high-class heists. They were military precise in their planning, research, strategizing, and delivery of everything they did. The job wouldn't be the most complex they'd done - not by a long shot.

In another part of town were the Leadbetters. Freshly having had a change in leadership, the person in charge now was violent and had no hesitation killing when people got in his way. Like most Leadbetters, Pete Leadbetter had always gotten away with what he'd done, no matter the depth of destruction he'd delivered. It was the way with the whole Leadbetter gang. Some were minor criminals who acted out of duty but with reluctance. Others were extreme criminals who acted with relish. The one thing they all had in common? An uncanny knack of hardly ever being charged with anything at all.

It was rare that the two groups took notice of the same target. Stonewardens aimed high. Leadbetters grabbed what they could. Each side knew there was someone out there who also wanted the same thing, but neither side was completely sure they knew who the other side was. In reality, if they ever came face to face, none of them would even know it.

CHAPTER 2

Sasha Leadbetter was a young woman with a long history of minor violence. She was the kid at school who hit and called others names. She was the teenager who initiated punch up scenes in the local park or mall. To anyone who met her, she oozed one feeling - anger. Sometimes it was mild anger. Sometimes it was extreme anger. The degree didn't matter. When someone came face to face with Sasha Leadbetter, they couldn't help but feel intimidated. At 24, her fast reflexes had caused many a person to experience a knife to their chest after simply asking an innocent question. No-one knew why Sasha Leadbetter was so angry. They just knew she was.

Through an unselfish act of heroism in earlier months, Sasha had finally found a friend. Nicky was just a kid. She was a ten-year-old kid who had been saved along with her mother after someone had attacked them in a nearby park. For weeks as Sasha had recovered in hospital, a cop had been stationed at her hospital room door. She'd been the suspected attacker. Not being able to remember what had happened hadn't helped her case. Fortunately, Nicky's mother had taken notice of what her rescuer looked like and had tracked her down to thank her and set the record straight about Sasha's involvement in the stabbing. From that, a special friendship had formed.

Anyone who'd ever met Sasha would never have guessed she could relate to anyone the way that she was relaxing around young Nicky. For the first time ever, it was becoming more and more frequent that people were starting to see Sasha Leadbetter smile.

"Can we walk down to the mall and get ice cream?" the young voice asked excitedly as its owner jumped up and down.

"Sure can, Nicky-kid," Sasha replied, still getting used to the strange feeling of her face moving and changing into a smile. "I even got enough moolah to get you your favorite caramel rocky road cookie."

"Yay!" Nicky said happily.

She, too, had always had issues making friends. She wasn't angry. She wasn't mean. There was no such reason that others wouldn't magnate toward her. She did, however, have an extreme lack of self-esteem. With Nicky, it was simply her constant thinking that they wouldn't *want* to that resulted in her emanating that she wasn't approachable. They were grown-up feelings for a ten-year-old. It had worried her mother Susan for years. Both were happy the anti-social young woman who'd saved them was giving them both a chance.

When Susan watched the two of them, she had to believe in fate or something like that. They were the two most unlikely pals she could imagine, and yet they fed off each other. They'd seemed to find a balance that let them both relax and just be themselves without having to worry about what anyone else thought.

Sasha led the young girl down the road. It had become almost a weekly thing now, the two of them spending time together. Despite the way people talked about Sasha, Susan hadn't felt any concern at letting her daughter spend time with the young woman. Sasha Leadbetter spending a couple of hours each week with Nicky was opening up the ten-year-old in a way no-one else had been able to. According to Sasha's brother, the same was happening to Sasha.

"Did you talk to a new kid at school this week?" Sasha asked.

She wasn't a sociable person. She'd *never* been a sociable person, but knowing the ten-year-old girl in her company hadn't yet become confident in making friends bugged her. She wanted to help any way she could to try and stop Nicky from feeling as alone as she herself had so often felt.

"I did," Nicky replied as she looked up into Sasha's eyes. "At playtime, I said hi to Tracy. We didn't play, but she did say hi back."

"Well, that's a great start, Nicky-kid," Sasha said, smiling. "Keep saying hi. Don't worry about whether they say hi back or not. Just keep practicing. It's scary, right? I get that, but you'll get there. You're awesome to hang out with. It won't take long, and other people will see that too."

Nicky smiled but said nothing. She liked Sasha. She was a grown-up, but she was cool. When she said words, they actually made sense. She didn't talk in little kid language like other grown-ups did. It had easily become the highlight of Nicky's week when she got to hang out with Sasha Leadbetter.

They walked on, equally as happy in silence as in chat. They were comfortable together. That was easier for both of them than spending time with other people had ever been.

When they reached the mall, Sasha bought their ice cream and they settled at a table. Sitting off to the side, they both liked to face inwards and watch the hoards of people. It wouldn't have been exciting to anyone else, but it sure was enjoyable to the two of them.

~~~~~~

James Stonewarden wandered through the mall. He hated shops, but he liked to always look and smell good. He had a plan he always adhered to when he had to go to the shop that sold his favorite men's facial moisturizer: get in, buy the product, and then get the hell out. He was far from oblivious to how his looks attracted women. On most days of the year, he loved that. When there was a job coming up, he was a professional in maintaining focus. Not even a woman could upset that.
~~~~~~

When he passed through the food court level, he was surprised to see a familiar face. He still didn't know her name. Every time he'd asked for it, she'd refused to give it. Still, for the moment, at least, he had to keep calling her his name for her: 'Sassy Girl'.

After first seeing her, he halted in his steps, surprised that she was in his view. He was further frozen in place when he noticed the child next to her. That stunned him. Sassy Girl was a mother? No. She couldn't be. She looked like she was only his age. If she had a child that age, she must have been a *really* young teen mother. Either that or she was much older than she looked. Was it possible?

For a moment, he wasn't sure what to do. Should he approach her and say hello? She hadn't been friendly when he'd tried it before. Was he in the mood for another rejection? It was a rare thing for him. Women always fell at his feet, eager to please him. Not Sassy Girl, though. She was different. *Really* different.

Committed to living every day in a 'what the hell' way, he resolved to at least try and say hello to her. He walked toward her. When he was a couple of meters away from their table, he saw her eyes focus on him.

Sasha saw that guy coming toward her. 'Seriously?' she asked herself in the peace of her mind. It felt like he kept turning up *everywhere*.

"Hey, hey, Sassy Girl," she heard him say as he continued to get closer.

Straight away, Sasha heard Nicky giggle.

"Sassy Girl? Why's he calling you that?" she asked.

Sasha turned to Nicky and put on the best smile she could.

"He's just a real a funny guy, Nicky."

James saw the interaction and felt slightly uncomfortable. Was he interrupting some mother and daughter moment? He quickly brushed the discomfort aside.

"Am I just? A *funny* guy?" he asked, making the child laugh even more. "Well, Sassy, how about you tell me your real name?"

Nicky began to speak.

"Her name's…"

Sasha laughed as she brought her finger to her mouth.

"Shhh, Nicky. It's a secret I'm keeping from him."

Nicky smiled and nodded, silently promising to not reveal the secret.

James looked on. It was the first time he'd seen happiness on the face of the woman before him. He'd only previously seen her real angry and a little angry. Perhaps motherhood was the one thing that could make her smile.

"I can give you a clue," Nicky said teasingly to him.

"Go on then," James said, really believing he was finally going to get the name of the young woman who had secured his attention weeks earlier. He couldn't help but grin widely in anticipation.

"You've got the first part right," Nicky continued.

She kept watching Sasha. She didn't want to make her mad. Sasha only smiled and winked. It was all good.

"Oh, *really?* Hmm, well, let me think about that. Is it … Sasparilla?" he asked, making Nicky giggle again.

"No!"

"Sasquatch?"

"No!" Nicky replied, laughing harder still.

"Saspidicious?"

Sasha listened to the stupid words coming out of his mouth but couldn't help but smile. He was making Nicky laugh, and that always made Sasha happy. The kid definitely deserved fun and happiness.

"Saskerella? Sas..pidon? Sas..tonic? Sas..tastic?"

James kept throwing out imaginative words as he could think of them. He was enjoying watching the kid laugh. It was something to see, especially since that, in turn, was making Sassy Girl smile and laugh softly.

"No! You're no good at this," Nicky said, smiling at James. "Oh well, I guess you won't know her name then."

James grinned broadly at her.

"I think you're right. Ah, well, you know I've been asking her for weeks, and she won't tell me. It might not happen today, but it *will* happen," he said and winked before beginning to move away. He looked directly at Sasha. "See you again soon, Sassy."

Sasha watched as he turned and walked away. She still didn't know what he wanted from her, but she knew guys always wanted to use chicks for sex. She wasn't going to give in to that. She'd tried it once. and it hadn't felt good. Not only that, but the jerk had never spoken to her again. He'd used her for some sick pleasure of his own and then thrown her away like she was a worthless piece of garbage. No way, she wasn't having sex again.

"I like him. He seems nice," she heard Nicky's voice say, breaking into her thoughts. "Who is he?"

"I have no idea, Nicky-kid. No idea at all."

Nicky watched Sasha's face but said nothing. She suspected the guy liked Sasha, but it was impossible to know if Sasha liked him back. That was grown-up stuff. She didn't need to worry about it.

~~~~~

James walked away with a smile on his face. It had been a nice surprise, seeing Sassy again. Since he'd last seen her, he'd spent time with a couple of different play friends. No matter how much he enjoyed their company, though, his mind still drifted back to Sassy now and then. Every other time they'd met, she'd exuded anger. He'd just seen a different side to her. He hadn't
~~~~~

even known she could *be* anything but angry. Her smile was something to see. He wanted to see it again.

But was she a mother? He hadn't factored that into his thoughts about her. He understood the bond between mother and daughter. Since his mother had died, he'd watched the struggles of his sister, Charlie. Their father had done a good job of raising her, James knew. He'd taken on all the girl things and dealt with it well enough, but Charlie had been a loner. It was only after she'd met her now-husband, Ash, that she'd truly opened up and found the ability to make a friend. Perhaps Sassy was the same. No matter what, he knew a mother was a special person. If she was a mum, she was someone very special indeed.

~~~~~

Sasha and Nicky walked back after enjoying their ice cream and a short look around the mall shops. If she'd been on her own, Sasha would have been tempted to do as she'd been taught to do - pickpocket and steal. But she wasn't doing any of that stuff in front of Nicky. To her, Sasha wanted to be a good example. She'd keep spending time with the kid because they did like each other, but she'd keep Nicky clear of the Leadbetter ways.

"Hey, you two," they both heard Nicky's mother Susan call out to them as they ventured into the gate of the Leadbetter family home. "Did you have fun?" she asked, scooping Nicky into her arms.

"Yep," Nicky replied, smiling. "We had ice cream, and I saw a guy who likes Sasha."

Susan turned to Sasha and gave her a smile.

"Ahh, some news to share?"

"No, nothing to share," Sasha said. "Just some random guy."

No more was said on the subject as Susan and Nicky said goodbye and began their journey home.

~~~~~

As she walked into her family home, Sasha was

greeted by her mother, Stacey.

"You like spending time with her," Stacey said.

Sasha looked at her mother. They hardly ever spoke to one another, and never on any level even closely resembling a friendship, but she felt okay responding to that statement.

"I do," she replied, nodding. "I really, really do."

"Maybe that's a sign that you'd like to be a mother yourself, Sasha," Stacey said quietly.

Until Sasha had met Nicky, such a thought would never have entered Stacey's head. She loved her daughter, but she'd never fooled herself. Sasha was angry. She always had been. Stacey had been as surprised as everyone else in seeing how well Sasha took to the child, and how much that child seemed to be changing Sasha.

Sasha smiled sadly at her mother. It was a rare act of expression for her. She knew she'd never have kids. Having kids came from having sex. Having sex came from letting some asshole touch her. That was never going to happen. But she didn't have to say all that to her mother. She knew there had been enough stress between her parents in recent times. They didn't say anything to her, but she could sense it. She was determined to keep trying to live differently than she had before. She still felt extreme anger inside of her when she was alone, but the times she was spending with someone like Nicky - someone who needed a boost in self-esteem - was helping her own anger to be more controllable. She didn't want to be angry anymore. It was far from being completely gone, but she could feel that slowly, over time, it was lessening, as was the need to keep her much-beloved blade in her pocket 24/7.

"Maybe," she said quietly before walking away from her mother and into her bedroom.

Once inside, she lay down on her bed. It had been a good few hours with the kid. It was always a relaxing and calming experience. It was good for her - even she knew that.

She let her mind cast back to the few minutes she'd seen that guy again. For all the attempts he'd now made to ask her name, she realized she didn't even know *his* name. He was still a stunner. Every time she saw him, she knew that. It wasn't enough to make her want to give him anything though. He was a guy. He'd want sex. That had nothing to do with him even liking her. Guys fucked girls and then never spoke to them again. She'd already had that experience. She wasn't going to have it again.

CHAPTER 3

James made his way to the Stonewarden family home. He hadn't lived there for ages, but each time he went there, it still felt like home.

"James," he heard his father, Mitchell, call out to him from the large staircase off the main foyer.

"Hey, Dad," James replied. "I was in the neighborhood, so I thought I'd see if Max is around. I might head out to the ranch and catch up with Charlie."

"I don't think Max is home. He's probably out with that new girl of his," Mitchell said, smiling. He could still remember the silky smoothness of the voice of his second youngest son, Max, when he'd chatted up the girl at the cop shop over the phone.

"Max is seeing someone?" James asked, surprised. All of the brothers did well in the women department, but Max was like James - a player. "*Seriously* seeing someone?"

"You'd have to ask him that," his father said. "It's only a suspicion of mine. I could be completely off base."

"Hmm," James replied, momentarily stupefied. "Okay, I'll drive over and see how Sis is doing. Do you want me to take anything to her?"

"No, I'll head out there tomorrow," said Mitchell. "But we're having another planning session tomorrow night. Make sure you're here."

"Yeah, yeah, I'll be here," James said. "You know we aren't going to let you down, Dad."

Mitchell nodded.

"I know. It's just this job feels a bit different. I can't put my finger on it, but I think we all need to be extra vigilant."

"You think something's off? Bad intel or something?"

"I don't know. It might just be an old age thing. I'm going to start training Vic to take over all of this stuff. How do you feel about that?"

James shrugged his shoulder.

"I don't feel anything about it," he said. "How do you think I *should* feel?"

"I wasn't sure if you had any wish to become the head of..."

"*Hell* no!" James exclaimed. "No way. Do I look like someone who wants that kind of responsibility? Geez, Dad, what the... no! I'll keep doing jobs you guys keep telling me to do, but there's no way I ever want to be in *that* position."

"Okay," Mitchell replied, relieved. "Well, as far as this job is concerned, for now, we just move forward but keep your ears and eyes open. If you hear of anything that sounds like it could be related to that gala night, make sure you let us all know."

James nodded.

"Will do," he said as he turned and walked out.

~~~~~

"Hey, Sis," James said to his baby sister when he arrived on the ranch she worked on with her husband, Ash, and her great aunt and uncle.

Immediately he found arms wrapped around him. It made him smile. They were eight years apart in age. When their mother had died, Charlie had only been nine. James had already been seventeen. There was little crossover in their lives, but since Max had been shot a year earlier, James had developed a stronger bond with his youngest sibling.

"Hell, that bump's getting huge. Can't be long now, huh?" he teased her as she pulled away from him.

"Eight weeks, apparently," Charlie replied.

James did the quick calculation in his head. Two
~~~~~

weeks *after* gala night/jewelry burglary. Perfect.

"How are you feeling about it? Are you ready?" he asked as the two of them settled on a small sofa. "Are you feeling okay?"

"Yeah, I'm fine," she said. "I'm still doing some work around here but Tom and Molly have told me they won't let me after another couple of weeks are gone. They suggested me and Ash go away and have some time together alone before the baby comes."

James smiled. He suspected he knew where and who that suggestion had *really* come from - their father, Mitchell.

"That sounds romantic," he said.

Charlie laughed.

"There's nothing romantic about having a bowling ball in your tummy, James, but it will be good. My life is going to be so different in only a couple of months. Do you think I'm crazy, having a baby at this age?"

James pulled her close and kissed her forehead.

"I think anyone *else* having a baby at your age would be crazy, but you and Ash have a real love thing going on," he said. "Even I can see that. Hell, you almost have *me* convinced this love thing is good."

"Ahh, my big brother is getting ready to find *luuurrve*."

"Hell, no! But I'm a little closer to believing in it, thanks to you and that husband of yours. Where is he, by the way? Shouldn't he be staying close to you in case something happens?"

"He's out with Tom and Molly, getting supplies," said Charlie. "I'm fine. We did all the morning chores together and we'll do the evening ones together. This part of the day, I'm using to just chill and read mostly."

"Cool," James said, nodding. "So tell me, what's this deal with Max having a proper girlfriend?"

Charlie's face revealed how surprised she was.

"Does he? I know he mentioned a girl, but he

didn't want to talk about it. He was only here last night and said nothing. Is it serious?"

"Well, *I* don't know. If I did, I wouldn't be asking you, would I?" he teased her quietly.

"Huh. I'll call him later and get the goss."

~~~~~~

Across town, Max Stonewarden was waiting in his car outside the police station. Being there always made him nervous, but that was where Christy worked. So far, he'd had lunch with her twice and had spent an evening helping her to serve meals to homeless people. Every time that he went to meet her, he told himself he'd see her that time and then he wouldn't again. Every time he walked away from her, he found the thought of not seeing her again just not something he liked.

Christy was different from all the other girls he'd dated. She wasn't tall. She wasn't slim. She wasn't confident. When he looked at her, he always considered her shape as similar to a little round apple. When he studied her, he couldn't figure out *why* he was so attracted to her, but he definitely was. His body told him that every single time he was around her. He loved looking at her, he loved listening to her laugh, and as she was slowly relaxing more and more around him, he was loving listening to her talk. It had taken a long while for her to even start to be relaxed around him. As perplexed as he was about why he was so drawn to her, she was perplexed about why he kept wanting to spend time with her.

As he gazed at the large building with his mind working overtime, he saw her walk out, look for his car, and then start walking toward him. Immediately he jumped out, ran around to the other side, and opened the door.

"Hi, Max," she said timidly.

Max smiled at her as she carefully climbed into his car. Every time she greeted him, she made him think
~~~~~~

of a shy little cinder girl being swept away in a royal coach by a dashing prince. He suspected that was the kind of situation she thought she was in. He didn't. She was definitely no cinder girl, and he was definitely no prince.

As he climbed in the driver side, he turned to her and gave her another brilliant smile. Whenever he saw her, he had to do it - smile.

"You know I'm sweeping you away for a quick dinner and then a movie, right?" he asked.

Christy looked at him. She still had no idea what he wanted from her, but she was at least finally reaching a point where she wasn't stressing about that.

"Okay."

Max chuckled slightly. Her shyness was blissfully refreshing.

"Do you want to go to your place first for anything?" he asked as he started the Mustang.

With it having been stolen on the same night of the supermarket shooting the year earlier, and then the car being held by police, he'd missed his Mustang baby. It was good to have her back. It felt even better having his baby back, *and* Christy sitting beside him in it.

"No," she said. She took a deep breath. Whenever she saw Max Stonewarden she had to work hard to simply breathe. "Take me where you will," she dared to say, feeling her face blush in the process.

Max saw the blush, so didn't tease her. Instead, he just smiled and pulled out. He didn't think she'd be comfortable somewhere too swanky, so he'd found a small place that would be quieter with fewer people. He was getting used to her needing a little time to relax around him. It would be a slow process, but he found he wasn't minding being patient. Some girls - many girls - he'd rushed to get to know intimately as quickly as he could. He didn't want to rush with her. Truth be told, he was kind of enjoying getting to know a woman on a friendship level without all the physical stuff getting in the way.

Christy sat and pondered things she could or should say or ask. Everything was just so new for her. Part of her was scared to say the wrong thing. Another part of her argued that she should ask whatever she wanted to. Wasn't it best that he see the real her, not the guarded one? She thought over their previous conversations. She still didn't know too much about him, but she did remember one topic of conversation that had come up before.

"How's your sister this week?" she asked, her face becoming heated in the process of asking a question.

Max turned to look at her briefly. Her asking questions was a new experience. Whenever she did, he felt the depth of determination in her forcing herself to speak to him. He smiled.

"Charlie's doing great. I went out and saw her last night. She's huge though," he said, laughing slightly. "I think she's got another couple of months until she pops."

"Will that be the first time you're an uncle?"

"Yeah," he replied. The tone of his voice revealed he had hardly considered that. "Charlie's the youngest of the six of us, but she's the first to have a kid - well, as far as I know anyway."

Christy processed that comment and instantly became worried. Was he saying *he* had kids somewhere? Max saw her facial expression change.

"What?" he asked, curious.

"I ... do you think *you* have some kids somewhere?"

"Oh, shit, no (excuse my French). No way," he said as he pulled into a restaurant carpark. He turned off the ignition, unbuckled his seatbelt, and turned to her. "Christy, I'm no angel. I've been with women - a lot of women. I'm not going to lie to you about that. But I'm a safe sex guy. There's no way I'd risk a baby being made unintentionally."

Christy unbuckled her seatbelt and turned to face him also.

"But you sounded unsure if somewhere there *were* some kids…"

Max smiled at her.

"I actually meant my brothers," he reassured her. "I have three older ones, and at least one of them gets around a *lot*. It wouldn't surprise me in the least if James had one or two kids somewhere," he said, watching her face studying his. "Not me, though. When I settle down, I'll want to be a dad, but I don't want a kid I'm not going to be an active dad to. Kids deserve better than that."

"You aren't trying to hide all these women you've been with…" Christy said quietly, casting her eyes downward. Whatever way he was going to humiliate her, just like all those guys in high school did, she was sure it was coming soon.

Max moved closer to her and gently raised her chin to make her look right at him.

"One thing my mother drummed into me before she died was that I should always be myself. We *all* should just be ourselves. Some people will like who we are. Others won't. It's no good to try and pretend to be someone you're not. Just find the people who like the real you."

"What about me?" she asked shyly.

"What *about* you?"

"I'm not the girl who gets to go out in a nice car with a gorgeous guy," she said. "This is all just pretend…"

"No, it's not," Max said, surprised at her words. "Christy, it's *not*. I get that you're shy, and I'm okay with that. I *like* that."

"But I have to force myself just to speak to you…"

Max laughed softly as he caressed her cheek. He

didn't think she was aware of it, but he could feel her moving her head slightly as if leaning into his hand. It was nice. *Real* nice.

"Do I look like I mind your shyness?" he asked quietly.

"No..." Christy conceded. Her head wanted to argue with her. She was used to her own mind putting her down. The more time she spent with him, the more she wanted to argue back with her mind. She wanted to believe his sincerity. She really did. She just didn't want to be made a fool of anymore in her lifetime. "I just..." she started to say as she forced herself to look into his eyes. It wasn't an easy thing for her to do. "This confuses me, Max. I don't know what you want from me."

"Well, neither do I," Max said. On seeing the confusion grow on her face, he spoke again. "All I know is that I like spending time with you. I like your blushing, I like your shyness, and when you relax with me and you start opening up, I like listening to you talk. I also really like what you look like, in case you were wondering."

Christy smiled sadly. She was hugely overweight. There was no fooling anyone about that.

"Now I know you're lying..." she started to say before he cut her off.

"Actually, I'm not," Max said. "You're not like any woman I've hung out with before, but I really like looking at you. I like your eyes, I love those long eyelashes ... and your mouth ... is very kissable. If I was sure you'd want me to kiss you, don't worry - I'd definitely be doing it."

He waited a long time. He didn't want to startle her and move any closer. They were already within reachable kissing distance. Normally, he would have kissed a girl long before the fourth date. Hell, he'd most likely have *bedded* a woman long before the fourth date.

"I'll wait as long as it takes," he said. "For now,

I'm happy to have you as a new friend. Personally, I think I'd quite like to explore the kissing thing with you, but I'm not going to push you. Friends is good enough."

"Can you kiss me once, and then we still just be friends?" she asked, wanting with all her heart to seize the moment even though she was still uncertain of everything.

Her face was hot. She knew it must be deep red, but she pushed that aside. The gorgeous guy sitting beside her was telling her he wanted to kiss her. Even if that was part of some weird disappointment or hurt that would come later, she needed to take that kiss!

Max heard the question and smiled broadly before nodding. Slowly he leaned in and placed his lips on hers. She wanted one kiss, and that was it. He could give her that. One kiss. He'd make sure it was the deepest, most loving and passionate kiss he possibly could give her.

Christy felt breathless. It was the first real kiss she'd ever had. She indulged in the feelings. Her lips found their own groove, moving in sync with his. She felt his hand still caressing her cheek before it moved back toward her hair like it wanted to make sure she stayed right where she was.

Max felt his body spring to life. Right from the moment he'd first met her, his body had screamed at him that it liked her and wanted to be closer to her. With his lips on hers, that feeling only intensified. He suspected she might not have kissed before since she seemed to be far too shy to have had relationships. He could have been wrong in that assumption but he thought he was probably right in that. Her lips, though, felt good against his. His jeans grew real tight, real quick. He had to fight to keep his hands from exploring.

Even though he was only 22, he'd loved a lot of women. Kissing always moved fairly quickly to groping. He didn't want that with her. She'd only asked for one kiss. He heard her request, and he respected it. He kept the kiss respectable. Even his tongue was behaved. Eventually, after a long while of finally learning what those kissable lips felt like, he pulled away.

He looked at her face as he distanced himself slightly. Her eyes remained closed, like she was savoring the moment and committing it to memory. When she finally opened them, she looked directly into his.

"Thanks," she breathed out.

Max laughed slightly and kissed her on the cheek.

"Anytime, Christy. Anytime."

"Should we go and have a friendly dinner now?" she asked as she felt her nervousness slip away quietly but forcefully.

"Good idea," Max said. "Come on. We'll just grab something small before we go to the movie."

Christy quietly assembled herself to get out of the car. As usual, before she'd even opened the door, Max was on her side of the car, doing it for her. She was relieved. Nothing had changed there. That was a good sign.

~~~~~

Throughout their meal, Max could see the difference in Christy. It was like the kiss had produced a magical effect on her. She sat more upright, she smiled more at him, and she talked.

Even though the conversation flowed, inside Christy's head was a little voice singing. She'd had her first real kiss! And it was from an absolutely gorgeous guy. Unfortunately, the gloriousness of that kiss only seemed to further cement in her mind that he'd move on from her soon. She was okay with that. She could still smile. At least she'd always remember that for a brief moment in time, someone gave her some attention.

Once their meals were out of the way, they made their way out of the restaurant and walked slowly the two blocks to the cinema. Both were silent on the outside. Both were thinking deeply on the inside.
~~~~~

At the ticket counter, Max turned to her. She had her face turned upwards as she looked up at the movie schedule. He'd enjoyed kissing her. He wanted to kiss her again. Fuck, he *really* wanted to kiss her again. She seemed okay since their last kiss. She seemed even a little more confident and open. Was that a good thing? Would she *want* him to kiss her again?

Christy felt his eyes on her. Knowing that flowed on to her then feeling her face get very heated. Finally, she turned and looked at him. He was full-on looking at her. She hadn't been imagining it.

"Are you okay, Max?" she asked tentatively.

The softness of her voice was enough to break Max out of his thoughts and stare.

"Yep," he replied. "So … what are our options?"

"Well, we could see a romantic comedy, or we could see an action movie. It has cars. Fast cars," she said, making Max laugh at her.

"Not a romantic comedy girl?"

Christy forced herself to smile.

"Not really," she said. "I do like cars, though."

"Done."

As they settled into their seats, both looked around. Max wanted to kiss her. He didn't want loads of people around when he attempted that, just in case she rejected him.

Christy looked around in wonder that she was in a dark cinema with a gorgeous guy beside her. Would people laugh at her if they saw? Would they also assume it was some kind of weird joke he was playing on her? He was the gorgeous guy with the beautiful body and the beautiful face. She was the short, ugly, fat girl. Other people would surely see them together as having to be a joke.

Max turned to her as they waited for even the previews to come on. The room was semi-dark with enough lighting for people to make their way to seats.

There were only a handful of people around, and they were rows in front of where he and Christy sat. He had to act. He leaned slightly toward her seat before he turned to her. He saw her turn and look at him. She wasn't smiling. He wasn't sure what her face was revealing.

Christy found a moment to let herself be a little bit cheeky. It didn't happen often. Leaning a little bit toward his seat, she smiled at him. He didn't move away. She moved a little bit more. He still didn't move away. She looked into his eyes before moving her face slightly closer. It was a nerve-wracking experience. She'd never kissed anyone before.

She knew there were only a few people in the room. If he told her to get lost, she probably wouldn't know them anyway. Finally, she took the plunge. She leaned right into him and placed her lips on his. When the initial moment passed, and he hadn't pulled away, she forgot everyone else. She let her lips explore even more than they had in the car earlier in the evening. She could feel him respond. She could hear his breathing change. It only drove her on more.

Max was surprised but very pleasantly so. Her lips on his again quickly made his jeans tighten. Holy hell, she turned him on easily. He raised a hand and let his fingers slide into her hair, pulling her to him. He didn't want her to pull away. Without any conscious thought on his part, his tongue ignored his wish to keep things safe and not pushy. He couldn't help it. It was a delicious kiss. His tongue needed to be in on the action. He tentatively let it slip quietly between her lips. It was welcomed by her own tongue. It surprised him, but that was his green light. He happily began a beautiful lips and tongue dance with her. He also felt like he was falling. He was in free fall, and it felt glorious.

Christy had her first experience of kissing. Now there was another part to it. Tongues were involved. It was a very strange feeling at first, having his work its way into her mouth. By the second, it was feeling better and better. She could feel a sense of being alive in parts of her body that usually remained asleep. She didn't know kissing could produce such physical feelings. They were new, they were odd, but they were nice. Still, she expected her time with Max Stonewarden was limited. It made her all the more determined to enjoy each moment and make sure it was well-secured into her memory.

CHAPTER 4

Mark Leadbetter held his wife Stacey tightly upon waking. He'd stepped down from being the head of the Leadbetter gang. Now he could enjoy waking up beside his wife every day without any concerns for making decisions that would affect the entire Leadbetter clan. Lying behind her, he edged as close against her back as he could. It took some realignment, allowing for the size of the erection he'd woken with.

"Hmm, is that for me?" he heard his wife ask softly. That was before he felt her move her hips and ease herself back onto him. Mark was instantly enclosed in her moist warmth.

"You're already wet, my beautiful wife. Were you dreaming about me before you woke up?" he teased her as he felt her start to rock her hips forwards and backward.

He remained still and let her control their connection. No matter how it happened, being inside his wife was always the most incredible feeling in the world.

Stacey chuckled softly.

"You've had this ready and waiting for me every single morning for the past thirty years," she said. "It should be no surprise that my body prepares itself for you before I even wake up."

She moved slowly at first, then more quickly as she felt Mark's finger begin to caress her clit at the same time. A well-tuned synchronicity in their lovemaking over their decades together resulted in them both exploding into orgasm within seconds of each other.

Mark moved his arms so he could hold her while remaining joined with her. In recent times he'd considered life without her. He couldn't bear that thought. They were made for each other. They always had been.

"I'll never get tired of waking up with you," Stacey said quietly.

She'd also worried about him recently. She'd truly believed that if he stayed in charge of the entire Leadbetter clan, he was going to either end up in prison or worse - killed. It hadn't been easy to tell him she wished he'd step down. She'd supported him in everything for three long decades. She'd accepted the criminal ways of his family when they'd first met. They had both been teenagers then. The Leadbetter lifestyle had been a world away from that of her own family, but in her love for him, she'd adapted and changed. Now she couldn't stand even considering life without him.

"I know," Mark replied quietly before kissing her softly on the back of her neck. "I feel the same."

He felt her start to pull away. He removed himself from her, instantly feeling the emptiness that always presented itself when he was distanced from her body. He watched her turn and move onto her other side, facing him. Finally, she kissed him. He loved her kisses. That was something he could do all day, every day.

They lay and looked at one another.

"Do you regret standing aside?" she asked him.

She had conflict inside of her. On one side, she was gloriously happy that he'd stepped aside and would no longer be dealing with so many crime-related decisions anymore. The flip side of that was guilt. She'd been the one to try and nudge him in giving it all up. For her, he had. A part of her still wondered if she really had any right to have asked that of him.

Mark lifted one hand and lightly ran his fingertips over her lips.

"No," he said as his eyes focused on that beautiful mouth. When he raised his eyes to hers, he saw them glistening, as if she were holding back tears. "What's wrong?"

Stacey said nothing. Instead, she moved her body closer to his and wrapped her arms around him, encouraging him to do the same to her.

"Stace?" Mark asked, instantly concerned. He pulled back far enough to still look into her eyes. "You're freaking me out. What's up?"

"I … I don't feel good knowing that you gave it up because I asked you to," she said.

Mark kissed her and pulled her back into a tight embrace again.

"I didn't give it up because you asked me to," he said. "I'd been thinking about it for ages. You know that. You mentioning your worries about this next job was just a final nudge I needed. That and that offer to fuck me three times a day."

Stacey burst out laughing. She nodded and pulled away from him.

"I *did* say something along those lines." Neither needed any nudging in that. She moved so she was lying on her back, legs spread wide. "Come here, big boy. I'm ready for your daily second round."

Mark grinned broadly. Hell, he loved his wife. His body was instantly at attention as he moved on top of her, kissed her deeply, then slid into her for another round of beautiful marital pleasure.

~~~~~

"Anyone home?" they heard as they later lay in their bed, quietly holding one another again. It was the voice of their oldest son, Phillip. He'd moved out at the request of his father. Mark still felt guilty over kicking his son out. Stacey still believed it was the best thing that could have happened. At 30 years old, it was well overdue that her oldest son was living independently.

Stacey jumped out of bed and got dressed quickly. She never wanted to miss any moment to see her kids. They'd never been a close or affectionate
~~~~~

family, but now that they were all slowly drifting away as adults, she wanted to know them better while she could.

"I haven't seen you move that quickly in a while," Mark teased her as he lay in bed, watching her dress.

"Don't talk rubbish. I was moving quickly when I was on your hard-on a couple of hours ago," she said, making him laugh softly. He'd loved her every day for thirty years. Whenever she spoke like that, he loved her even more. "Are you going to come out and see him?" she asked softly with a more serious tone. She didn't want her kids feeling deserted by her or their father.

"Yeah. I'm gonna lie here for a few more minutes, then I'll get up and come out," he said as he saw her put on her final layers and start to move toward the door. "Hey," he said, making her turn. "I really love you, Stace."

Stacey heard the words and was a little surprised. She'd always known he did love her, but they were words that no-one in their household ever really shared. She walked back toward the bed, moved around to his side, and leaned down to kiss him softly. "I love you too, my gorgeous husband."

~~~~~

"Ma," Phillip said quietly as his mother made her way into his bedroom. Nothing had changed in the room since he'd moved out.

"It's good to see you," Stacey said quietly as she moved close to him. They weren't traditionally huggy, although more affection had been shared in recent months.

Phillip saw the expectation on his mother's face. He moved to her and pulled her into his arms.

"How are you doing?" he asked her. "Is everything okay?"

Stacey pulled away, nodding.

"Yeah, everything's good here," she said. "I miss
~~~~~

seeing you here, though. Are you still at Greg's?"

"Officially, yes, but I have been spending more and more time at Daisy's," he replied. He couldn't miss the smile on his mother's face when he'd said that.

"Sounds like it might be getting serious," Stacey said.

"Maybe."

"Phillip," she said, the tone of her voice sharpening his attention. "If you have a chance to live with love and harmony, do seize it. Don't wait too long."

Phillip kissed her forehead.

"I know," he said. "I'm working on that. Don't worry. I'm gonna take her away that weekend the job's on. I don't want to be pulled into it, and I don't want her to become a target if anyone's pissed off about that."

"I'm glad," Stacey said, nodding in relief.

"Is Dad going to be part of it?" Phillip asked.

"No," Phillip heard his father say from the doorway. He looked up and saw Mark walking in. "It's all in Pete's hands now. It's time for another part of the Leadbetter family to take the reign. He'll do what he wants. I don't want to be anywhere near him when he does."

Phillip nodded but said nothing. He hoped for his mother's sake that his father was telling the truth.

"Well, I just came home to get a few more things. I'll head off now."

"Stay…" Stacey said.

It wasn't intentional. She just had a sudden horrible thought that she might not see her son again once he walked out the door.

"Hey, what's everyone doing in… hey, hey, big bro!" Anya's fifteen-year-old voice threw into the mix.

She ran up to him and threw her arms around him in her well known theatrical hug. Phillip couldn't help but laugh. Of all his siblings, she was the one he missed the most.

"Hey, baby sister," he said, teasing her as he always did.

"I'm not a *baby*," she replied, just as *she* always did. The two of them then laughed. Mark and Stacey left the room, leaving their oldest and youngest to catch up. "What's new with you?" Anya asked, sitting on the bed.

Phillip sat beside her. "Well, I'm working full time, so finally I've got some cash rolling in. And ... how would you feel about being an aunt?"

Anya jumped up, shrieking. "What?? You're having a baby?"

Phillip laughed.

"Well, no, *I'm* not," he teased her. "But Daisy and I have been talking about it. I think it's time for me to settle down and do the boring dad thing."

"You'd never be a boring dad," Anya said. "You'll be a great dad. But when are we even going to meet this flower of yours? I don't even know what she *looks* like."

"I know," said Phillip. "It's a bit of a hairy situation. I don't know how it will go down with everyone, who she really is."

Anya showed her confusion.

"She's your girlfriend," she said. "What else matters? She knows who *you* are, right?"

"Oh, yeah, she knows all about *our* family."

"Well, if she accepts you with all of our rubbish, surely everyone can accept hers."

"In a perfect world, Anya, but not necessarily in this one," Phillip said as he kissed her forehead. "I gotta go. Hey, keep yourself out of trouble, huh?" he threw at her as he reached the bedroom door.

"Always, big bro. Always."

Phillip walked to the kitchen to say goodbye to his parents. They looked close. He liked that. It had only become evident in recent times since his youngest brother had been arrested for stealing a car. Phillip liked seeing his mother receive affection so openly.

"I'm off. I'll catch you next time," he said before walking toward the front door.

Before he reached it, he heard his father behind him.

"Phillip," the deep voice said. Phillip turned to face Mark. "For what it's worth, I'm glad you're getting things together and setting up a life away from us. You deserve better."

In an extremely rare move, Phillip stepped up to his father and gave him a manly hug.

"My setting up my own life has nothing to do with me deserving better, Dad," he said. "I just want a chance to have a life away from things that make me constantly worry about getting arrested. I wanna have kids. I know you and Ma had all of us in this kind of life, but I want to be further away from it - *much* further away. Not away from you and Ma. I want *you* to be a part of my life still, and of my kids' lives if I'm lucky enough to have any."

Mark felt slightly emotional at his oldest son's statement. He nodded but said nothing more. Instead, he just watched as Phillip turned and walked out.

~~~~~~

"Phillip!" he heard his sister Sasha call out to him as he walked down the sidewalk from their home.

Just hearing her use his name was enough to surprise him, let alone that she was using it to seemingly stop him. Generally, she only snapped at him.

Sasha ran up to her oldest brother. She'd never in her life wanted to be mean to him, but she had *always* been mean to him. It was a constant cycle with her - snap at someone and then instantly regret it. Part of learning to finally control her anger was determining to try and be friendly in situations just like she was presently in.

"Hey," she said to him when she reached him.

"Hi. How's things with you?" Phillip asked.

The words seemed weird coming from him. No-
~~~~~~

one asked Sasha how she was. If they did, they either got an earful of abuse or a knife to their chest. Surprisingly, neither of those happened.

"I'm okay," Sasha said. "How are you?"

"Fine," he responded, finding the interaction *really* weird.

"I have to talk to Greg," Sasha said. "Are you walking there now?"

"Yep," Phillip replied as they started walking together.

"They're still doing this big job. Greg's a part of that. So am I," she said, trying hard to make conversation.

She'd been trying to help Nicky with that. It seemed hypocritical to try and tell a ten-year-old how to make friends when Sasha herself couldn't do it. She had to try harder if she wanted to be able to help Nicky.

"What?" Phillip asked, halting his steps. "Why are *you* on that?"

"Don't panic," she replied. "I'm just a decoy. I'm not touching the goods. I just have to walk around in some stupid dress and watch what's going on. If I see anything, I let them know. That's all."

They resumed walking again.

"And Dad?" Phillip dared ask. He wanted to believe his father. He really did.

"Nah, he's out of it," said Sasha. "Pete's going to be running it. Dad's taking Ma away that week so they can't be caught up in it. It'll just be me and Rex."

"*Rex?!*" Phillip asked, stopping again. That was absurd. Rex was too impulsive. He'd be the exact *wrong* person to put on a job that needed subtlety.

"Yeah, he's keen as. We'll be alright. It's just a quick smash and grab. Nothing major."

Phillip said nothing. Inside he was groaning at the news. It was a great thing that his father had stepped down - except in the reality that someone far less savvy and far more violent and criminally-minded had stepped in to replace him.

He had to refocus. He couldn't get caught up in the news about the job. He *wouldn't*. He had found an incredible woman who lived for the law. Even if Daisy gave her job up, she would still have those beliefs and standards. He was determined to live a life that she could support, that wouldn't change her.

Phillip and Sasha walked in silence the rest of the way. Once in the house, he said a quick hello and goodbye to Greg around grabbing some more stuff, and then he left. He didn't want to hear anything more about the upcoming job. It was getting closer, and even though he wasn't a part of it, it definitely had him on edge.

~~~~~

"This is the dress you're going to wear," Sasha heard Greg say as he held up what looked like a flimsy piece of fabric.

"You have got to be fucking *kidding* me!" she said as she grabbed it from him. Holding it up, she could see it was a full-length gown, made of some kind of shimmery fabric. It had a halter neck and a huge slit up one side of the skirt. There was no back to it. "What the *fuck* is Pete thinking? Do I really look like I could pull off wearing something like *this*?"

Greg shrugged. He'd been questioning everything about the upcoming job. He was glad he was just the getaway driver. Everything felt wrong in his view.

"It's the dress Pete wants you to wear," he said. "He wants you to catch people's attention, so they won't notice him and the boys."

"Fuck *me*," Sasha said, rolling her eyes. "And what about this?" she asked, putting the dress down and pointing to her full arm tattoo. "It kinda clashes with *that*, doesn't it."

"Which is why," Greg said, pulling a second item out of his bag of magic. "I have this for you. Don't ask
~~~~~

me anything about it. All I know is that it's supposed to hide tatts."

Sasha sighed and sat down in the kitchen table chair.

"Okay, whatever," she said. "I'll do as I'm told."

Greg watched her. They were cousins of a sort. He was almost fifty. She was in her mid-twenties. He'd watched her grow up right from when she'd been a baby. She was a strange one, with her extreme anger and moods. He was surprised to see her today so talkative … and defeated, as if she had no fight in her at all.

"What's up with you?" he dared to ask.

He knew asking any question of Sasha was a recipe for anything to happen, but he didn't care.

"I don't know," Sasha replied. "I feel like something's going on in me, like I'm changing. And I *want* that. I've always hated who I am. I want to be a better person, Greg. I really do."

"But?"

"But … why am I doing a job like this when I want to change?" she asked. "Phillip and Dad have walked away. Why can't I find the motivation to do that too?"

"You have to do what's right for you," Greg said.

"Do you?" she asked. Immediately she saw his eyebrows raise in question. "Do *you* do what's right for you?"

Greg smiled sadly.

"My life is almost over," he said. "Yours is just beginning. Make better choices, and live your life, Sasha. It starts to pass more and more quickly, believe me. It's easy to reach a point where you look back and wish you'd taken a chance and done something you wanted to do - or said something you wanted to say."

Sasha smiled sadly back at him but didn't ask anything more. Quietly she rose, gave him a rare hug, and then just walked out. She had a job to do. It was that simple.

~~~~~~~

Greg sat alone in his home. Phillip still officially lived there, but he was hardly ever there. He'd found love. Greg was happy for him. He liked having his home to himself. Sometimes, though, he found himself wishing he'd shared a life properly with someone he really wanted to be with. His heart was secured. No other living person knew that. It was a well-guarded secret. It had to be. Anyone learning the object of his affection and talking of it to the wrong person could lead to disaster and horror of the worst kind, given how some people in the Leadbetter clan felt about certain things.

A knock on his front door pulled him out of his reverie.

"Hey," Rhett said as he was welcomed into the home. "Did you give the stuff to Sasha?"

"Yep," said Greg. "She's all good."

"Do you think she'll come through?"

The two men walked to the table and sat.

"Yeah, she's got no issue with her part. All she has to do is look pretty and chat up guys to keep them occupied. She's tough, but she'll do fine."

Rhett nodded.

"And you?" he asked. "You're okay with just being a getaway driver?"

"Hell, yeah. I haven't worked directly with Pete before but I know his temper," Greg said. "I don't want to be really in on a job he's running. What about you?"

"I'm just one of the witnesses," Rhett said. "Pete's lined up others to do the grabbing. I'm kinda glad about that, too, for the same reason. He's a bit of a ticking time bomb, I think."

"Well, just use your gut, right? If it's not right, get the fuck out of there. You'll know where I'll be sitting. Get out and come to me."

"No worries. It'll all be good," Rhett replied. He
~~~~~~~

wasn't convinced the job was going to be a success either. Maybe if Mark had planned it since he had a level temperament, but Pete was rash and unthinking at the best of times. At the worst of times, he was a killer. "I'm glad Mark and Stacey are getting out of dodge, though. If something goes wrong…"

"Agreed. Who knows who Pete'll blame if things don't go to plan."

CHAPTER 5

The Stonewarden boys sat in the living room of their family home. On the coffee table in front of them were pages that the youngest brother, Fitz, had produced. He was the tech expert. Usually, he was the one who came up with intel on potential jobs. He was also the one who researched and sussed out security systems. Nothing was too much of a challenge for Fitz. The more complex the security, the more the adrenaline flowed through him.

For hours they talked. They'd been doing it for weeks. The gala event the jewels would be at was getting closer with only three weeks to go. The planning and talking would continue right up until the actual night. One of their reasons for success was their determination to keep talking and keep thinking up scenarios where things could go wrong. Each person in the room proactively tried to think up something else they hadn't considered. The concern was voiced, then everyone contributed to a solution that worked and everyone was aware of. Nothing was ever taken for granted.

Mitchell looked at the faces of each of his sons. The biggest downside to living like they did and doing what they did was the fear of losing one of them. He'd been a soldier in horrific war situations. He'd seen men lose their lives in the most unthinkable ways. It scared him more to think of losing one of his sons.

He listened to them talk among themselves. It wouldn't be long before he'd let his oldest son, Vic, take over the Stonewarden legacy and handle doing all of the job planning himself. It was time. Vic was old enough to be in power. Mitchell was old enough to retire and enjoy whatever life he had left. The biggest problem with that was that his kids *were* his life. Since Caroline had died a decade earlier, his sons and his daughter had been the rock he'd held onto. They were his whole existence. What would he do when they no longer needed him?

His mind cast briefly to his youngest, Charlie. She was the youngest but the first to find love. It was only weeks till she was due to give birth to the first Stonewarden grandchild. Mitchell was happy at the thought. Perhaps there would be another little one who might need him after all. It was past time his sons had kids too - Vic, James, and Regan anyway.

Mitchell silently scoffed at that idea. Although Regan had been serious about his girlfriend for a while, he didn't seem to be in any hurry to move things to the next level. Vic lived a life that even Mitchell was too afraid to ask about. He had no idea to what degree his oldest son enjoyed women, but he certainly expected he did. In his early twenties, Vic had been just like James was. He'd always had a woman hanging off his arm - or in his bed. And James … yeah, well, Mitchell gave up there. James was the biggest womanizer on the planet. Plain and simple. It would take someone like Wonder Woman to catch his heart.

He turned his attention back to the conversation. They were all good kids, and they all had a job to do. That had to be the focus of each of them in the coming weeks - more so as every day passed and the gala night drew closer.

~~~~~

After walking out of his family home, James drove to the beach. Whenever he left a planning session, he had to refocus on reality and normal life again before actually returning to it. His favorite place when the sun was out was the beach. He wasn't a surfer. He wasn't a swimmer. What he liked about it was the solitude and the lack of any noise other than the water and the sea birds.

After parking his car, he stood and scanned the
~~~~~

area. He wanted a slice of sand that no-one was close to. His eyes rested on the playground between where he stood and where the sand began. There he was treated to a sexy surprise. Sassy Girl was there. She was sitting on a bench, half looking at the water and half looking at the climbing frame. James followed her eye sight and saw the young girl on there. When he looked back at Sassy Girl, he could see her smiling at the young girl, but then look sad as she glanced out at the water.

He didn't hesitate. He moved forward.

"Hey, Sassy," he said quietly.

She was usually boisterous, but even she seemed to have a thoughtful aura coming off her at that moment. James didn't assume she'd want him to sit with her. He remained standing as he watched her face, looking for any clue about whether she'd want him there or not.

Sasha recognized the voice before she even turned to look up at him. He was a persistent bugger, that was for sure, but she was in Nicky's presence, and she wanted to be a better person for her.

"I'm beginning to wonder if you're stalking me," she said.

James was amused at her statement.

"Well, you're the one who's everywhere I'm going. Maybe it's *you* who's stalking *me*." He waited for a response but got none. "Can I sit?" he asked, pointing at the space beside her on the bench.

"I get the feeling that you'd sit even if I said no," Sasha said.

"No way, Sassy Girl," James replied, shaking his head with a serious look on his face. "No means no. There's never any question in that. Tell me to go, and I'll go. You don't need to worry there."

Sasha didn't know what she wanted. She didn't want sex - that, she *did* know - but that guy kept turning up everywhere, and he kept talking to her. She knew he was slowly chipping away at the ice around her heart.

Hearing her silence, James resolved to walk away and not look back. She didn't want anything from him. He had known that from the first moment they'd met in the local bakery months earlier. He just hadn't wanted to believe it. He turned and began to walk toward the beach.

"Hey," he heard her yell out. When he turned, she was patting the place next to her. "The seat's here, not there."

James smiled and almost ran back to her. Happily, he sat down next to her, leaving a polite space between them. He hadn't forgotten that knife she carried. He hadn't forgotten how quick she was with it, or the fact that she'd seemed to use it without any consciousness of doing so.

Neither spoke as they watched Nicky on the climbing frame. When she saw James, she climbed down carefully and ran over.

"Hey, it's funny boy," she said, making James and Sasha both laugh.

"Yeah, that's me," said James, grinning at her. "I can't remember your name, though."

"I'm Nicky," she said, holding out her hand to him after glancing at Sasha and receiving a small nod.

"Nicky. I am very pleased to meet you," James replied as he shook the young girl's hand. "I'm just hanging out here with Sasperocious."

Nicky burst out laughing.

"You still don't know her name, do you?"

"Nah, she won't tell me," said James. "It's very cruel of her, isn't it, Nicky."

"Well, does she know *your* name?" Nicky asked.

James smiled in response.

"Of course. She absolutely knows that my name is…" he started to say before turning to the woman beside him and holding out his hand to her. "James."

Sasha couldn't help but smile. He was a cocky

asshole, but he kept making her want to smile. She reached out her hand and shook his.

"See, Nicky? Even now, she says nothing," James said. "It's okay. I'll just keep calling her Saspodimus. If she's okay with that, so am I."

Nicky laughed at him before shaking her head, turning and returning to the climbing frame. James sat silently. If they sat in silence, that was okay. At least Sassy Girl didn't look as angry as she had previously.

Sasha said nothing. She knew she was growing a familiarity with him that could burst into something weird like liking him. She couldn't risk that. If he wanted to sit near her, that was fine. If he wanted to talk to her, that was fine too, but she had nothing at all that she wanted to say to him. He was a guy. He wanted one thing. She wasn't at all interested in giving it.

After a long time, James stood up and looked down at her.

"Alright, Sassy Girl, I'm off to find a square of sandy solitude to do some thinking," he said. "See ya."

As he walked away, a little piece of him hoped he'd see her again, and at some point, she might open up to him about who she really was. For the present moment and the weeks ahead, he had a job to keep thinking about. During the final weeks building up to it, he wouldn't give any attention to women. It was the one time when they held no place in his mind, in his bed, and definitely not in his heart.

Sasha watched him walk down and along the beach. A little piece of her wanted to talk to him. It really did. It just couldn't.

Not yet.

"Hey," she heard Nicky's mother, Susan say as she sat down. "Thanks for watching her again, Sasha."

"No problem. I love hanging with Nicky. She's a great kid."

"I saw that guy who was sitting here," Susan said.

"If you don't want me to ever ask about this stuff, tell me, but is that the guy who apparently likes you?"

Sasha chuckled softly.

"I don't know about that, but he does turn up a lot," she said.

"Don't you like him?"

"Actually, he's starting to grow on me a bit," Sasha said. "I just don't want to be anyone's … sorry, I can't think of any other word than bitch."

Susan laughed. She wasn't like Sasha, but she did *like* Sasha. She was a breath of fresh air among all the stuffy people Susan knew and worked with.

"Maybe he doesn't want you to be his *bitch*," she said. "Maybe he'd like to be your friend."

Sasha looked at Susan and smiled sadly.

"Maybe."

"Okay," Susan said. "I am going take this little lady of mine and whisk her away for a dinner out. You're welcome to join us…"

"Thanks," Sasha said. "Another time I'd like that, but today I've got things on my mind. Do you want me to watch Nicky again next week?"

"Mummy!" both women heard Nicky yell as she ran toward them.

Sasha watched as Susan scooped her daughter up into her arms. She wondered briefly why her own mother had never done that to her.

"Sasha and I are just talking about next week," Susan said.

"Okay, but you asked her about dinner tonight, right?"

"Yeah, your mum did, Nicky-kid, but I'm going to pass today," said Sasha. "Next time, though, okay? See you next week?"

She watched as Nicky nodded, Susan smiled, and then both walked off. Once alone, Sasha looked down the beach. She could see that guy sitting on the sand.

Even with his sunglasses on, he looked like he was looking out toward the ocean. For a moment, Sasha considered it might be nice to sit beside him and look out at the ocean too.

Resolved that doing that was a stupid idea, she stood and began to walk in the other direction. Then she thought of Nicky again. She kept trying to help her to be more at ease with simply saying hello to people. She hated that she preached that, but she didn't live it.

She turned and began to walk toward the sand. It was only sitting beside him. They were in public. They weren't going to have sex. He wasn't even going to expect sex, there in front of everyone. What could it hurt to just sit with him?

~~~~~

James closed his eyes and lifted his face toward the sun. It felt good having the heat pound down on him. That, combined with the sound of the waves crashing on the shore in front of him, made for a perfect thinking place. The job they had coming up wasn't a huge job, but something about it felt off. It was almost like it was too easy or something. He trusted his brother, Fitz, in intel. He had nothing else in common with his kid brother, but he was good at the business.

He sensed someone walking close to him. That sense grew as he felt someone sit beside him. He opened his eyes in surprise. He was stunned to see Sassy Girl sitting beside him.

"It's a welcome surprise, having you sit beside me, but still a surprise," he said, looking at her in confusion.

"I know," Sasha said. "Do you mind?"

"No! Not at all. I was just doing some thinking. You are very welcome to think with me," he said, making her smile. He liked that smile. "Did you lose something, though?"

"What?"
~~~~~

"Your daughter," James said.

Sasha thought she'd not heard right until she realized the mistake he'd made.

"Oh, Nicky isn't my *daughter!* She's just a kid who I hang out with every week," Sasha explained. "Her mum's just come and taken her away. Shit, how old do you think I *am?*"

James laughed softly as he breathed out deeply.

"I have no idea," he said. "I don't know anything about you. I don't even know your *name.*"

Sasha laughed. She couldn't help it. Finally, she held out her hand to him.

"I'm Sasha."

James grinned broadly as he shook her hand.

"Sasha. Hmm, that wasn't one of my guesses," he said. "In fact, I don't think that *ever* would have been one of my guesses! I am very pleased to make your acquaintance, Sasha."

They said nothing more. He was glad to just know her name and to have her happy enough to want to sit beside him.

Sasha was glad she'd taken a bit of her own advice and reached out to introduce herself to someone.

Nothing more was needed.

At least for the moment.

~~~~~

As he made his way into his apartment that night, James realized how little he felt like his usual self. He sat on the sofa and closed his eyes. For a moment, he could see the face of Sassy Girl - Sasha. He now knew her name. He did smile at that. It had taken quite a while, but she finally trusted him enough to tell him.

Unless it *wasn't* her name.

"Oh, *hell* no!" he yelled out to no-one. The thought that she might have just given him a fake name to shut him up became all-consuming. "Ugh, fuck, can't do anything about that now," he mumbled to himself. He
~~~~~

thought he was probably right. Of course, it wouldn't be her real name.

He quickly pushed her from his mind. He couldn't concentrate on her or any other woman at that moment. His libido would be non-existent in the final weeks before the job. It always was. Usually, he could summon some thoughts about some woman or other. It wasn't happening then. At that moment, there was only one woman who was at the forefront of his mind. All others seemed utterly forgotten. Once again, James Stonewarden desperately tried to push Sasha Leadbetter not only from the forefront of his mind but completely *out* of his mind.

CHAPTER 6

"Are you sure about us heading away together next week?" Phillip Leadbetter asked Daisy as they lay in bed early on a Saturday morning. It was exactly two weeks until the job that the rough part of his family was going to take part in. He hadn't had any word or heard any rumor that Pete even cared that Phillip and his father weren't going to be part of the job. That didn't stop both of them being on high alert, just in case. Pete was a murderer. He'd never been convicted, but the family knew things he'd done. He wasn't a guy to get on the wrong side of. Phillip didn't want to think about his parents. His father had to do that. Phillip needed to concentrate on the beautiful woman lying underneath him, with her legs still wrapped around his ass.

"Of course," Daisy replied happily. She suspected there was an actual reason he wanted to get out of town, but she didn't ask. They'd set up their boundaries. She wouldn't talk about cases she worked on. He wouldn't talk about his family and their criminal ways. Even as she resolved to give up the law completely, she still appreciated those boundaries. "I want to lie around with you like this all day every day in a beautiful hotel room."

Phillip laughed softly. "*All* day, every day? I am a very lucky man indeed."

Daisy pulled him down to her and kissed him passionately.

"I want you to make me pregnant," she said.

"I want that too," he replied as he started to move in her again. "But it ain't going to happen until you agree to become my wife."

Daisy felt him growing inside of her. He'd only recently climaxed. She loved feeling him grow while still inside her. She instinctively started to raise and lower her hips, meeting his thrusts. He moaned as they began to move together in beautiful harmony.

He lifted his upper torso high and looked down at her. As she lifted her arms above her head, he looked at her breasts, her lips, her eyes. He couldn't help but thrust faster.

"Touch yourself," he whispered and watched her hand creep downward. With every thrust into her, he could feel her hand there. He could hear her moaning heavily and then felt her tense up underneath him. The sensation pushed him into his own sweet release. "Oh, fuck," he breathed out as the climax crept up, hitting him hard and fast. He lay still and then looked down at her. "You'd kill me if you wanted me to do this all day every day."

Daisy laughed. "What a way to die, though."

Phillip grinned and pulled out of her. He lay beside her and faced her, encouraging her to do the same.

"I really do want to get away with you," Daisy said softly. Whatever his real reason was for going out of town, she trusted his need to do it.

"It's another week off work, though," Phillip replied.

"I know, but soon I'll be off work full time anyway."

"Are you sure you want to do that? Your job is your life," he said to her, still not sure what had prompted her to resign from her job as a lawyer.

"No, it isn't," Daisy said. "Being with you has made me see that. I love being a lawyer, but it isn't my life. I want more, Phillip. I want love, and I want babies. I want to be a mother."

"You already have love," he said before kissing her softly. "Never question that."

"I know. Now I just need babies," she said

suggestively, making him laugh.

"You really do want to kill me."

They laughed together.

"I want to marry you," he said after he kissed her again. "If I have kids, Daisy, I want them to be part of a stable, loving family home - with a mum *and* a dad."

"I know. It isn't the being with you that's stopping me from saying yes."

"Well, what is it?"

"It's … it's just that … I don't want to say, Phillip."

He pondered what her reason could be.

"Do you love me?" he asked.

"Yes! Of course I do. I wouldn't be wanting babies with a guy I don't love. I want the mum and dad thing too."

"Do you see us being together forever?"

"Yes," Daisy reassured him.

"And you want us to make babies together…"

"Yes."

"And raise them together? In the same house?"

"Yes."

"Then what … why won't you *marry* me?"

Daisy wished the conversation would stop. She didn't want to say the truth out loud. It wasn't even a valid reason. She knew that. She also knew how she felt.

"Your name," she finally said.

"My name … Phillip?" he asked and saw her giggle. He then thought about her reason and instantly became serious again. "Leadbetter. Seriously, Daisy? You won't marry me because of my last name?"

"It wouldn't just be *your* last name, Phillip. It would be *my* last name too. And it would be the last name of our kids."

Phillip pulled away from her and lay on his back. Sometimes it was easier to look at the embossed ceiling than look at her.

Daisy watched his face. She'd hurt him. That was exactly what she'd expected. That was why she hadn't wanted to voice her reason for avoiding getting married. She was surprised when he turned and looked at her.

"Then I'll take *your* name," he said.

"*What?*"

"Why not? It's the law, right? When two people get married, one can take the other's surname. There's no legal law that says the woman has to take the guy's name. It *can* be the other way around, can't it?"

"Yes … but Phillip, it's your name. It's your family and your heritage."

"Forget that for the moment. Daisy Leefton, please, will you marry me and allow me to become your husband, Phillip Leefton, and have lots of little Leeftons running around our ankles?"

Daisy looked at him for a long while. The plan was an okay one. It certainly would remove all concern she had about having an entire family who had the Leadbetter name. Not only could her kids be safer with her surname, but Phillip could be too.

"Are you sure?"

"I am if you are," he replied. "Do you want to? Was that your only reason, or are there others?"

"No, it really was the Leadbetter name that worried me."

"Then…?"

"Yes. Phillip Leadbetter, I want to become your wife and have lots of kids with you."

"So you *will* become my wife and have lots of kids with me, you mean?"

She laughed at him. "Yes. I am saying yes."

Phillip kissed her deeply. "When?"

"Well, that, I need to leave up to you. You're still worried about your family knowing I was a lawyer associated with Rex's case…"

"Yeah, I don't anticipate there ever being a good

time for me to introduce them to you, but I know I have to. The worst-case scenario is that they get angry at me, and they don't welcome you into the family. That isn't such a bad thing though, is it."

"Maybe not for us, but our kids would be their grandkids. Your mum and dad would be our kids' grandparents."

Phillip let out a deep sigh. Everything about being a Leadbetter was fucked up. Inwardly he was glad of the opportunity to get rid of his name.

"Alright. I can at least talk to my mother and see how she goes first, but let's wait till we get back from this week away. I think they're stressed enough right now with some family stuff going on."

"Okay," Daisy replied.

His words were the cue for them to stop talking. Family stuff in Leadbetter terms meant stuff she *really* didn't want to know about.

CHAPTER 7

"Rex, you're a welcome sight," Pete Leadbetter said as he saw Mark's youngest son walking up the path at his home.

Rex saw Pete step out of his large garage. Pete Leadbetter's property had never been a place Rex had been to. He'd met Pete a handful of times at family gatherings, but it had always been on neutral ground.

"Hey, Pete," Rex said. He'd felt confident as he'd made his way to the address he'd been provided. He felt hugely intimidated as he stood in front of a man he'd heard was a killer. "I wanted to talk to you about next Saturday night."

"Come inside," Pete said, leading Rex back into the depths of the garage. "I hope you haven't decided to bail…"

"No!" Rex exclaimed. "Hell, no. I'm looking forward to it. I just wanted more information about what you want me to do and stuff. I'd rather know what you wanted before we turn up there."

Pete nodded. He'd purposely kept Rex out of the loop. He and Sasha were Mark's kids, and Mark had recently turned his back on the family. Could they really be trusted? Pete took a long time looking at the young face before him. He was good at reading people. With Sasha, it didn't matter. She would be there only to look good and report on what she saw. Nothing could go too wrong there. But Rex - he was a different story. Pete knew he'd gotten caught and charged for a car theft not too long before.

"That's a fair call, Rex," said Pete. "The lads are coming over in an hour, and we're going to be talking about stuff then. You wanna sit in on that?"

"Yeah, ah … if that's okay with you."

Pete could see the nervousness on Rex's face. He wasn't sure if that was a good thing or a bad thing. Nervousness could drive someone to excel. It could also drive someone to fuck up - badly.

"Sure. While you're here, you wanna help me replace the brakes on this beauty?" he asked, shifting their conversation to neutral ground.

Rex looked at the classic car beside them.

"Sure," he replied even though he didn't yet know much about cars. "You'll have to tell me what to do."

Pete smiled. Perfect. He needed something - even just one little thing - that he could give instructions to Rex for. That was a perfect way for him to assess one simple thing - if Rex could *follow* instructions. Of all the skills a criminal needed, that was surely one of the most important ones as far as Pete was concerned. He wanted every person on his crew to hear, understand, and do what they were told, without fault or hesitation. If they even hesitated, there'd be hell to pay.

CHAPTER 8

"Does she know what's going on?" Mitchell Stonewarden asked Tom as they together walked out over the fields of the ranch toward the donkeys. Tom was the oldest living Stonewarden that Mitchell knew of, and his uncle. He'd been tending the family ranch for most of his life. His discretion was paramount, especially since the ranch was a hideout for any Stonewardens on the run and needing refuge.

"No, young Charlie has no knowledge of the upcoming job, as far as I can tell," Tom replied. "She believes Ash is sweeping her away for romance, nothing more."

"And Ash?"

"I told him, Mitchell. He knew something was up. He won't say anything. He agrees that she needs to not hear about any of it. I know in my heart that he wouldn't tell her what you guys are doing. He loves her too much. With the baby so close, he'd wrap her up in cotton wool if he thought it would keep her safe. No, he's a good lad. You don't have anything to worry about there."

Mitchell nodded. He trusted Ash. Of course he did. If he didn't, he sure wouldn't have approved of him marrying Mitchell's 19-year-old daughter.

"When will they go?" he asked.

"Wednesday," said Tom. "I told Ash the job was Saturday night. He's happy to get her out of here Wednesday and be well gone before the weekend. They aren't going far. I suggested the next town over that has a good hospital. Then she'll be within reach of you if you need to get to her, but she'll also have access to good medical care if the baby decides to come early. They'll be back before her due date, but babies come when they want to come."

"Don't I know it. All of my sons were at least a month early. Then Charlie decided to come two weeks late," Mitchell said, laughing slightly at memories of each of his children being born.

"And now everything's reversed," Tom said, chuckling. "She's the first to fall in love, marry *and* start a family. But I have hope for those lads of yours, Mitchell. Sometime one of them is going to fall…"

Mitchell burst out laughing.

"You keep thinking that, Tom," he said. "I have no expectations for any kids from any of my sons. I love to them to bits, but hell, they're lovers, that's for sure."

"We'll see," said Tom. "The ones that love women the most might be the ones who turn out to be the next to fall."

~~~~~

Inside the house, Ash was lying down on their large bed beside Charlie. It had been a crazy year, and soon he would become a father. He lovingly reached out and softly touched her belly.

Charlie watched his face as he caressed the large bump.

"Are you happy, Ash?" she asked. She was instantly greeted with the broadest smile.

"Of course," Ash said. "I'm lying on a bed beside my beautiful wife, and inside this incredible big *bulge* is our son or our daughter. What's not to be happy about?" He leaned in and kissed her softly. "I am happy in this life with you, Charlie. I love living here with you. I love working on the ranch. I love being around Tom and Molly. Everything is amazing."

"You don't wish we'd waited before doing this?" she asked as she pointed to her tummy.

"No," he said. "I think the timing of children should be just your choice. Whether we have heaps now or we space them out, or if this is the only one we have,
~~~~~

I'll still be happy. I just want to be with you. I want you to be happy and healthy."

"I *am* happy," she said as she raised his hand to her lips. "But I do look forward to having my energy back."

Ash smiled at her. She was teasing him suggestively. He had no reply that could even fit the way he felt at that.

"Do you want to go down and see your father before he leaves? I think he and Tom just came back through the paddock gate," Ash asked.

"Yes. Can you help me up? I'm a bit fat today," Charlie said, smiling all the while.

Ash grinned and helped her up. She was awesome, and he loved her. It was that easy.

~~~~~

"Charlie, I'm going to head home," Mitchell said as he wrapped his arms around his daughter. No matter how much he saw her with her big belly, he was always surprised by it. "You guys have a great holiday. The next time I see you, there might be three of you. Please be careful. Ash, take care of my little girl."

Ash shook his father in law's hand and nodded.

"I will," he said.

Nothing was said directly between him and Mitchell about the job they were doing that weekend. It was an unspoken acknowledgment on both sides that neither side would mention it even though both sides knew about it. They were in agreement that regardless of what Ash thought of what the Stonewardens did, the most important thing was keeping Charlie safe and calm, and seeing her through a safe delivery.
~~~~~

CHAPTER 9

On Wednesday, as Ash and Charlie made their way out of town, Mark Leadbetter and his wife Stacey were doing the same. Nothing had been said about anything negative to do with Mark since Pete had taken over the helm of the Leadbetter family. It didn't hurt to be extra cautious, though.

Stacey was glad Mark was traveling away with her. It was a preventative measure in case something bad happened in the weekend around the robbery. For her, it was also the first time she'd had a romantic holiday with her husband without any kids. Anya was the only one she worried about leaving behind, but she'd managed to find a friend to stay with for the remainder of the week and over the weekend. She'd be alright.

"How are you feeling?" Mark asked his wife when he saw how thoughtful she appeared.

Stacey leaned close to him and lay her head on his shoulder. They were on the very first train trip they'd taken together.

"I'm glad to be away with you," she said as she took his hand in hers. "I was just thinking that this will be the first time we've had time without any kids around since before they came along. That's a really long time."

Mark slipped his arm around her shoulder.

"It is," he said before kissing her forehead. "It kind of feels like a second honeymoon."

Stacey sat up and smiled at him.

"Well, since we didn't actually have a *first* one, maybe we can make *this* our honeymoon."

He laughed at her and pulled her to him to kiss her.

"What exactly does a honeymoon entail?"

"Lots and lots of *loving*," she said in a whispered voice close to his ear.

Mark grinned. He was looking forward to *that*.

~~~~~

The oldies were gone. Rex sat in his room in the Leadbetter home and rejoiced. He had the house to himself, and on Saturday, he was going to be part of Pete's crew. He'd attended a couple of planning sessions with them, and he knew his role to play. He was going to be celebrated as a main player in the robbery. Hell, *everyone* would want to know him. Everything was looking good.

The house seemed quiet - too quiet. It was good but at the same time a bit spooky. His oldest brother, Phillip, had long moved out. That had been good. He'd always been too much in Rex's face. His next brother, David, was never around. He was pretty much shacked up with his girlfriend. He wouldn't be home. Great. Brat Anya was away with friends. He was glad to be rid of her, stupid baby sister she was. That only left Sasha. She was okay. She was going to be doing the job with him on Saturday. He didn't mind Sasha. She was one tough bitch. He much preferred that to squeaky clean, super happy Anya. Yeah, the only one even remotely cool was Sasha. The rest of his family could go to hell for all he cared.

Fuck. Them. All.

~~~~~

Greg was getting nervous. He was set up to be the getaway driver for Rhett, Rex, and Pete. There would be a number of cars and drivers at the ready, but that would be his passenger list for the night. He'd tried to get Sasha assigned to his car too. Pete was having none of that. He wanted her to not be seen as a part of anything that went down, so it would be up to her to grab a cab and make her own way home. Greg didn't like it, but he'd follow the instruction. If there was one woman on the planet who he absolutely knew could look after herself, it was Sasha.

Contemplating how the evening might go, he automatically began to pack a bag of clothes and stock up his car with food and water supplies. He had a cabin in the woods an hour out of town. It had come into his possession from his mother's family so it wasn't a Leadbetter asset. He'd purposely kept it a secret from the family. He had often wondered if he might one day feel like just getting away to it and closing his eyes and his ears to the rest of the world. He currently felt like that time had come. Saturday night, he would do his job, but then he was going to just drive away. He might go for a week. He might go for a month. Hell, he might go and never be heard from again. He'd consider that option once the robbery was over, and he was on the road.

Thinking ahead to others he cared about, he grabbed a handful of unopened burner phones he'd had in stock for ages. If he left town, he'd ditch his usual phone and use a new one with a new number. He was going to give one to Sasha and one to Rhett too. He'd make sure they didn't give the numbers to Pete. If he was honest with himself, Pete Leadbetter scared the crap out of him. They'd all grown up together in the same crime family, but that guy was psycho. Nothing was too extreme for him, and that made Greg nervous.

Working through a hypothetical list in his mind, he jumped in his car and drove off to purchase other just-in-case supplies. Matches, firewood, coal, and spare fuel all filled his car boot, along with blankets, sleeping bags, and pillows. He hadn't been out to the cabin for months. It could have been looted to hell. He was taking no chances.

CHAPTER 10

The day had come. At 7pm, doors to a high-class gala would open, and people would ascend in their tuxedos and gowns. On display but under semi-heavy guard would be jewels that were the actual center of attention for a select few.

At the Stonewarden house, everything was checked and re-checked. Everything was questioned, answered, and then re-questioned. Nothing could be left to chance. The Stonewardens had an advanced plan in place to make sure they could get what they wanted with precision and discretion. That was their way. They'd done burglaries where stolen items hadn't been noticed as missing for months after they'd disappeared. They were masters of something being there one moment and quietly gone the next.

All boys had their tuxedos at the ready. Even James and Vic, who lived in their own homes, were getting ready at their family home. It was a night of work, but it was also a night of charm. That was part of their illusion.

When all were showered, dressed, and ready, Mitchell looked around at all of his sons. Everyone was working, as was normal. They all had their specific parts to play. One by one, he got each of them to recite their individual codes to everyone else. Through advanced microphones and earpieces, they would be able to hear one another, but they were too professional to actually talk to each other. Nothing stood out more than people standing around talking to themselves when it came to crime. The boys each had their lines that they would deliver to someone else - preferably a stranger - if anything seemed off. No-one was too proud in their crew to call a job doubtful and suggest an abort. To do so was far more intelligent than continuing in a plan and everything going to hell.

Vic thought through his part as he sat on the living room sofa. Soon he would be the one planning jobs. For the moment, however, he knew they had sound plans in place. It wasn't going to be the hardest theft they'd done, but it was going to be incredibly rewarding when it was over with. After that, his father would start handing over the Stonewarden reign to him. He looked forward to that. He'd been waiting for it for a long time.

James stood in front of the large mirror in his old bedroom and focused. He was looking good. He was smelling good. He would easily do his part to watch everyone and make a judgment call if it was needed, all the while being simply a charmer who loved women.

Regan just waited for everyone else. He just wanted it over with. He wanted the job to be done, and then he wanted to get back to his girlfriend. She had no idea who he was really. He liked living the mirage he hid in when he was with her. It was a nicer place to be than the reality of what he was about to do in the name of family honor.

Max hoped everything would go well. He'd experienced being shot and being confined in a coma the year before. It had put him off criminal behavior, but he would step up and do his part for his father. He no longer had any desire for it, but he'd do as was expected of him. For a brief moment, he thought about Christy. What would she think of what he was about to do and had always done? The thought wasn't good. It created a slight panic in him. He quickly pushed her from his mind. He couldn't think about her. To be distracted on that night would be a recipe for disaster.

And finally, there was Fitz. Always the planner and initiator, he was fired up and ready to go. His adrenaline was flowing through his veins. He couldn't wait to get into that building and see his ideas take shape.

"Right," Mitchell said as he looked around them all one more time as they assembled in the living room again. "Does anyone want to stop this? Speak up if you do."

No-one said a word.

CHAPTER 11

In the Leadbetter household, Sasha had showered and was spending time putting on the thick makeup that Greg had given her. It was supposed to hide her tattoos. It seemed a fruitless effort given how far up her arm they went, but she'd do as she had to. As she applied it to her skin, she thought about all she'd been told. She'd have no active role except to walk among the people, be approachable, smile, and keep her eyes open. She had a communication link to go into her ear, and she was to report the movements of security as they moved around. That was it. She had no other part to play. She was glad.

The whole thing had made her father and mother nervous. That, in turn, made her nervous. She knew she was an adult and able to stand on her own two feet, but for a sliver of a moment, she wished her mother had pulled her into her arms and told her to go with them out of town. She wished someone had said to her that she shouldn't do what Pete had asked her to do. Did anyone even consider anything happening to her? Anyone at all?

Satisfied with the images on her skin being successfully hidden from view, she ventured to put on the dress Greg had given her. As it slipped down over her body, she was well aware that she had never worn anything like it before. She'd worn dresses. The gown was more than a dress. She'd never been enthusiastic about girl stuff like hair, makeup or clothes, but she did like the feeling she got as the gown slipped over her and settled on her slight curves.

She looked in the mirror. With the bare back and halter neck, she could see the level of skinniness she possessed. She didn't think about it day to day, but she had to admit, she didn't look healthy. She wanted to look better - not for some asshole - just for her.

Her body wasn't changeable in the immediate future, but her face was. She hated makeup with a vengeance, but she knew how to apply it to create something resembling sultry. She got to work. Why Pete thought *she* was the best person to try and draw people's attention, she didn't know. The fact was that he did, and that was all that mattered.

Finally, she sat back, slipped on the high heels, and looked at herself. She was a different person. For one night, that couldn't be a bad thing.

She'd wanted to be a different person for a very long time.

~~~~~

In the bedroom next to hers, Rex was getting ready. He was fired up and wound up. His heart was already pounding in his chest. He was eager to get to the finish line - even before he got to the starting line. Everyone was always giving him a hard time about everything he did, but tonight he'd show them all. He'd do great, and he'd be a hero for it. No-one would ever talk down to him again.

Quietly he did as no-one knew he would do. He'd found the gun in David's room weeks earlier. His brother was hardly ever home. Even though David was supposed to also be working the job that night, he wouldn't need it. Rex picked it up and carefully tucked it into the back of his pants. Turning to look in the mirror, he made sure no-one would see it. It was well hidden. Perfect.

"Hey! You ready?" he called out to Sasha after he entered the hallway.

"Yeah," she said as she grabbed the stupid little piece of fabric someone thought was suitable for a handbag. All it held was her house key, her ATM card, and her burner phone. The only other thing she needed was the communication piece that was already in place. The only other thing she *wanted* was her knife. That was
~~~~~

strapped inside her thigh. It would hardly be an easy place to grab it from, but she was limited in where else it could go. It would have to do.

The two siblings faced each other in the hallway.

"Whoa," Rex said, stunned at the sight of her. "Pete is going to be *really* happy with *you*."

Outside they heard a car approach and then a voice in their ears.

"If you can hear me, come on out," Greg said in a soft sing-song voice, making them both smile.

"Hey, Rex, be careful tonight," Sasha said to her youngest brother. In many ways, he was like her but he was far more rash. She knew the one thing that might bring her brother down, in the end, would be his inability to walk before he ran. He could be like a bull in a china store with his impatience and stubbornness. She hoped to hell he wouldn't be like that inside the gala.

~~~~~

"Hey," Sasha said as she climbed into the back of Greg's car. It wasn't his day to day car. It was one that only made an appearance on nights when they'd do a job.

"Jesus, girl," Rhett said as he looked at her. "I was wondering what Pete was thinking to give you this job, but fuck, you are going to make heads turn."

Sasha rolled her eyes at him but said nothing. No more was said as the four of them drove off, each with their heart pounding more and more heavily by the minute.
~~~~~

CHAPTER 12

James and Vic made their way independently to the venue. They would be lookouts, but their part included being playboys for the evening. That meant they needed a car each to sweep away a woman if that was what was needed to cover anyone's tracks and have an alibi.

As he pulled into the car park, James forced himself to take deep breaths. It was a trick he'd learned from Charlie when she had her panic attacks. A panic attack wasn't what James was having, but it felt good to breathe deeply. His adrenaline was running. He'd been in the family business for seven years. He knew how to put that adrenaline to good use.

He sat in the car for a long while before stepping out, holding his head up high, and making his way with the crowd through the large entry doors.

At different times the rest of the boys made their way in. Max was paired with Regan. They looked like two young lads eager to make a score with women for the evening. That was the hardest part for Regan to play, but he always did it well. It was just an act, but it still felt like a betrayal to his girl.

Vic entered alone and immediately sussed out someone to approach. He had a job to do, and he'd get on and do it well. There was nothing more to his thoughts. The job just had to be done.

Mitchell and Fitz entered together. They hardly ever spoke to one another, but standing side by side, anyone could see that they were father and son. They would attract mothers with daughters. It was always the way.

All circled and socialized. There was no hurry for anything more. They would take their time and remain observant about who was there and what each person was doing. They would watch security. They would watch the guests. It would be a long while before they moved toward doing anything else.

CHAPTER 13

"I'll be right here, Rex," Greg said to the youngest person in the car as they parked. He then turned to Sasha. "You know you're to make your way home in a cab," he said and saw her nod. For a fleeting moment, he thought she looked like a scared child. That look was quickly replaced with her unique look of fierce determination. "But Sasha, if you need me, I'm here. I know it's not the plan but fuck if I'm going to desert you if you need me."

Sasha nodded, thankful he'd said that. She wouldn't go against Pete's plan, but it was sure nice to hear someone express *some* kind of concern for her.

"Thanks," she replied.

Rex and Sasha climbed out. As Rhett went to do the same, he heard Greg's voice.

"Hey, be careful in there."

Rhett looked at him and nodded.

"You know I always am," he said quietly.

The three of them began their entry into the large structure before them.

~~~~~

As they moved inside, each went in their own direction. Sasha was supposed to be a woman on her own. That was the image she had to present so she could draw the most attention. She glanced around and took note of the paintings on the walls. She hadn't been in the building before, but it was clearly some kind of gallery. She wondered why she hadn't even been told what the inside of the building was like. It seemed kind of a major detail to have been left out. Not that it mattered. She just had to look pretty. Ha! Pretty. Yeah, *right.*

She moved to a painting and glanced at it before
~~~~~

looking around. To others, it might have looked like she was looking at other paintings on the walls, but her work had begun. She started to take note of security guards - where they were and how many there were. She'd been slightly worried about how the night would go, but as she sank into her role for the evening, she felt calm flow over her.

Everything was going to be alright.

CHAPTER 14

James walked around, chatting with people. It was a strange sensation, talking to people while hearing his brothers and father talking to people at the same time through the earpiece. He remembered his earlier days in the business, practicing to get used to it. His father had made him take the communication piece out to a mall. The two of them had walked around on different sides of the large building that was packed. It had felt like an overload of voices those first few times. It had now been a long time since he'd honed his skills in hearing what he needed to take notice of and blocking the rest out.

He wasn't out for a night of woman gazing, but he knew how to charm. He took his time and walked around, all the while keeping his eyes well open and alert. When he spotted a woman standing alone, looking at the artwork, he was startled.

From the distance he was at, he couldn't be entirely certain, but if it wasn't Sassy Girl, it was a woman who certainly looked like her. He held down the impulse to go up to her. Instead, he stood off to the side, partially out of view near a large column. He watched her. When she turned, he could see her face clearly. She had a lot of makeup on, and there was no sign of her tattoos, but he was pretty sure it was her. She looked outstanding. Fuck, she looked like an entirely different *person*.

He decided to just keep watching her. Over time he started to see her lips moving. The more he watched her, the more a shiver started to flow down his spine. He watched her eyes darting here and there, particularly toward security. He watched her speaking. It was subtle, but his eyes were trained to notice every little thing.

After observing for a good long while, James became nervous. She was there for a reason. She was watching, and she was reporting. That took his nervousness up a great deal.

Before she saw him, he readied to make the call and use his code for abort. Just as he was going to, he heard Max use his. Then Regan. Then Vic. He walked to a woman close to him and said the line that was all his own. To her, it was polite conversation. To each of the Stonewardens, it was as important as a neon sign glaring out the words, 'this is dirty. Get the hell out.'

Each boy heard Mitchell speak, his voice the final word.

"Fitz, I think I've seen enough. Are you ready? We should catch up with Max and Regan while we can."

James stepped forward to the banister that enabled him to look out over the entire main foyer of the gallery. He watched discretely as his father and three of his brothers quietly and peacefully left. Something was off. His father's wording had plainly stated that James and Vic would stay and just be regular guests. Nothing would be done. They were to do nothing except look perfectly at ease in the gallery environment. They wouldn't go anywhere near the jewels on display. They would turn the evening into a social occasion as if that was all it ever had been.

He looked around. In the distance, he could see Vic, but they didn't interact. He turned back to where he knew Sassy Girl was. Watching her face carefully, he approached her. Even the amount of makeup she was wearing couldn't hide the surprise on her face when she saw him.

"Sassy," James said quietly as he approached her. The surprise on her face turned quickly to concern and then fear.

Sasha looked at him. What the *fuck?!* How did this guy keep finding her? She'd enjoyed sitting with him on the beach, but she was working, and one floor down from them was Pete. One floor down from them was someone who would kill if things didn't go his way.

She moved him away from the crowd.

"What are you doing here?" she asked, panicked.

James shrugged his shoulders.

"I like art."

"Sasha, what's going on?" Sasha heard Pete ask in her ear. "I need you to tell me what's happening."

James saw her wince as if in pain. Anyone else might not have had any idea of anything that was going on. To him, with his years of training and experience in high tech gadgetry and military-style heists, he could see everything as it was happening. He wouldn't tell *her* that, but she wasn't being anywhere near as subtle as she should have been for what she was doing.

~~~~~

As they made their way outside, Mitchell and Fitz both became aware that something wasn't just a little off about the evening. They made their way quietly to the car they shared, but their eyes were trained. There were cops everywhere. Most were in plain clothes, but there was no mistaking them.

Mitchell looked to his left and his right and saw Regan and Max both safely heading toward their individual cars. Once he and Fitz sat in their car, he spoke.

"James, Vic, get the hell out of there *now!*"

Vic heard the instruction and immediately walked out without hesitation. He didn't even look at James. For that evening, they were on their own.

James heard the words and knew he had to leave. He looked at Sassy - Sasha she'd told him her name was. He had no idea if that was really her name. He decided to test her. He discretely turned off his comms and then approached her.

"Sasha," he said quietly. Instantly she turned and
~~~~~

looked right at him with an incredibly sad look on her face. She looked frozen, unable to move or speak. "Come with me," he said further, desperately not wanting to leave her there if something was going to happen.

She turned her head away and glanced at the security guards again. Her eyes followed the same route: guards then around four or five guys in the lower level of the large open space.

"I can't," she whispered to him, distraught.

James could see her eyes watering. He had no idea what was driving that emotion in her. He had hardly thought she was capable of *feeling* any emotion.

A loud sound from the ground level caused both of them to turn their heads sharply toward it. James was quick enough to see who was doing what. That was enough for him to run to Sasha, put his arm forcefully around her waist, and pull her back toward the back staircase.

"What are you...?" she started to ask until she heard more sounds. She'd first thought someone had dropped something on the shiny hard floor. With every step James pulled her, it sounded more and more like gunfire.

"Shut up and walk beside me as if I've picked you up, and I'm taking you home with me," he said to her. He didn't care what part she'd played in whatever was happening. He just wanted to get the fuck out of there, and he couldn't leave her there to do any more for her part. He just couldn't.

Sasha looked at his face. She was good at reading expressions. His said that he wasn't kidding. Something serious was happening, and it was best they get out of there. She cast her mind back to the others. Pete, Rex, and a handful of other guys from her family's wide circle were in there. Then she remembered that Greg was sitting in the car, ready to drive off as soon as Rhett,

Rex, and Pete reached him. They'd all be okay. Everything would be okay.

She said nothing but did as James had suggested. She didn't even know him, but she felt safer with him than she would have felt alone.

As they approached the front entranceway, he took her hand in his. She didn't even stop him. She knew when to act. She leaned into him and kissed him on the cheek. He smiled back at her. They passed through the doorway and toward his car. With every step, he kept thinking to himself, 'one more step', 'one more step.' He, too, had noticed the high number of cops around. He had no idea what was happening inside, but the gunfire hadn't yet stopped. It would go quiet for a few seconds, and then another round would go off.

Finally, they reached his car. He unlocked the doors and watched as she climbed in without any prompting from him. Inside she turned to him.

"What..."

Before she could say another word, Sasha saw James hold his finger to his lips then point to her ear. She looked surprised, stunned, and then resigned. She nodded as she pulled the comms unit away.

James held out his hand, and she handed it to him. He'd seen the type before. It was short range. Her communication with whoever was inside would have been severed almost as soon as they'd walked down the first staircase. He was taking no chances, though. He deactivated it and placed it in a thick-walled tin he kept inside the car's glove box. It was a move he'd done a thousand times before.

"I don't know what you're *supposed* to be doing, but right now, I have to get out of here, and so do you," he said as he started his car. Sasha said nothing. She just looked at him, confused. "I'm not leading anyone to my place or yours so how do you feel about parking up at the beach for a while?" he asked.

She could have read it as some kind of pick-up line, but the way he was looking in all of the car mirrors told her that was far from his thoughts.

"Sure," she said simply.

CHAPTER 15

From his car outside the building, Greg could see and hear confrontation. Guns were being used. His well-tuned ears could tell that. He was on edge with not knowing what to do. He'd seen Sasha come out with some guy. He had to hope she would be okay there. Really he should have run after them and dragged her away, but he didn't dare stray from the car. He had a job to do, and she was a tough chick. The guy hadn't looked menacing. Greg hoped that Sasha would be able to look after herself.

He was broken out of his thoughts as he saw Rhett walking quickly toward the car.

"Drive," he said as he climbed in.

"But Pete…"

"Dead. *Drive,*" said Rhett.

"Rex?"

"*Drive!!*" Rhett said as forcefully as he could.

Greg reacted. That was his role in that particular job. Whatever went down, he was there for the purpose of driving to get people safely away. He had to push out of his mind that he only had one of the two people he was supposed to have. He had so many questions but seeing the stress on Rhett's face, he kept quiet and focused on getting them to safety.

"I'm heading to a cabin an hour out of town," Greg finally said quietly after deactivating his comms piece, and seeing Rhett do the same. "I can drop you off somewhere or you can come with me."

Rhett felt like he was was overloading on emotion. Fuck that stupid job. Fuck, fuck, fuck! He turned and looked at Greg. His emotions were more than overloading. They were at a critical level.

"Pull over. There's something I gotta do," he said forcefully. There was a fear inside of him that the cops were going to catch up with him, and Pete wouldn't be the only one dead by the time the sun rose again. He'd held something back for a long time, and fuck if he was going to hold back anymore.

"Here?" Greg asked, his voice full of confusion.

One assessment of the way Rhett was looking at him, and he immediately pulled over. There was no-one around. He could see that as he turned and looked through the rear window…

The observation was cut short. In an instant, he felt Rhett's hands reach out and pull his head closer, and his lips come down on his own. Greg was surprised, and relieved, and confused, and stunned, but they couldn't just sit there like they were. If cops were after either of them for whatever reason, they had to keep moving.

He pulled back from Rhett and could see the emotion in his eyes.

"We'll have to talk about that later," Greg said quietly. Seeing Rhett nod and move to withdraw backward, Greg leaned further and kissed the lips back. He'd been silently dreaming about kissing those lips for years. He wanted to kiss those lips more, but they would have to wait. "Are you coming with me, or do you want me to drive you somewhere?"

Rhett was more confused by being kissed back, but neither said anything more about that.

"Let's just go. I don't have to be anywhere."

Greg nodded, started the car, and they drove away, not looking back.

Fuck.

What a night.

CHAPTER 16

Mitchell drove around for a long while. None of the boys would go to their homes straight away. It wasn't a situation they were caught up in, *hopefully*. There wasn't anything about their actions of the night that would have caused any suspicion, and they'd left before anything went down - *if* it went down. He still needed to check in and make sure they were all safe.

He pulled over and sent a coded text to James, Max, Regan, and Victor. Within a few minutes, three of them had messaged back with their individually coded response that looked like nothing but shouted 'I'm good.'

~~~~~

James pulled into the carpark at the beachfront. The weather was too cold to suggest they get out and walk. He left the heater running as he and Sasha sat for a long while, just looking forward out toward the ocean. Even over the sound of the car heater, they could hear the waves. It should have been a reassuring sound. For Sasha, it didn't hide the noise in her head.

The sound of his phone alerting again made James finally pick it up. He'd missed his check-in, so his father had sent a follow-up. Quickly James keyed in the right response. Immediately he received his father's code for 'all of you have reported in and are okay'. James put the phone safely in his pocket.

When he turned to Sasha, he could see she was shaking. He reached over to the back seat and grabbed an old sweater.

"It's old and probably smelly, but put it on. You look like you're freezing in that thing," he said, pointing at her flimsy dress.

"You wouldn't rather I was dressed and looked
~~~~~

like this than how you've seen me before?" she dared to ask. All guys wanted pretty princesses with perfect hair and makeup … didn't they?

"Hell, no," replied James. "I'd rather see the real you than a pretty picture borrowed from how other people present themselves. You look good in that dress, don't get me wrong, but my mother always told us that we have to just be ourselves."

"Myself is ugly," she mumbled. She hardly ever looked in the mirror. It seemed a pointless exercise that never brought any joy.

"Yeah, well, you might like telling yourself that, but to be completely honest, I think you're sexy as fuck."

Sasha almost had a sliver of a gut reaction like she'd always had. In the couple of seconds after he spoke to her, she could have pulled out the knife at her thigh. She didn't want to hear anything like that coming from any guy's mouth. It said to her that they saw her as a piece of meat, to be used and then tossed aside.

As she looked at his face, she argued with herself. He didn't act like he was going to treat her like that. She dispelled thoughts of grabbing her knife and holding it to his throat. Instead, she accepted the sweater and put it on, not saying a word. She had to admit it felt amazing to put on something that was so warm and comforting.

"I'm not going to ask you questions about whatever you were part of tonight. If you wanna talk you can, but I don't need to know," James said, trying to calm her down. He was used to his sister having panic attacks that would make her hyperventilate when she got too stressed. It wasn't the same thing as was happening in front of him, but the young woman before him did look stressed. He at least had the skills to try and soothe the young woman sitting with him.

"Thanks. I need to check my brother's okay…" she started to say as she pulled out the burner phone Greg had given her earlier.

James put his hand over hers.

"Are you sure that's wise?" he asked. "Is anyone going to be looking for that phone, who might search for its location?"

Sasha was confused. He had a valid point, but that side of things wasn't what she knew. She was just an active participant, doing what she'd been told to. She didn't know who to call or *if* she should call. She wished her mother wasn't so far away. They weren't close, but Sasha had no doubt she'd know what to do in situations like that.

"It's a burner," she said quietly. "I just need to know he's okay."

She decided not to call the phone Rex had on him. As far as she knew, he was still inside the building when she'd left. If he'd done something stupid, the cops would have him *and* his burner phone. At least Greg would be able to confirm he was okay.

As if sensing her confusion, Sasha saw the screen on the phone light up with Greg's name.

"Greg?"

"No, it's me, Rhett. Are you alright? Are you safe?"

"Yeah. Yeah, I'm okay," she said as she glanced toward James. He didn't look like he was going to try anything that guys did. She'd be fine. She had her knife. It never let her down. "Are you guys?"

"I'll call you again when I have more news," Rhett replied. "Just be safe. If you have anywhere you can go other than home tonight, go there."

"Okay," Sasha said to ease his mind. Of course she had nowhere else to go. She didn't tell him that. He sounded worried enough. She hung up without saying goodbye. She knew the phone call had come from a place of caring, but for all the people her parents had drummed into her were her 'family', she felt completely abandoned and alone.

"Is everything okay?" James asked her. He wouldn't ask her too much. He knew how hard it was to keep a certain level of information secret from people. It was all the harder when the only option was to downright lie to them in response to a question.

"Yeah," she replied with a tone of defeat and desolation evident in her voice. She was worried about Rex. They'd never really gotten on, but he was her kid brother, and she'd just left him there. Sure, he'd been left with a handful of men who had the power to not let anything happen to him. They had the power to protect him and keep him safe, but had they?

"You do look really different tonight," James said softly in an attempt to veer her thoughts away from whatever was worrying her. "No tatts?"

Sasha smiled sadly but in appreciation of his attempt to divert her.

"They're under there," she said. "I've just got some magic tattoo-hiding crap on my skin."

"I'm gonna really look at those tatts one day. When I do, I don't want a knife to my throat."

Sasha chuckled. He was teasing her. In the moment, it felt good to have someone say something stupid.

"Deal."

"You hungry?" he asked.

"No, I don't think I could eat right now."

James kept checking the rear and side-view mirrors of his car. There was no reason anyone should have followed him, but he was savvy enough to at least consider they might have.

"Who do you think is after us?" Sasha asked, very aware of his actions and the seriousness on his face.

"I'm pretty sure it was guns going off in that building. Who knows what the cops think. Maybe they think someone who isn't there is related to whatever was going on. I don't think anyone *is* coming after us. It won't hurt to wait a while, though. I don't want cops coming to my door," he replied as he turned and did another full look through the rear window.

"Someone else might have been worried about people being hurt inside," Sasha wondered to herself, not realizing she was speaking out loud. She looked at him and saw the surprise on his face. "Who are you, James? Why is your first thought cops coming after you instead of people being hurt?"

James was speechless. He hadn't given any thought at all to where all those bullets had flown to. His only concern had been getting himself out of there. Following that thought had been his father and brothers. He was alarmed to have someone present a snapshot of his inward focus. She had a valid point.

"I don't know," he said quietly as he faced her. Feeling ashamed, he decided he couldn't face her so squarely on after all. He turned away and looked out at the ocean again. "I'm just me."

Sasha felt weary. She'd always pushed her mother away when she'd tried to be affectionate toward her. Now she wished she could feel her arms around her. She felt isolated and incredibly vulnerable and lonely.

"I think we're all good," James said, wanting the subject changed. "If you think there's any chance your home might not be safe, you can come back to my place and stay there the night," he continued. Her look of fear was evident. He laughed softly. "Sassy, if I was going to do anything to you, I'd probably do it on that beach rather than in my apartment. And if you're thinking about sex, forget it. That is the last thing on *my* mind tonight, so if you're thinking that me taking you to my place will give you the chance to adore my body, it ain't happening."

Sasha felt a deep breath flow out of her. She was uncertain about what to do. He was making light of the situation but was he being honest?

"I have my knife with me," she said.

"I have no doubt about that whatsoever," James said and turned back to face her again. "Look, all I'm offering is somewhere to sleep for the night. You can have a shower there if you want. If you're not too proud to wear guys' track pants and t-shirts, you can change into some of mine there. At least you'll be warmer and more comfortable. I mean it, Sasha. You're safe with me. These hands," he said, holding them up. "They're not working tonight. But I can drop you home if you want. Your choice."

"No," she said quickly. She didn't want to be on her own, and she had no idea what might or might not be happening in the Leadbetter household. She didn't know the guy next to her, but he had already proved he wouldn't push her too much in whatever it was he really wanted. "No, I'll come with you if you really mean it about not expecting sex."

James smiled sadly at her.

"Even if I wasn't too wound up for that, you haven't given me any clues you want anything like that from me," he said. "I'd never try and get sex from a woman who doesn't want it. Don't stress, Sassy. All's cool."

Sasha relaxed and smiled. She wasn't sure if he was aware he was drifting back and using his nickname for her now and then, but she didn't point it out to him. She kind of liked it. It was unique. It gave her a strange sense of feeling like she was someone special. That was something she'd rarely ever felt.

"You sure?" he asked one more time as he started the engine.

She nodded. That was all the answer she could provide. She was nervous, she was worried about Rex, and she was alone with no member of her family anywhere nearby. Everyone had scattered and just left her hanging. She'd always fought to prove she was independent. Now she wished she hadn't done that to quite the degree she had. She wished *someone* considered that maybe she did need someone close by after all.

~~~~~

They drove in silence. James was alert and Sasha could tell. She didn't want to interrupt or distract him. He was trying to keep them both safe. That was a huge thing in her head, like a large neon sign flashing, 'he's an okay guy'.

When they finally pulled into an underground carpark, Sasha felt her heart start pounding. Visions of horror movies she'd watched kept trying to enter her head. She fought to keep them at bay. Like he'd said, if he was going to hurt her in any way, it made no sense he'd take her to his apartment to do it.

"Are you all good?" he asked her once parked and had turned the ignition off. "You look scared."

Sasha couldn't say anything. He was right. That was how she felt. She watched as he climbed out of the car and then opened her door for her.

"You got your knife firmly planted somewhere?" he asked, trying to tease her to get her to relax. It worked. He got the small smile he'd hoped for.

"Oh, yeah," she said, making him laugh softly.

"Good," he said. "Just promise me you don't do things in your sleep like sleepwalk and sleep-knife."

"You'll be safe, so long as you keep a distance from me," she said, *half* kidding.

"Fair deal," James replied, nodding and smiling.

~~~~~

When they entered the small apartment, Sasha was surprised. She lived in a decent family home with multiple bedrooms. Where he lived was compact, but she liked it. She stood still and waited as he walked into one doorway. When he came out, he had clothes in his hands.

"Here, take these," he said, handing them to her. "The bathroom's here," he then said, walking toward another doorway. "If you want to grab a shower, use whatever's in there. I'm going to get changed."

Sasha saw him move through the first doorway and then close the door. She walked into the bathroom and closed and locked the door behind her. Seeing towels on a rack, she grabbed one and turned on the water. Finally alone, her mind wandered back to the events in the gallery. What had happened to everyone else who'd been in there? The only one she knew was okay was Rhett. Where was everyone else?

She looked in the mirror. Who was that woman looking back at her? The reflection revealed a woman who could be thirty or more. She was dressed well, and she wore makeup that made her look confident and mature. Sasha felt neither of those things. Glad she'd not chosen waterproof mascara, she bent over the hand basin and began to rinse her face. As she watched black intermingle with the water going down the drain, she felt sobbing coming on. A week earlier, everything had seemed normal. Now her parents were who knows where on their holiday and she didn't know where anyone else was either. She had no idea if she was safe or if someone might have seen her and be looking for the woman who left the gallery at such a precise moment. She had no idea if the guy in the next room intended to rape her - or worse. She let herself slide to the floor. She didn't even try to stop the tears.

When she'd cried herself out, she stood, undressed, and climbed under the water spray. It was hot. It felt good on her skin. She got to work with soap, scrubbing off the makeup that hid her tattoos. She used shampoo to rinse away the hair product that had seemed essential earlier in the evening. She lifted her face to let the force of the shower flow drive heavily into her face, ridding her of the remaining makeup. After that, she stood under the flow for longer, just feeling the hot water over her back and her front. Finally aware that she was using someone else's hot water, she turned the taps off and climbed out. She was bare again, and it felt good. That was who she truly was, not that woman dressed up with pretty hair and pretty makeup.

She slowly dried off and dressed in the track pants, t-shirt and hoodie she'd been provided with. Of most importance was her knife. She grabbed that and secured it in the pocket of her pants. She wasn't going to let that sit anywhere away from her. It had been a long while since she'd felt she needed it so much. Spending time with Nicky had started to mellow her in that regard. The events of the night had prompted her need for it again.

~~~~~

James quickly changed out of his tuxedo and into jeans and t-shirt. As he hung the tux up, he looked at it. It had been a wasted effort. Nothing had been gained by going to the gala at all, but that wasn't a big deal. His father and brothers had been through the process before. When something felt off, it was always better to walk away and not give it another thought.

He considered that for him, something good *had* come out of the evening, though. Sassy Girl was in his apartment. Nothing was going to happen there, but it felt good anyway. He must have secured at least a minor amount of trust for her to have let herself be alone with him. There was no way she was a chick who'd get in a car with someone she feared or hated.

He smiled at the thought.

~~~~~

When Sasha walked out of the bathroom, she saw him in the kitchen part of his small living area. As his eyes focused on hers, he smiled at her.

"There's the sassy girl I've been slowly getting to know," he said.

Sasha was quiet. She didn't know how to handle the situation with the guy who'd been turning up all over town when she'd been in different places. She saw him approach her. She stood tall and refused to give in to the natural instinct to pull her beloved knife out of her pocket.

"Can I look today?" he asked as he pointed to her arm.

She nodded and pulled up the long sleeve of the hoodie. She watched his eyes as he reached out slowly and tentatively touched her skin. It was a big thing for her, to let him do that.

"I'm not going to hurt you, Sasha," he said in almost a whisper.

"I know," she replied quietly as she held her breath. She didn't want to be so afraid of touch, but she was. Even her mother hardly ever touched her.

James slid the sleeve up further so he could see more. Ideally, it would have been easier for her to take the long-sleeved top off, but he wasn't going to suggest that. He knew women, and he was well aware that the woman in front of him was afraid of touch. He didn't want to ponder why that was. It was acceptable to him that it was just a part of who she was, and he'd respect that.

"It's really beautiful," James said as he pulled his hands away. For a moment, they looked at one another. Sensing she didn't much like that either, he turned away. "Are you hungry? I don't usually eat this late at night, but I'm gonna just throw together a toasted sandwich. Do you want one?"

Sasha nodded, realizing she hadn't eaten since breakfast.

"Tomato? Cheese? Ham?" he further asked.

When she silently nodded again, James smiled. He wasn't going to push her in any way.

After making the sandwiches, he invited her to sit

on the sofa with him to eat. He made sure to sit a decent distance from her. If that was what she needed, that was what he'd give her - distance.

~~~~~

Long after eating and then sitting quietly, both in their own thoughts, James stood.

"I'll show you where you can sleep if you want to crash," he said.

"Where are *you* going to sleep?" she asked.

James could hear the fear in her voice again.

"I'll be right here on that there sofa," he reassured her. "Don't worry. You'll be safe in the bedroom."

Sasha stood and nodded. She had to start trusting people. She knew she'd already made good progress in changing a little since she'd been spending time with Nicky and Susan. She had much further to go in her own desire to change.

As she walked through the bedroom doorway, James saw her turn and look back at him.

"Thanks," she said quietly before closing the door.

James settled into an old sleeping bag. It wasn't going to be a comfortable sleep, but he believed that suggesting they both share his bed would be too much for her. As he lay back along the length of the sofa, he wondered what she'd been at the gala for, who she'd been there with, and where the hell any other participants had gone. He'd heard the gunshots. Something had gone wrong somewhere. But how? Who? And why?

He was just drifting off to sleep when he heard the sobbing coming from his bedroom. If she'd been anyone else - someone approachable - he would have quietly gone to them and soothed them. He couldn't try it with her. In her case, he'd let her cry it all out. It was probably long overdue.
~~~~~

CHAPTER 17

The next morning Sasha woke and was initially startled by confusion over where she was and whose bed she was in. As she lay still, everything slowly filled her mind again. Things had gone wrong at the gala, and now she was in that guy's apartment. James. What was she to make of him? If he wanted sex from her, he was going to be in for a shock. She wasn't having sex with anyone ever again.

As she lay on her back and looked at the ceiling, she had to admit that he hadn't done anything to deserve any anger toward him. He'd only acted with kindness and attempted friendship so far. She didn't mind his company. It was kind of nice to be able to just sit with him and not make up conversation for the sake of it. Two times they'd sat together without having to talk. It really was just nice.

With her senses all slowly awakening, she could hear the clattering of dishes beyond the bedroom door. She could also hear something resembling singing. She was new to smiling, but she let herself - just this once.

She lifted her head and looked around the room. Everything was where she'd left it - the dress and high heels, the track pants and hoodie, and the pitiful excuse for a bag. When she focused on that, she left the warmth of the bed, grabbed the bag, and returned to under the covers.

Pulling out the burner phone, she hoped there would be some news there - *something* from *someone*. There was nothing. She wished she had her own phone. All that was keyed into the burner were numbers for Rex, Greg, and Rhett. She wondered why she'd never made a point of actually remembering the phone numbers of people in her life. She'd relied on technology too much. Now she had no way of contacting her parents or any of her siblings, except perhaps Rex. She was scared to call him, afraid that the cops had him *and* his phone.

For a moment, she felt incredibly angry at her father. If he hadn't stepped down, he could have stopped the robbery from ever becoming an actual plan. Putting someone crazy like Pete in charge wasn't her father's finest decision. She understood that he'd wanted to be away from everything but what a fucking *mess*. She had no idea what had happened but guns going off was a pretty good indicator that nothing went as it was meant to.

The sound of singing came through the door again. This time the pitch was higher, and it wasn't pretty. He did make her want to laugh. That was something because few people in her life ever had.

~~~~~

James had woken after a surprisingly good sleep. The night before, he'd lay awake until the sound of crying had stopped, then he'd turned over and finally relaxed. When he'd woken up, he'd been glad to hear silence. That meant she was probably sleeping. He suspected it might have been a while since Sassy Girl had been truly at peace.

He'd quickly dressed and begun to make some breakfast. Pancakes and coffee. That was it. That was all she was getting. His mouth was already watering from the thought of pancakes. So easy to make but *so* satisfying to eat.

When the bedroom door opened, he looked up to see her looking pretty much as she had when she'd gone through that door the night before - except for her hair. It was refreshing to see a girl who didn't care her hair was in a real state of messiness.

"Are you hungry, Sassy?" he asked. He was
~~~~~

greeted by a half-smile.

"You do know I told you my real name, right?" she asked him, holding back a larger smile that wanted to burst forth.

James grinned widely at her.

"Yeah, but I like Sassy. Can I keep using it? Can I? Can I?" he asked.

Sasha gave no reply except for raising her eyebrows and smiling. That odd feeling of her face moving into such a shape was still relatively new, but she was settling in to liking it.

James had just thrown pancakes on two plates and handed her one when his phone beeped. He pulled it out of his pocket. At first glance, he could see it was from his father. Opening the text, the words that appeared almost made him jump.

'Your sister's in labor. I'm heading to the hospital now.'

"Holy fuck," James said out loud. *That* wasn't supposed to happen for another couple of weeks.

"What?"

James looked at her. She still surprised him when she seemed to want to actually interact in two-way conversation.

"My sister's having a baby," he said.

"Like *now?*"

"Yep. Eat up, then you're coming with me to the next town over."

Sasha froze.

"Why would I do that?"

"You don't have to, but to be honest, I'd really like you to," said James. "If there's somewhere else you need to be, I'm happy to drop you off on the way."

"I don't *know* your sister."

James shrugged his shoulders.

"Well, she doesn't know you either, so you'll both be in the same boat, won't you."

Sasha couldn't find any actual logic in that statement, but it did relax her.

"Okay."

James grinned. She was a tough nut to crack, but he was enjoying seeing her relax and seem more at ease.

They both ate quickly and then were on their way.

~~~~~

The hour-long journey to the hospital was indeed long. It gave Sasha time to worry more about her family. It gave James time to wonder how they could even move forward as friends when they both obviously had things to hide from one another. The night before was still an unspoken thing, but they were both happy to avoid the conversation.

When they arrived at the hospital, she turned to him.

"Are you sure you want me here?" she asked. "I mean it's a family thing…"

"I'm not going to *make* you come in."

"Oh, alright. I'll come," Sasha said reluctantly, making him smile.

They made their way to the birthing ward. Already James's father Mitchell was there, along with Max and Regan.

"Hey," James greeted them all. "What's news?"

Mitchell looked at the young woman beside James. He knew his son was a player and loved women. That didn't mean James had ever let any of those women meet his *father*.

James caught the look and turned to Sasha.

"Oh, this is Sas … *sha*." He didn't elaborate, but everyone said hi to her.

Sasha kept quiet. She'd noticed two of the other men at the gala the night before. She suspected they wouldn't have noticed her. If they had, they probably wouldn't recognize her in her current au natural state. It didn't really matter if they did. It was probably normal
~~~~~

for James to take women home with him after a night out. The brothers wouldn't think anything of a woman being attached to his arm after a night like that.

Looking at them standing together, it was easy for Sasha to see that all the men in her company were related. James was by far the hottest - not that she cared about that, of course. No asshole was getting his claws into her, so it didn't matter how pretty he was.

"I'm going to see what's happening," Mitchell said and strode off.

Sasha moved to one of the seats. She didn't know how to handle the situation she was in. She'd never made any friends in her lifetime. Standing among four men was overwhelming.

When Mitchell came back, he invited them all to go with him to visit Charlie. He was excited. His sons were considerably less so at the thought of seeing their sister in pain and gut-wrenching agony.

"Stop being cowards," Mitchell teased them. "It's only a few liters of blood pouring out of her."

He watched as their faces went pale. When he laughed, they relaxed. Haha, their father was teasing them.

"Do you wanna come?" James asked Sasha, seeing her looking uncomfortable and off to one side.

"No, I'll wait right here."

"Okay," he replied quietly. In hindsight, he thought it probably would have been better to drop her off somewhere. It was too late for that.

~~~~~

Sasha sat in the waiting room. In one corner was an old television. She gazed at it, willing it to suck her into a trance of oblivion. When she focused on what was on, she recognized the outside of the gallery she'd been in the night before. She walked over to the TV and turned the volume up enough for her to hear. It was a news report.
~~~~~

"A charity fundraising event last night at the Gallalaya Gallery turned into a tragedy with blood spilled from police and gala attendees. Police are expected to make a formal announcement later today, but witnesses have reported two men - one in his twenties and one in his forties - pulling out guns and shooting into the crowd. It is believed their intention was to steal the Falimar Diamonds, worth more than a million dollars. The two perpetrators were shot and killed shortly after their rampage began. We'll have more on this story as police release further details of the tragic shooting throughout the day."

Sasha stared at the screen. Two people were dead. Who were they? Who were the two people? People who'd had guns, the reporter said. That narrowed it down then. Rex didn't own a gun. She was certain of that - fairly certain anyway.

She pulled out the burner phone and dialed Greg's number.

"Sasha," his voice said almost immediately. "Are you alright?"

"Yeah, but I just saw the news on TV," she said.

"I haven't seen it. What are they saying?" Greg asked.

"They're saying … they're saying two people pulled guns and started shooting at the crowd. It can't be us, right? It can't be…"

"Calm down and listen to me. I don't know what happened," he said carefully. He wasn't going to let on that Rhett was with him. It was possible he was going to need to be hidden for a while. "All I can tell you is that Pete was shot and killed."

"Pete's … *dead?*" she asked. She didn't really care. Everyone had always expressed hatred for the guy even though he was part of the family. That thinking didn't stop her from feeling something in the knowledge that he'd died the night before. She'd never dealt with anyone dying.

"Apparently," Greg continued. "That's all I know. I'm not in range of news right now, and I'm going to go silent. Tell me you're definitely okay."

His concern roused her focus.

"Yeah," she said. "Yeah, I'm okay. I'm out of town right now, and I haven't been home."

"Good girl."

"But I don't know how to contact anyone. Where *is* everyone?"

Greg took a deep breath. He had no idea where Phillip, David, or Rex were. Questioning Rhett the night before hadn't been a happening thing. As far as Greg knew, Phillip had gotten out of town and hadn't played any part in the robbery attempt. But David and Rex? Both had been there. As yet, both were unaccounted for.

"Wait another night before going home if you can. When you talk to your dad, tell him I'm taking time out, and I'll be in touch. Can you do that for me, Sasha?"

Yet again, Sasha felt like she was being abandoned, like everyone else mattered except her. Regardless, she wasn't going to voice that.

"Yeah, of course," she said quietly.

"Thanks," Greg said. "I gotta go. You take care and keep safe. Your parents are due home tomorrow night. Steer clear of the house till then."

The line went dead. That was it. That was the extent of answers for her. Pete was dead. He must have been one of the shooters, but who was the other one? There had been a handful of people. Any of them could have been the other one with the gun. It probably wasn't Rex or David. They were both safe, she was sure. They'd be in hiding too, so of course she wouldn't see or hear from them.

"Hey," she heard the now familiar voice say softly from behind her. She turned around and looked at him. She wanted to not look worried, but when he spoke again, she guessed she'd looked worried enough. "Are you okay?"

James studied her face. His alert eyes saw the phone in her hands. He wanted to provide support to her, but how was he supposed to do that?

Sasha nodded. Him asking her that question pushed her to release emotion that had built up in previous minutes. She willed the tears to not come, but she couldn't stop them. She wanted to be strong, but she just felt so weak all of a sudden.

Right before his eyes, James could see the usually fierce young woman start to crumble. He took a tentative step closer to her, then another, and then another. She didn't move away when he slowly raised his arms and wrapped them around her. She didn't flinch. She didn't pull out her knife. Instead, she stood perfectly still. James could tell she wasn't likely to wrap her arms around him, but he didn't care. He suspected it was a major thing for her to allow anyone to simply hug her. He found that belief an incredibly sad one.

Sasha let him hold her. It felt comforting, warm, and secure to be in his arms. She couldn't reciprocate, but she did welcome him sharing his strength with her. That was all that she needed - just someone to provide her with some support. Just one person. While her family were wherever they were, doing whatever they were doing, he was right there, holding her.

She pulled away from him and rubbed her eyes.

"How's your sister?" she asked.

James let her change the subject.

"She's okay," he answered. "It's gonna be at least a few more hours, they're saying. I don't know whether to stay or go..."

"Stay," she said forwardly. "She's family. She'll need family right now. Don't leave. Don't abandon her right when she needs you."

James heard the words and accurately perceived

them to be how *she* was feeling rather than how Charlie would feel, but she had a valid point.

"You're right. I guess I'll just keep hanging around."

"Thanks," Sasha said. It seemed out of context, and James's facial expression showed it. "Thanks for helping me."

James opened his arms up as an open invitation to her. She forced herself to step against him and receive his arms around her again.

"It's no problem, Sasha. Lean on me however you need to."

To that, she said nothing. Instead, she closed her eyes and rested her cheek against his shoulder. She never let people be that close to her. With him, it felt okay.

~~~~~

In a room down the long sterile hallway, Charlie lay in a bed. Ash sat beside her, holding her hand firmly. She could see tears in his eyes. It touched her to see him so emotional. That was until she felt a contraction pound through her body. Then she didn't think about him again for a long while.

Max and Regan swiftly got out of there. Seeing her in that kind of gut-wrenching pain wasn't something they particularly wanted to witness. Her father remained even though he'd been strictly told he would have to leave when the contractions increased.

Mitchell sat on the side of her bed and stroked her forehead. His baby was having a baby. That brought out mixed feelings in him. On one side, there was the fact that she seemed far too young to be in such a position yet. On the other side, he remembered when Caroline had delivered each of their children into the world. She had been Charlie's age when Vic had been born, and nothing had gone wrong. There was no reason to expect anything to not go to plan with Charlie.

The evening before had already left Mitchell's
~~~~~

mind. It had been a non-happening job, that one. That was okay. They happened now and then. He didn't know what had gone down in the building after he'd made sure the boys were all out. All he cared about at that moment was Charlie and the delivery of his first grandchild.

Tears threatened as he wished his wife was still alive and going through the experience with him and with Charlie. Perhaps she was right there, looking down on them. It was a nice thought.

"I love you, Dad," he heard his daughter say, bringing him back in his focus. It wasn't something she often said to him, but he reached over and kissed her forehead.

"I love you too, Charlie," he replied, smiling at her. He knew some fathers wouldn't have been happy for their baby girl to wed at 19. Mitchell had no concerns. Ash loved Charlie. It was simple, and it was good. He'd stayed with her every day when Max had been in the coma after the shooting. Now he was staying with her during her time of pain, even though Mitchell could see how pale he was.

"Do you want to go and get a coffee or something to eat, Ash? I'll stay here with Charlie," he offered.

"Thanks," Ash replied. "But I'm not leaving. I want to stay right here."

Mitchell nodded. He wasn't surprised in the least.

"How about I go and get something for you then?"

Ash looked at his father-in-law. Sometimes, Mitchell Stonewarden still scared the hell out of him, seeming so formal and seriously dangerous.

"Okay. I've got some money…"

"Ash," Mitchell said, cutting him off. "I got this. Tell me what you want. A sandwich? Pie? Burger?"

"Anything's fine," Ash replied. "Thanks."

"Charlie? You want something?"

Charlie rolled her eyes at her father.

"Yes. This baby out of me," she said.

Mitchell was relieved to see a look of amusement on her face. How she could look like that when she was in labor was beyond him. She was an amazing young woman, his daughter.

After he left the room, Charlie turned her full attention to her husband.

"If something happens to me, you'll take care of him or her, right?"

"Charlie, please don't say such a thing…"

"*Promise* me."

"Of course I would take care of our baby, but don't think like that," Ash said. "This is only baby number one. You want dozens, remember?"

Charlie laughed.

"I think it was *you* who wanted dozens."

Ash smiled at her. It was beautiful to hear her laugh.

"Yeah, maybe," he said. "I don't care. I just want you to be okay."

Charlie felt him squeeze her hand harder just as another contraction came on. She closed her eyes and rode it out. Seeing Ash almost in tears every time she was the one feeling the pain was almost as unbearable as the pain itself.

~~~~~

In the waiting area, Sasha found herself among the three brothers again. She was briefly envious of the girl having a baby. At least she had family who were there for her. As Sasha looked at James standing and talking with his brothers, she saw him smile at her. It was a small gesture, but it helped to keep her calm.

Her mind kept wanting to jump back to the same questions. Pete - dead. Rex - where? David - where? Had her parents heard about the shooting? If they had, surely they'd come home straight away to check up on their kids. And Phillip - where was he? The only one she
~~~~~

didn't give any real thought to was her teenage sister, Anya. She was off at a friend's house for the whole weekend. She probably didn't even know about the intended robbery. That was good. She might be saved from the worry Sasha had.

James, Max and Regan made small talk among themselves. It was a well-practiced rule that no matter where they were or who was around, they never said anything out loud about a job, even if it had gone wrong. There was no way of knowing who was after information. It was best to not risk comparing notes or discussing how things went, whether in a good way or not.

"Sorry. This isn't much fun for you," Sasha heard the deep voice say, breaking her out of her thoughts.

"It's okay," she replied. "Actually, it's good to be somewhere else, away from home. Thanks for bringing me with you."

James studied her face. Something had seriously changed in her between the first few times he'd seen her, and when he'd run into her again this time. She'd been so quick with that knife the first time he'd met her, and that had only been over a bag of baked goods in a local bakery. Now she had things far more stressful happening to her, but she couldn't be any more different from the knife-wielding chick she'd been then.

They sat beside one another in silence for a long time. It felt a bit like it was becoming their thing. Silence but company. Quiet but strength.

"I don't want to ask you any questions, but if you want to talk about anything, I am here," he said quietly. The look he received said she wanted to talk. The words he heard said she didn't.

"I'm good, but thanks."

James held out his hand. He didn't think she was someone who would ever like someone just grabbing hers. He watched her eyes as they seemed to assess the gesture offered to her. It took a while, but he was patient. Eventually, Sasha raised her hand and placed it in his, her eyes not leaving their two hands as they entwined.

As she felt her hand being held tightly, Sasha felt a surge of comfort roll through her. As a general rule, she hated people touching her. With him, it felt okay. It felt alright.

It felt … nice.

~~~~~

News came that the baby had been delivered. It hadn't taken as many hours as had been predicted. Like in anything, Charlie had to do things much earlier than everyone else.

When Mitchell entered the room after the birth and tidy up, he thought of his wife, Caroline. In many ways, Charlie looked like her. Seeing her sitting in bed holding a small bundle reminded Mitchell of every time one of their kids had been born. Six they'd had in total, all of whom were still alive and healthy. He knew they'd been blessed in that. Not everyone was so fortunate.

He held back tears and made his way forward. Ten years had passed since Caroline had left them. He sometimes wondered if he would ever have a day again where tears didn't threaten when he thought of her.

"Dad, come and see our daughter - your granddaughter," Charlie said when she saw him enter. He had that look on his face again. She knew that look. It was how he looked when he was thinking about her mother.

It was nice that he'd loved Caroline so much that he still thought about her so often, but Charlie hoped that at least one more time in his lifetime, he would find love with someone else. It didn't seem like a betrayal to her. It seemed natural. Her father was an incredible man. As strict as he was, he was caring and incredibly supportive. His heart needed someone to love. Charlie believed someone else must be out there who *deserved* his love.
~~~~~

Mitchell looked down into the baby blanket. The last time he'd seen a newborn had been when Charlie had been born almost twenty years earlier. None of his sons had become fathers despite their active love of women. He didn't expect that to change in the near future.

"I thought we might name her … after Mum. Would that be too painful for you, though?" Charlie asked.

Instantly she saw tears flow faster in her father's eyes. He raised a hand and wiped the first away.

"No, that wouldn't be painful, Charlie," Mitchell said. "I think that would be nice if both of you feel it's a good name for her."

Charlie smiled and sat up further, holding out the bundle.

"Here," she said. "Take her. Meet Caroline Patricia Thomson, named after both of her grandmothers."

Mitchell tentatively accepted the parcel into his arms. He felt an overwhelming blend of emotions. He wondered how it was possible that humans could feel such strength of happiness and sadness all at the same time. Looking down into the tiny face, he felt the happiness emotion start to take over and push aside the sadness. It was another day that Caroline should have been present at but wasn't. Regardless, Charlie looked fine. She'd had a safe delivery of a healthy baby. There couldn't be any sadness in that.

"Are your parents coming, Ash?" he turned and asked his son-in-law as a distraction.

"Yes, they'll be here shortly," Ash replied. It would be the second time his parents were in the same space as the people who had broken into their penthouse apartment in the city and stolen jewelry. He had to keep that thought hidden. He still believed that only Mitchell knew of the unfortunate coincidence that had happened the year before. He would never ever speak of it. It would only bring grief to his own parents if they ever found out who had robbed them.

Mitchell saw the look that passed quickly on Ash's face. He understood fully how difficult the situation was for them all. In his years in the family business, he'd never had something so unlikely happen. That would be the one job that haunted him for the remainder of his days.

"I'll round these boys up and get them to come and meet this little one, and then we'll leave you in peace," Mitchell said, not wanting to make things awkward for Ash.

"You don't have to leave…" Ash started to say.

Mitchell could see it was a polite statement. The words were contrasted with a look of relief on Ash's face.

"I think we do, but I'll come back tomorrow, baby girl," Mitchell replied and then chuckled softly. "I guess you're not the baby girl now, Charlie," he said as he handed the baby back to her and kissed her forehead.

Mitchell left the room and returned to the waiting area to address his sons.

"Each of you go and meet your niece and then we'll give them some peace and time with Ash's family."

As their father seemed to say the words and then just leave, no-one questioned why such a strict order was made on such a happy day. James and Max were oblivious to any discomfort between their father and Ash's parents. Only Regan knew about the robbery, and he said nothing. He'd endured being in the same room with them at Charlie's wedding. If he could avoid ever being around them again, that would make him real happy.

James watched his brothers go into the room.

"Aren't you going in?" he heard Sasha ask.

"Come with me," he dared to suggest. "You're obviously good with kids…"

Sasha laughed.

"Why would you think *that?*"

"Because I've seen you with little Nicky…"

"Oh, yeah, well, she's like ten years old," Sasha said. "I've never even seen a baby."

James smiled and stood up. From there, he looked down at her in her seat and held out his hand again.

"Neither have I since Charlie was born, and that's different," he said. "Come on, let's do something brand new for both of us."

Sasha contemplated for a long while. She was already doing things outside her comfort zone. One part of her wanted to shut down and not do any more. Another part of her wanted to keep moving forward with challenging herself to keep putting herself out there just a little bit more each day.

She stood and placed her hand in his.

"I'll wait for Max and Regan to leave, and then we'll go in if you feel comfortable," said James."You'll like Charlie and Ash. They're okay."

Sasha stood still. It felt awkward to just stand there with her one hand interlaced with his but them doing nothing. She remembered how much more she'd liked leaning against his chest. After taking a deep breath, that's what she did.

James felt her move against him and happily wrapped his arms around her. She was unique, that was for sure. With some women, such a move would be a seductive attempt to make him want them physically. With Sasha, he knew it was completely not that. He kind of liked the feeling he got from just providing support and comfort to her. It was new to him, but it definitely felt good.

~~~~~

Max stood in the room with his sister. He couldn't help grinning at the tiny being in his arms. He'd never seen a baby, that he could remember. With there being
~~~~~

three years difference in age between them, he supposed he must have seen Charlie as a baby when he was a toddler. He was sure he'd never known anyone who'd had a baby since then.

"Will you stop looking like an utter idiot?!" Regan teased his younger brother.

Max lifted his head and poked his tongue out in an effort to look as childish as he felt.

"I'm gonna go, Sis," Regan said, dismissing Max altogether. "I'm glad you're okay." He turned to his brother-in-law. "Congratulations, Ash. I'm really happy for you."

"Thanks," Ash replied as he shook Regan's hand.

After Regan left the room, Charlie turned to Max.

"So what's the gossip? What's happening with that girl who 'is but isn't'?" she asked, making Max laugh.

"We hang out a bit. That's all," he said as he handed the tiny bundle to Ash.

"That's all? Have you kissed her yet?" Charlie asked.

Max grinned.

"You know I'm the big brother, and you're the little sister," he said, teasing her. "I don't think you get to ask me things like that."

"Oh, I'm taking that a big fat yes then."

"Speaking of which, I better get going," he said as he leaned over and kissed her forehead. "Will you text me tomorrow and let me know if you're going to still be here or back at the ranch?"

"Yep," Charlie replied as she watched him walk toward the door. "Make sure you kiss her!" she yelled out as a final dig. She was greeted by another incredible grin from Max before he walked out completely.

Minutes after Max had left, Charlie saw James enter. She was more than a little stunned that he had a woman with him. She knew her brother always had women around. She'd never before actually *seen* any of them.

"Hey, I thought you would have left already," Charlie said as James approached the bed.

"I'm gonna leave soon. I just wanted to meet my niece," he said as he looked down into the tiny human wrapped in her mother's arms. "What are you going to call her?"

"Caroline," Charlie said softly.

"You're naming her after Mum?" James said, feeling a little emotional all of a sudden.

"Yeah, I think it's only right," Charlie replied. "She has Ash's mum's name as a middle name too."

James turned and smiled at his brother-in-law. "Nice."

"Um, James?" he heard Charlie ask.

"What?"

"Are you going to introduce us to your friend, who is standing looking uncomfortable since you haven't introduced us?"

James smiled sheepishly at Sasha, embarrassed at having been called out yet again for being unthinking.

"Charlie, this is Sasha. Sasha, this is my sister Charlie and her husband, Ash."

Sasha felt her anxiety rise but fought to keep it at bay. Visualizing kicking it in the guts seemed to be working every time she was presented with a new situation. She stepped forward and smiled as much as she could smile.

"Sasha, it's nice to meet you," Charlie said in her usual carefree manner. She eyed up the woman in front of her. Sasha was *not* how Charlie had imagined a woman of James's to be. Charlie had always thought he'd go for perfect women wearing perfect girlie clothes, with perfect hair and perfect makeup. The girl he was with was natural and wearing guys' sweat gear. She had no makeup on, and her hair was clean but not styled in any particular way. On sight, Charlie instantly liked her.

"Hey," Sasha said quietly as she looked at Charlie and then Ash. She couldn't help but notice the way he was looking at the woman in the bed. Love was something Sasha didn't seek, but if she did, surely it would be nice to have a guy look at her like he was looking at his wife.

"Alright, we're gonna leave you in peace now," James said, smiling down at the baby. He'd never wanted kids, but he didn't mind looking at that one. His niece. He was an uncle. That was kind of cool. "How long are you in here for?"

"I don't know," Charlie said. "They said they'll watch me for a few hours and then decide if I need to stay or not."

"Okay. Text me if you need anything," James said as he reached over and shook Ash's hand. "Congratulations."

Sasha was relieved when they finally left. She also felt a little bit proud. She felt like she'd walked into a lair and only held her head up high. Not bad at all. She could get used to the being-around-people thing. She'd keep working at it, but all in all, it was definitely getting easier - not necessarily easier to *talk* to people, but being near them was a start. She was happy with that.

"How about I pick us up some lunch, and we head down to the coastline to eat it before we head back home?" James asked.

Home. The word instantly brought on stress in Sasha again. She fought to push it aside as she nodded in reply to his question.

"Yeah, that sounds good."

CHAPTER 18

Sitting on the top of a large flat rock formation with seawater on three sides of them, James and Sasha once again enjoyed the simplicity of each other's company while no words were spoken. The food provided a good excuse for not talking over a long period of time. Eventually, James heard her speak. What she said surprised and kept him in silence for even longer.

"I don't want to have sex," Sasha said. She knew she was possibly saying something that wouldn't be relevant anyway. Maybe that wasn't even something he wanted from her. The more time she spent with him, the more she was questioning her own beliefs about her categorization of 'all men'. She just wanted to be sure he knew that they weren't working toward sex.

James processed the words. It felt like a little bit of context was missing. The words could be interpreted in so many ways.

"I hadn't thought that you wanted to have sex with *me*, Sassy," he said quietly, reverting to his pet name for her again. "Your vibe about that is pretty strong."

"Well, why do you keep approaching me then?" Sasha asked. "You're a guy. You want sex, right?"

James repositioned himself so that he was facing her fully. It was an intriguing conversation she'd begun.

"Yes and no. I want to have sex with women who want to have sex with me," he said. "I'd never try and have sex with someone who clearly *didn't* want to have sex with me, though."

"But why else do you talk to me?"

"Because I like you," James said, smiling at her.

"You don't know me."

"Well, people can only get to know each other by

actively engaging with each other," he said. "For me to know you, I have to talk to you. We don't know anything about each other. That's okay. That just gives us loads to talk about, right?"

He saw her lower her head in frustration or sadness. He wasn't sure which.

"But what if the things about me are things that I *can't* talk about?"

James nodded.

"Oh, I get *that*, believe me," he said. "But I like being around you. I even like just sitting with you. You don't need constant conversation, and that's really cool. If you're okay with us just sitting together now and then and not talking, I'm all up for that."

Once again, they sat and looked out at the ocean with no words spoken. After a further long period of silence, James heard her speak again.

"I'm scared to go back to my home today," Sasha said. It took courage, but she had to say it. It was the truth.

James lookcd at her and waited until finally, she raised her eyes to look into his.

"If you feel alright staying at my place for another night, you can. Or I can drop you somewhere else. What do you want to do?"

Sasha felt her eyes water. He could have tried to dismiss her fears as stupid. He could have told her that her time with him was up. He could have just said no. It felt like all of her family had abandoned her. He hadn't, and he hadn't said any of those things that he could have.

"Yes, please let me stay at your place again. I felt safe there," she said as she felt her fortitude fall away. She didn't want to cry in front of him. She didn't want to cry in front of *anyone*. The tears were too strong to hold back.

James watched and waited a moment. Seeing her wiping her eyes in an attempt to look normal when she was obviously upset pushed him to extend one arm out. He saw her assess for a moment before she repositioned herself a little closer and into his hold.

She wasn't so afraid of human touch anymore. It felt good to have someone right beside her, comforting her. Why had she pushed people away over the years whenever they'd wanted to hug her? That thought drove the tears to flow even faster.

A long time later, the tears softened and then stopped. Sasha felt like she should be ashamed. At the same time, she knew that she didn't feel ashamed at all. Being with him didn't inspire any such feeling in her. While she'd let her emotions flow out of her in the form of tears, he had sat quietly with his arm firmly around her shoulder. He hadn't spoken. He hadn't told her to harden up. He had simply accepted what was happening. To Sasha, that was incredible.

She pulled away and looked at him as she wiped her eyes.

"Sorry," she said.

"You don't have to be sorry for being sad," James said. "We all have sad times."

"It's hard for me to imagine that *you* do," she said with a sad smile on her face.

James looked at her with curiosity.

"Why would you think that?" he asked.

"You are ... so ... *confident*."

"I am," he said, nodding. "My mother always told me to stand tall in who I am, so I do. She's been dead for a long time now, but I still feel sad when I remember back to when she was dying. I feel sad that she isn't still here. Days like today with something big happening in my family like Charlie having a baby, I feel sad that our mother isn't here to see things like that." He paused and looked at her. She was truly listening to him. That was a welcome change from girls pretending to listen to him as some weird way to get his attention. "I have my share of sad days, don't you worry about that. I don't know about you but after I let my emotions loose like that, I always feel heaps better. It makes me feel calm after a good old cry."

Sasha thought he must be kidding. His words seemed doubtful. The look on his face made her believe what he was saying.

"I feel like I'm changing," Sasha said quietly as she looked out over the water.

"Are you happy about that?"

"I think so. For a long time, I've been angry at the world. I don't feel like that as much now." She paused and looked at him. "Spending time with Nicky has made me feel different about some things."

"Like what?"

"Like … simple things … saying hello to people … *smiling*."

James pondered her words for a long while. How could anyone be so unfamiliar with smiling? What kind of life did they live to not bring something into their life at any time that would make a smile appear naturally without any effort?

"Do you think it's Nicky herself that's making things change in you, or something about the situation of you being around a child?" he asked.

Sasha looked at him with confusion evident on her face. She had no idea what he meant.

James saw the look and reformulated his question.

"I mean, if she wasn't Nicky," he said. "If, instead of her, there was some other ten-year-old kid who wanted to spend time with you, would you still be affected the same way? Is it you being close to a child that you're reacting to - *any* child? Or is it being close to Nicky as an individual person that you're reacting to?"

"I think … I think it's her specifically," Sasha answered. "Her mum told me that Nicky often feels alone and has problems making friends. I want to help her get past that…"

"Because you're the same…"

Sasha focused on his eyes and saw the intensity in them. She'd never had a proper conversation of such depth before other than with the multitudes of counselors she'd seen when she was a kid. Even that had been different because they hadn't talked to her - they'd only listened. Maybe that worked for other people - people who wanted to talk. For someone like her who couldn't speak to people, it hadn't helped at all.

"Yes," she said.

She watched his face and wondered what he really thought of her. Not that it mattered. They'd broached the no-sex subject. It was out there. He'd be sure to stop approaching her, knowing her feelings on the subject. After he dropped her home, she wouldn't hear his voice call out to her again. She wasn't sure how she felt about that.

"Do you have lots of women friends?" she asked.

James was caught off guard. In what way did she use the word 'friends'?

"If you mean real friends, like people I talk to about things, then no," he said.

"What other kinds of friends are there?"

"The kind who meet up now and then to have sex," he replied, smiling at her.

Sasha was surprised and embarrassed. She felt her face warm up. She must be a complete idiot to not know something like that. She just didn't understand the whole enthusiasm-for-sex thing. Maybe she never would.

"That's not to say I don't *want* to have women as friends," James continued. "It's more that they don't seem to want me to be *their* friend."

"Why?"

James laughed softly. "You tell me."

"You're a guy. You want sex," Sasha replied. It seemed so simple in her mind.

"Okay, I want to ask you something. When I do, I don't want you to freak out on me and think I'm working towards getting in your pants. The no-sex thing is out there in the open between us, so don't go reading anything wrong from this point forward, right?" he asked and saw her nod. "Do you just not want to have sex with me, or are you talking about the entire male population when you say you don't want sex?"

Sasha took a deep breath. She could see on his face it was a serious question, and he was eager for her answer.

"I don't want someone to do that to me again," she finally answered.

"So you have *had* sex before?"

"Yes."

"Did he force himself on you?"

"No."

"So … it was … something you just didn't enjoy? Did he hurt you?"

There was silence for a long time. Sasha had never spoken of her one and only time of having sex. Nobody else on the planet knew how she'd felt ever since that had happened. Only one person knew it *had* happened, and he was the one who'd screwed her and then never spoke to her again.

"You don't have to answer..." James started to say. He could sense that she was wound up. He wasn't sure if it was because she didn't want to talk about it … or she did. Her words cut him off mid-sentence.

"He put his dick in me and did what he did, and then he told me to leave."

There. She'd said it. For the first time, she'd put that out there. That was hard, but fuck, it felt good to say the words out loud.

"That's what guys do, right?" she went on. "Spread a woman's legs and fuck her and she should just lie there, shut the hell up and take it."

"Whoa!" James said, probably far more loudly than he would have if he'd considered anything before letting words tumble from his mouth. "No *way*! Sassy, that's *not* how sex is … or at least not how it *should* be. No - *fuck no!* Who was this asshole? Was he a boyfriend? Was it his first time too? It takes a while for us guys to learn how to ple…"

"He was older - like 30 or something. I thought he liked me. I was so stupid. No-one's treating me again like that," she said.

As she spoke, James could see the same wildfire in her eyes that he'd seen when he'd first met her. She was aiming her words right at him, but what bothered him most of all was what had happened to her.

"Abso-fucking-*lutely* no asshole's treating you like that again!" he exclaimed. "Holy fucking crap. Sasha, you … he … *fuck* that makes me angry!"

Sasha watched his face. He wasn't kidding. It was the first time she'd seen him anything other than happy, and he was downright *pissed*. She had no idea what he was angry about, but it sure was interesting seeing a different side to him than his perfect one. Despite him being so angered, she found she didn't feel in any way threatened by him. It was like he was real angry, and he was with her, but that anger wasn't directed *at* her. She also noticed that although she had her knife in her pocket, she didn't feel like she was going to need it in that moment.

"I don't…" she started to say. "I don't get what has you so riled up," she finally said quietly.

When James looked at her, he could see her confusion over his reaction. It calmed him enough to take a deep breath before he spoke.

"No, I don't think you do. Fuck, Sasha," he said as he gently reached out with one hand. He left his palm up at a safe distance and waited to see if she would put her hand in his. The last thing he wanted to do right at that moment was make her feel like he was pushing her into anything.

Sasha slowly placed her hand over his. She'd held his hand at the hospital. It had felt okay. It hadn't hurt in any way. As soon as her skin touched his, she felt his fingers wrap around hers. It gave her that same feeling of comfort.

"No woman should feel like you do," James said quietly. "No guy should ever leave a woman feeling like you do after he's touched her. I'm sorry that your first time was with such an asshole to treat you like that. I hope ... I hope that some time in your life you give someone a chance to prove to you that it isn't really like that - not with someone who really likes and respects you anyway. Don't let that one time stop you from enjoying good times. Thinking of you spending your entire life feeling like this and never experiencing actual pleasure and the niceness that comes from being with someone ... that fucking pisses me off."

Sasha could see the passion in his face as he spoke. It really was a different side to him. She wasn't naïve. He was probably saying the right thing to make her relax and let him fuck her too. Maybe. When she pondered that option, she wasn't sure. He did seem sincere and honest, but then, didn't all guys who wanted to get into a woman's pants know how to appear sincere and honest?

She lowered her eyes to their hands. It wasn't scary or horrible to feel his palm against hers or his fingers gripping hers. What if he was telling the truth? What if there was something in sex that was nice with the right person? What if she was turning her back on something that truly could be enjoyable? As quickly as she considered those questions, she felt her negative side kick in. There was nothing nice about sex. No, she wasn't letting any asshole near her again - in that, she was resolved. It had been a nice speech, but she knew the truth. She wasn't being fooled twice.

James could feel a change come over her. She was shutting down again. It saddened him but he respected it. All he could hope was that she still saw him as being someone she could be safe with.

"We should get going. I think this water's rising, and I don't want a wet butt," he said in an attempt to take them back to a light-hearted place.

Sasha smiled sadly at him and withdrew her hand before nodding and standing. It had been nice sitting where they had. He did seem to find good spots to sit and think about things, that was for sure.

After walking back to the car, they settled inside. James turned on the heater for a while. It was a soothing heat, and that was what he wanted for her - to feel soothed, safe, and secure. When the car was a nice steady heat, he started the engine.

"Hey," he said, encouraging her to raise her eyes from her hands and look at him. "I like spending this time with you, and I'm not going to try and have sex with you. Believe that."

Sasha nodded. Her feelings were veering strongly toward believing what he'd said. Her doubts were still strong enough to be trying to push her beliefs back in the other direction. It resulted in conflict in her mind and her heart. She said nothing. He seemed to sense she'd say nothing. Both remained quiet as he pulled out of the carpark, and they began the rest of their journey home.

~~~~~

As they made their way down the final stretch of road to their small home city, Sasha turned to him.

"Could you drop me at my home?"

James was startled.

"Are you sure?" he asked. "Is it safe?"

"I dunno, but there's only one way to find out..."

"Have you changed your mind because of the things we talked about? You said you didn't want to go
~~~~~

ho…"

"I just want to go there now, okay?!" she said, her confusion starting to work its way into the anger inside of her.

"Okay," he replied gently. "Tell me which way."

Sasha directed him through the streets until they approached the Leadbetter home. Her heart was pounding. Anyone could be inside. She didn't know why they would be, but she'd sensed enough from enough people in earlier weeks to know that people feared *something*.

"Pull over here," she said, moving to open the door before the car even came to a complete halt. She was stopped by James gripping her wrist.

"Wait," he said, holding her in place as he maneuvered the car into a park. Right in front of him was a black Chrysler Valiant. His mind cast back to the day of the supermarket shooting that Max and Charlie had been caught up in. Wasn't that the description of the car Charlie thought she'd seen outside the supermarket that day?

"Whose car is that?" he asked.

Sasha looked at the car and then back at James. She was confused. She must have been. Otherwise, she wouldn't have instantly spoken with honesty before getting out of the car.

"Chill. It's my brother David's," she said before pulling her wrist away from his grip.

"I'm going to wait here for five minutes, Sasha. If there's anything in there that you need to get away from, run back here."

Sasha felt her heart ache. Greg had said the same thing the night before. He'd said if she needed him, he'd break rules, and he'd be there for her. He wasn't. He'd called her and told her to pass on a message to her father.

She nodded and climbed out. She'd be fine if David was home. He was hardly ever there, so most likely wouldn't be staying, but if he was there, all would be fine.

Walking into the house, it initially seemed deadly quiet. After a few hours of being caught up in pretty-boy's conversation, she remembered she'd been worried about Rex in particular. She still had no idea where he was. She hoped he was inside.

Carefully and quietly walking down the hallway, she could see David's bedroom door was open. She could hear noise from inside, as if things were being tossed around. At first, she feared someone else was inside, going through his stuff. When she peered around his doorframe, she was relieved to see that it was him. He wasn't his usual calm and peaceful self. He was clearly panicked about something.

"David?" she asked softly. Straight away, she saw him startled and reach behind him as if to grab…

"Sasha," he breathed out before his hand found anything. "Are you alright?" he forced himself to ask. He had to seem normal.

Sasha walked into the room a little way, but she was wary.

"What are you doing?" she asked as she saw him begin tossing things aside again.

"My gun … I can't find it…" he said, unthinking. If he had been thinking, he would have considered that no-one actually knew he *owned* a gun. Nor did they know when and where he'd used it…

Finally, he seemed to realize what he'd just said. As he did, he looked at her. In that very moment, he saw her eyes grow wide.

Sasha was surprised. David had a gun. Someone had been shooting into the crowd at the gallery, and he owned a gun. But that made no sense - if he'd used his gun to shoot into people the night before, he wouldn't be looking for it in his bedroom.

David was panicked. She was his sister, but could

she be trusted? Fuck, he had to find that gun. He would have been seen on any footage from the night before. He wanted to get out of town quickly. First, he wanted to make sure that the gun he'd seen in Rex's hands when a horror scene had begun right in front of him wasn't *his*. For now, though, what to do about Sasha? Fuck! She was his sister. They'd all done stupid shit, and none of them ever reported anything they learned about each other to anyone. He had to trust her. He could feel something in his soul. It was dark and trying to push out of him.

"Get out of here, Sasha. Grab whatever you need and get the fuck out of here," he said, hoping she'd heed his warning to her. "*Now!*"

It was pulling at him deeply. He'd had the feeling before - that feeling of need to kill. He'd never spoken of it to anyone, but it had always been there. For the most part, he pulled off being a calm and quiet guy. No-one knew of the conflict that resided throughout his mind.

Sasha didn't need telling twice. She could see something wasn't right with him. David was the quiet one. David was the one who hardly said anything. He could sit in a room and never say a word. She'd always thought that out of all them, he was the *good* one. The sane one. The one who could most be relied upon.

Without asking or saying anything more, she ran into her bedroom, grabbed a bag, and shoved some clothes in it along with her regular phone. All she wanted to do was get the hell out of there. Glad that James was still parked outside her home, she jumped in his car and told him to drive.

Having sat there for a few minutes, contemplating the knowledge that the car from the supermarket shooting might be sitting right in front of his face, James needed no further instruction to drive. He said nothing. He asked nothing. He was just glad she was in his car, safe with him.

Sasha didn't think about him at all. She reached into her bag and pulled out her phone. When it didn't turn on, she almost lost control. "*FUCK!!*"

James was slightly startled but glad he'd met her angry and had since seen her calm, and not the other way around. Her anger wasn't new to him. He could handle it. Seeing the dead phone in her hand, he reached under his seat.

"Here," he said as he handed her one end of a long charge cable.

Sasha accepted it and tried it, hoping it was the right connector. It was. Thank fucking god. She gave it a couple of seconds of initial charge and then turned the power on. Another few minutes later, she saw text messages appearing - seven of them.

Eagerly she opened them one by one. *Finally -* something from her family. She started reading them.

'Mum: 7.03am: Just saw news. Are you and Rex ok?'

'Phillip: 9.23am: Let me know you guys are alright.'

'Mum: 9.54am: Pls txt me.'

'Dad: 10.34am: Is Greg with you? Are you all safe?'

'Mum: 11.02am: Can't get hold of anyone. Where are you?'

'Phillip: 11.43am: I'm coming back to town now. Where are you?'

'Phillip: 2.21pm: In town now. Tell me where you & Rex are and I'll come get you.'

Sasha looked at the time on her phone. It was just after 4pm. She looked through a new lot of messages that had come in, this time reporting missed calls. Her father had been trying to call her over and over. That knowledge almost made her burst into tears. They *did* care about her. They *were* worried about her. She wasn't completely abandoned.

Having read through everyone's messages, she knew she had to make decisions. She sent a quick text to Phillip. He would be most reliable in letting the others know she was okay.

'Just got msgs. I'm okay. Don't know where Rex is.'

His message back was instantaneous. 'Are you safe?'

'Yeah. Don't go to house for a while. Stall Ma & Dad from going there. Is important.'

Phillip received that message and had to look at it twice. What the fuck did *that* mean? He obliged. Sasha was short with words but what words she used usually were important.

'I'll keep them away. You got somewhere safe for the night?'

'Yeah. Don't worry about me. I'll call you tomorrow.'

'Ok.'

While her fingers eagerly were working, James sat quietly as he drove them toward his apartment. He could easily identify things that were going on with her, and had been since they'd been at the gala. It made it effortless for him to sit and be quiet, leaving her to it - much more so than someone else might have been able to.

When he pulled into his apartment carpark and stopped the car, she looked up at him.

"I'm only asking one question. Do you still want to stay here tonight?" he asked.

"Yes," Sasha said quietly.

Her heartbeat was finally returning to normal. She'd done what she could to try and ensure her mother and father didn't enter the house while David was there. Whatever he intended to do, she was pretty sure it was something she didn't want anyone else caught up in. The equation of David + gun + their mother was an awful one. Sasha would keep worrying about that situation, but she knew she could trust Phillip to play his part. If nothing else, he was reliable, and he was strong. He'd walked away from the family and said no to their father. He had to have incredible strength to do that.

Looking at James, she was grateful. He'd had the gut instinct to sit outside her house for those few minutes. If he hadn't, she would now be walking around the streets, and that was far too open when you might be a target for someone with a gun.

"Thanks," she said.

James smiled and nodded before opening his door and climbing out.

Sasha followed him into his apartment. She had some of her own clothes finally. It was a small thing, but it was a nice thing.

"Can I have a shower?" she asked.

The softness of her voice almost made James laugh. She sure did have extremes.

"Yeah, help yourself," he said as he fell into his sofa. Fucking hell. The entire 24 hour period - now heading toward 48 hours - had been insane. At least whatever was happening all around him, Charlie couldn't get wrapped up in. She was a safe distance from the gala, from the city, from *him*. That gave him peace of mind.

Thinking over everything, he was pretty sure he had nothing to worry about. It could be on footage that he'd left with Sasha. She, in turn, could be discovered to be associated with whoever did what inside. That was his only real connection. He hoped like hell it wasn't enough to bring the police to his door. If that happened, they could be knocking on the door of *all* the Stonewardens.

Of other note was that car. Was the one outside her house the same one from the shooting? He chose to believe that there must be more than one black Chrysler Valiant around. Fuck he hoped so.

~~~~~

Once under the water, Sasha worked hard to try and turn her mind off. She still had no idea where Rex was, but her parents were going to be back in town. They would find him and deal with him if that was required. He'd scared them when he'd stolen that car. Their father had, in turn, scared the hell out of Rex. He'd be sure to scare him again if that was what was needed to get Rex to stop doing the stupid things he kept doing.

Now she had David to worry about too. What the fuck was up with him? He'd looked crazed even though he'd told her to get away from him. And he had a gun? Well, he *owned* one, he seemed to have said, but he didn't *have* it. Then who did?

She wanted her mind to turn off, but it refused. Only a few hours earlier, she'd been sitting on a rock surrounded by water, having an interesting conversation with a guy she hardly knew. That had felt stressful enough. Everything felt like it was all becoming more than she could bear. She wanted everything to just stop. She wanted it all to go away. She wanted an easier life. Why was life always just so hard for her? Other people made it seem easy. Why wasn't it easy for *her*?

She thought about the conversation she'd had with James. He reckoned sex wasn't horrible. He'd sounded pretty sure in those words. They hadn't sounded like he was saying it just to get into her. He had made it sound like it was something good for men *and* women. She wanted that theory tested. She was in the mood for anything to take her mind off all the crap going on. She talked herself into it. She'd changed her mind. She was going to be someone's bitch.

After stepping out of the shower, she wrapped a towel around her body and opened the door.

James had been sitting back on his sofa with his eyes closed. When he heard the bathroom door open, he opened his eyes. Sasha was walking toward him with
~~~~~

just a towel on. In any other situation, that might have made him smile. He wasn't smiling at the sight.

"What are you doing?" he asked her. Before him, she removed the towel and let it drop to the floor. James didn't think before standing and rushing to her.

Sasha was sure that was all she'd have to do. He'd push her to the ground, take his clothes off and fuck her. She couldn't have been more surprised when he stood, rushed to her … and then picked up the towel and wrapped it around her again.

"If you're trying to get me wanting to have sex with you, that ain't happening. We already talked about this…" he said while making sure the towel was tight and secure around her. As he then walked toward the bathroom to bring out her clothes, he heard her speak.

"I want it," he heard her voice say. It sounded confident. He didn't care.

"Yeah? Well, if you really do want to have sex with me, you'll be more than happy to wait, won't you," he said as he pulled out her briefs, knelt, and coaxed her to step into them.

Sasha was surprised by so many things. He was saying no. Even seeing her naked hadn't tempted him. And now he was kneeling in front of her, trying to put her undies on her? She did as he suggested and let him pull them up. She felt his hands move up the outside of her legs until her briefs were in place. His hands moved nowhere else. She also noticed she didn't mind his hands moving over the outside of her legs. She was pretty relaxed about it considering she'd always hated anyone touching her.

The process repeated with the track pants she'd put in the bathroom earlier. Again his hands helped them up via her outer leg. There was nothing sexual in his touch.

"Right," James said, confronted with the challenge of dressing her top half. He looked around to see if she had a bra. She hadn't worn one under the dress from the gala, and she was so skinny that he suspected she didn't need one. On seeing none in the clothes she'd had in the bathroom, he went straight to a t-shirt. "Raise your arms," he said. He wasn't taking any risks in her doing it herself - not when she'd just dropped that towel in front of him. He raised her t-shirt and settled it down over her body before reaching under and removing the towel. Once done, he started to dry her hair.

Sasha reveled in the feeling of someone dressing her and rubbing her head. It felt in no way like he intended to fuck her. It did, however, feel incredibly safe and comforting. Sensing she was liking it, James toned down his voice of authority and spoke gently to her.

"Come and sit on the sofa."

Sasha did as he bid.

"I was naked," she said. "Why didn't you just fuck me?"

James looked at her with a mixture of sadness and disbelief on his face.

"Sasha ... turn around."

She turned so her back was to him. Immediately she felt the towel on her head again, gently stroking her hair.

"I just don't get it," she said quietly. She heard him sigh.

"I know you don't."

"Do you think you would one day?"

James laughed softly.

"Do you think we could just get through *this* day without wondering about one other day?" he asked. "There's already enough crazy shit happening in your world, I'm guessing. Let's not add *that* into the mix."

"Okay," she said remarkably meekly. Inside, she was kind of relieved. It had been a fleeting thought, wanting him to do that to her. She suspected he knew even before she figured it out that she'd wanted it only as a way to turn off pain and stop thinking about other things. She relaxed in one other discovery. He'd been telling her the truth. He didn't want to have sex with her. He hadn't been lying with full intention of actually doing that to her. That pushed her feeling of safety and security up another notch.

James took his time stroking her hair with the towel. It was probably as dry as it was going to get through his rubbing, but he could sense her relaxing, and he didn't want that to stop. She was a funny thing, especially with that towel drop trick, but he didn't mind. She had pain. Anyone who saw her would openly see that. Pain always had to be dealt with one way or another. He wasn't against the idea of her 'one-day' plan either. He felt like she was turning his life upside down … in a very good way.

"I think your hair's pretty dry," he said softly after a long while of listening to her breathing deepen and slow.

Sasha turned around and faced him.

"Thanks," she said. She felt a bit of a longing she hadn't before. They were sitting close, but that wasn't new. What *was* new was her attention going to his lips.

James could see her eyes focusing there and inside let out a sigh that no-one heard but him. He hoped she wasn't going to go for another attempt at seducing him.

Sasha watched his face, his eyes, and his lips for a moment longer before leaning in a little and then kissing his cheek. It was a big thing for her - *another* big thing. He didn't move, and she was glad. He accepted the kiss and said nothing in return. Sasha stood, grabbed the towel from him, then returned to the bathroom to tidy up and grab a hoodie to put on. As she did, James turned on the television. He rarely watched the thing, but it was news time. He still had no idea what the night before had been all about.

'Police have released the details of one of the shooters from last night's horror at the Gallalaya Gallery," James heard as a picture appeared on the screen. It was clearly a photo of someone with a strong criminal background. The face he was looking at oozed it. *"Witnesses have reported that 45-year-old Pete Leadbetter pulled a gun out and started shooting into the crowd shortly after the charity evening began. A second man was also involved, but as yet, no details of his identity have been released. It's believed the men pulled guns in an effort to force security guards to open the glass case housing the Falimar Diamonds. When police arrived, Leadbetter shot directly at officers and was immediately shot and killed."*

Holy fuck. James was in shock about so many things. He'd known Sasha was part of something. He didn't expect…

He turned and saw her standing. She'd also seen the news broadcast. She was white. He didn't know whether to be angry, sad, or sympathetic.

"You're a Leadbetter," he said quietly.

Sasha turned her face from the screen and looked at him. Seeing the photo of Pete had shaken her up. So had the story. She was in disbelief that Pete had just walked in there and pulled a gun out to try and get the case opened so he could simply grab jewels and walk out. She had no job planning in such things, but the idea seemed completely absurd to her. Surely he couldn't have expected it would be that simple?

James stood and walked to her.

"It was your family who shot my brother," he said, his emotions intensifying.

Sasha was in a daze, but she sure heard that.

"No. I don't know what…"

"My brother and sister were in the supermarket and you shot at them through the windows…"

Sasha felt fear coming on. Fear and confusion.

"No!"

"Leadbetter," James said. "Rex Leadbetter stole my brother's car. He was found guilty of that. Who is he to you?" James asked and could see the confusion growing on her face. He didn't care. "Who *is* he?"

"He's my baby brother," she said quietly. Too many things were getting out of hand. How could the guy in front of her be brother to the guy who got shot and the guy who Rex stole a car from? What the *fuck* was the universe doing to her, screwing with her like it was? As if life wasn't hard enough without all this *crap* going on. "But *he* didn't shoot at them. The cops found proof that he wasn't there during the day…"

"The car that was at your house - it's exactly as my sister described the car she saw the gun come from…"

"No," Sasha said, shaking her head.

James watched her. He believed she had no idea what he was talking about. That didn't mean anything. It was still her family.

"No, that car is David's," said Sasha. "He wouldn't…"

Suddenly her mind was cast back to seeing him at their home. He'd been a different David then, and he'd been looking for his gun. She'd thought it strange he'd be looking for that if he'd used it the night before. She didn't want to believe it, but something clicked into place. He wouldn't be looking for the gun if he'd been the gunman the night before. But he *would* be if it had been used by someone else the night before … *and* it was the same gun that had been used months earlier in something as equally big in the eyes of the cops…

James watched as she walked to the sofa and sat down.

"No, it can't be … he … he wouldn't," she said, trying to process the possibility. "He's quiet and he's happy. Why would he have…?"

Looking at her, James felt another sliver of sympathy. He thought he could read people pretty well. Generally, he was good at knowing when someone was lying. He didn't think she was. He really did believe that she was just finding out that it could have been her brother who had let bullets fly into the supermarket that day.

Suddenly she looked up at him.

"I have to go. I'm so sorry. I didn't know…" she said as she moved quickly to gather her things. Her phone was half charged. That was something. All she had to do was call Phillip…

"Sasha," James said quietly as she began to walk toward the door. He kind of wanted her to stay but fuck, he also really wanted to never see her again. The contrast between the two feelings and desires was unbearable. He didn't say anything more. He watched as she opened the door and walked out, bare feet and all. He was angry, but he was also sad, and despite what it looked like her family had done to his, he hoped like hell that she was going to be alright.

~~~~~

"Sasha?" Phillip asked when he answered her call.

"Can you come and get me?" she asked, trying desperately to hold back tears.

In her voice, he could hear her cry for help. "Tell me where you are."

She gave instructions and then hung up. Out on the street, she felt vulnerable. Thinking about James and his family, she felt like she could be gunned down in the street by two sides - his family *or* hers. She hadn't often been scared in her lifetime. Now she was terrified.

It was only a few minutes before Phillip turned up in a car she'd never seen before.

Phillip looked at her. She was worked up in a way he'd never seen her. She'd always been angry. Utter terror was on her face.
~~~~~

"What's wrong?" he asked her.

"The world is fucked up," she managed to say, tears pushing out of her eyes and making their way down her cheek. She didn't even bother to try and hide them. She was beyond being able to control them at that moment.

"Yeah, well, you're gonna have to give me a better description than that."

"Where are you taking me?"

"You're coming back to Daisy's," Phillip said. "It's unknown to anyone else in our family so it's safe."

Sasha nodded. She wanted safe.

"Who's this Daisy?" she asked. "Do I know her?"

"Nope. No-one does. She's gone out for a few hours so that you and I can talk … if you want to."

Sasha nodded again. "Thanks."

They pulled into an unfamiliar carpark, and Sasha followed her oldest brother through the doorway, up the stairs, and through another doorway. Seeing floors, walls, and ceilings covered in greenery momentarily distracted her and made her smile. "Wow."

"Yeah, it's something," said Phillip. "Right, first, dump your stuff there. I'm gonna make something to eat…"

"I'm not hungry…"

"I don't care. You're gonna eat. You look like you haven't eaten since the *last* time I saw you, and that was weeks ago."

Sasha didn't argue anymore.

"While I do this, tell me what happened last night," Phillip continued.

"Have you seen the news?"

"Yeah, I saw Pete's face on there," he replied. "I know they shot him. I can't say I'm surprised or even saddened by that news. From what I've heard, he's always been a bit psycho and killed a heap of people. All I cared about was you, Rex and David. And Greg and

Rhett. Nothing was said about any of you. I didn't know if you'd gotten out or not."

Sasha sat on a bar stool on one side of the bench he was working at.

"I … fuck, Phillip, it was a fucked up night from the moment I got there."

Phillip looked up at her. The two of them talking to one another was a relatively new thing. He was still getting used to hearing her use whole sentences.

"Why? What was wrong?"

"Just … everything."

"Sasha! Tell me what happened," he said, starting to get frustrated.

"Okay! Fuck," she said. "I was there. I had a comms link, and I was watching the movement of the guards and saying what they were doing. That was all my job was supposed to be. Then out of nowhere, this guy I'd been seeing all over town appears…"

"What guy?"

"I didn't know then…"

"Was he a cop? Has he been following you under investigation?" he asked. Sasha was stunned into silence. She hadn't even considered that was who James was. How did Phillip so easily and quickly see that as a possibility?

"No, he's not a cop," she said, the uncertainty clear in her voice. "Anyway, he told me to go with him, and I told him I couldn't. Then there was a sound like something being dropped. When it happened again and again, it sounded more like guns going off. This guy pulled me away and offered to get me out of there, so I went with him. I didn't know what the other guys were doing. I just wanted to be out of there."

Phillip listened as he finished his sandwich making and handed one to her.

"Did you see Rex and the others leave?"

"No," Sasha replied, shaking her head. "The plan

was that I leave alone without giving away that I knew any of them. I couldn't even go near Greg's car..."

"Did Greg get away?"

"Yes. I spoke to him and Rhett both," she said. "They're fine, but they didn't mention anyone else - only Pete. They said he was dead."

"But the news said there's another gunman who fired and was killed. We don't know who that is. You know it could be David or Rex..."

"No, it's not David," Sasha said as she followed him to a small sofa.

"How can you be sure?"

"I saw him..." she said and put her head down, feeling tears come on again.

Phillip was startled. For the tough girl she'd always been, the stupid job sure had made her cry a lot.

"What aren't you telling me?" he asked.

"He ... he scared me when I saw him," she replied. "Today at the house. He was crazy. He was looking for his gun..."

"He has a gun...?"

"That's not the worst part, Phillip! That guy who gave me a ride? He's the brother of the guy who was shot in the supermarket. This guy saw David's car. He thinks it's the same car the gunner used that day..."

Phillip processed what was being said to him.

"Yeah, we knew it looked the same," he said. "That was what brought the cops around when it happened, but they didn't find anyone guilty. You think David *was* the shooter in the supermarket shoot up?"

"Yes! I think it was him in his car with his gun."

"Wait. Give me a minute," Phillip said. He took a few minutes to assemble his thoughts. David was only a couple of years younger than him. He hardly ever spoke. He was the only one the law hadn't really had any issues with in his family. "Why do you think it's him, though, apart from the car? I mean, there must be a few cars that look the same…"

"I know, but he was at the house looking for his gun," Sasha said. "Think about it, Phillip. Why would he look for his gun today? If he was the other gunman last night, he would have already had it with him. If it was used in the supermarket shootout and it wasn't used after that, he would have left it wherever he'd hidden it. The only thing that makes sense is that his gun was used last night by someone else, and he's now afraid it's going to get into the cops' hands - if it isn't already - and it's going to bring them straight to him for that other shooting."

Phillip nodded. "They've never found who did that…"

"Because they've never found the gun…"

Phillip groaned. Everything his sister was presenting to him made sound logical sense.

"But that means that the other shooter might be…"

Sasha nodded. "Rex."

Phillip stood up. Fuck. His baby brother?

"You think he's…?"

"I think we have to be prepared," she said, nodding. "Rex might have taken a gun that belonged to David and pulled it out at that gala. He might have used it. The cops might have shot him. And they might not be releasing his details yet because they haven't contacted Dad or Ma about it yet."

Phillip thought about his mother. Fuck, that hurt even more than considering his own brother might now be dead.

Sasha watched as her oldest brother paced the room, his hands over his eyes. She'd not wanted to believe Rex was likely the other shooter who'd been killed. Now she had to open up to that possibility. It seemed not only possible, but entirely likely. Rex had always been too impulsive. He'd barge at something he should have been subtle in approaching. If it hadn't happened now, everyone would have expected Rex to die an early death. His approach to everything had always pushed that possibility pretty high.

CHAPTER 19

In a café a couple of blocks away from her apartment, Daisy sat quietly and enjoyed the large cup of hot chocolate in her hands. In her apartment, she knew Phillip was with his sister, Sasha. Daisy knew everything that had ever been recorded by the law about Sasha. That hadn't prompted her to leave them alone. She'd heard the worry in Phillip's voice, and she was happy to let them have her apartment for a few hours. From all that she'd read about Sasha Leadbetter, she'd come away feeling more sorry for the girl than scared of her. Living with intense anger every day of her life - what could that possibly be like for a young girl, a teenage girl, and then a young adult?

Daisy became aware of her phone buzzing. She pulled it out and saw her boss's name on the screen.

"Daisy?" she heard when she answered. "It's another Leadbetter. Another brother. The cops are on their tail, and that kid Rex was shot…"

"Stop!" Daisy said out loud. "Stop talking." Fuck, she didn't want to talk to her boss like that, but she couldn't hear whatever they were about to say. "I need to tell you I am involved with someone in that family, and I can't work on any case you have been chosen to work on that's related to them. Please, don't say anything more to me. You'll need to find someone else for this one."

The line was silent for a long time.

"You're involved … with … a Leadbetter?"

"I'm not saying anything more," Daisy replied. "I'm now hanging up."

She pressed the call-end button.

She maintained calm, taking deep breaths while she drank the rest of her hot chocolate. Then she stood and walked quickly back to her apartment. Phillip's time alone with his sister had to come to an end.

When she opened the door, her eyes fell immediately to the woman on the sofa. Sasha Leadbetter - the young woman she'd read so much about in preceding months - was right in front of her.

"I got a call," she said. "Rex was shot, and they're after another one of your brothers," Daisy blurted out.

"You shouldn't have told me th…" Phillip started to say.

Daisy moved quickly to him and kissed him deeply.

"I know. I've told them I can't hear anything else, but I heard that before I informed them I'm involved with one of you. Phillip, they are *really* after you guys."

Phillip looked at Sasha.

"We need to go."

"What?" Daisy asked. "Phillip, you're safe here…"

"No, we're not, and neither are you," he replied. "Daisy, the law now know that you know us…"

"Wait," Sasha said, standing up. "Are you … a *cop*? Is that why he's kept you a secret?"

"No, Sasha," Daisy said, moving so that she stood in front of the young woman. "I'm a lawyer. I'm one of the lawyers from the case of Rex stealing that car."

"You were on his … defense…"

Daisy shook her head. "No."

Sasha felt the news sink deep inside her. Phillip was involved with a woman who'd tried to get Rex put in prison. She turned to him with a very evident look of disbelief.

"Not now, Sasha," Phillip said. "Did you hear what Daisy just said? The cops are after David, and Rex *was* shot."

Sasha fought to realign her thinking. At a logical level, she knew he was right. The fucked up situation of him dating his lawyer flower chick just wasn't anything to think about in the current moment. She nodded.

"Yeah, sorry," she said. "I'm mostly worried about Ma. Where are they? Are they home yet?"

"I don't know. They should be."

"We can't go in there. Tell me you won't go in there, Phillip," she pleaded with her brother. "David could still be there, and he could have the gun…"

"I'll go and see your mother," Daisy said. She'd read the files on all the Leadbetters. She was pretty sure she'd identify Stacey Leadbetter if she saw her.

"No!"

"Phillip, text your mother. Find out where she is right now."

He did as she suggested. He didn't like it, but it felt like options were reducing by the minute. The text came back. 'Almost at the house.'

'Stop. Turn around and come to Café Rue instead. You and Dad both. Don't go in the house.'

He sent her an address and hoped she would follow his suggestion.

"I've asked her and Dad to go to the café."

Daisy nodded. "Stay here. I'll be back soon."

Phillip followed her to the door. There he pulled her into a tight embrace and kissed her passionately.

"Someone might be following my parents," he said. "Be aware and keep yourself safe."

Daisy smiled and took a deep breath. She was well aware of how close the law could be to Phillip's parents. It didn't matter. She had to do something.

CHAPTER 20

Mark Leadbetter looked at the text. He could read the urgency in it. He could also read the warning. It was as big as a billboard in his eyes. He immediately changed course, and they made their way to the café. Before approaching it, they looked around. He considered he was pretty good at spotting plainclothes cops. He didn't think any were there.

They ordered coffee and sat to wait. They expected Phillip to turn up. They were both surprised when a young woman sat down beside them. Stacey looked at her. She'd seen her somewhere before.

"Hi," Daisy said. She saw Stacey smile even though her face revealed the puzzle she wasn't sure about. She then saw Mark hold out his hand to her. "I'm Daisy. Phillip and Sasha are safe, but your other sons aren't," she said quietly.

"Who are you really, Daisy?" Mark asked. He saw her take a deep breath. On her face was sadness - utter, extreme sadness.

"I'm a lawyer," Daisy replied. "I was on the periphery of the case that charged Rex with the theft of that car."

Stacey stood up sharply.

"I'm not listening to anything you say…" she started to say.

Mark grabbed her wrist and pulled her back down.

"Don't," he said to his wife before turning back to Daisy. "You tried to put my son away," he said and saw her nod. "But you are here to what? Threaten us?"

"No!" Daisy exclaimed. "I'm here to give you advance warning. They are after your other son right now."

"Not Rex?" Mark asked and saw her shake her head. "Not Phillip?" Again she shook her head. "Maybe you mean Pete?" Daisy shook her head again. "David?"

Daisy nodded.

"Why are you telling us this?"

"Because I love Phillip, and I fully intend to have his children - your grandchildren. Believe me, there's little I don't know about everyone in your family, but I don't care. I want to be his wife, and I'm not going to just sit back and be quiet about what I was just told. If you need to help your son David, right now is the time to do it."

Mark looked at her.

"But Rex…" As he quietly asked, he saw her face. "You know something about him too."

Daisy nodded.

"You haven't been informed of anything?"

Mark shook his head.

"No, we've been gone for days," he said.

"I don't know for sure. I heard something in a rush. It could be completely wrong…"

"What?" Mark asked, dreading what he was about to hear.

"He might have been shot, but I can't confirm that," said Daisy. "I told my boss I couldn't - wouldn't - work on this case, so I don't have access to official information."

Stacey broke down. She'd heard on the news that there was a second gunman who had been shot and killed by the cops. She'd not wanted to even consider it might be her baby boy. Suddenly she focused on Daisy.

"This is *your* fault," she said. "If you'd done things right, he'd be in prison right now. He wouldn't have done that job. He would still be alive."

"I … I don't know that he's not alive. I just heard that he was shot," Daisy said, feeling her own tears come on. The words she'd just heard were the logic of a mother deep in pain. Daisy could hardly be upset at Stacey Leadbetter for anything. She must have been living some kind of hell watching all of her kids get picked up by the cops at some time or other over the years. No matter how they'd decided to raise their kids, she and Mark had also produced Phillip, and Daisy still believed he was a good man. Some of that goodness must have come from his parents. It *must* have.

"I want to see my kids," Stacey said.

This time Mark didn't argue with her.

"I'm here," they heard Sasha's voice call out.

Stacey stood and was surprised to find her normally-anti-hug daughter launching herself into her arms.

When Sasha pulled away, she turned to Daisy.

"Phillip wants you home," she said. "Please go. I know you love him, and he loves you. I can see that. He wouldn't survive if something happened to you. I'll tell Dad and Ma everything. You need to leave so that you don't hear what I'm going to tell them."

Daisy opened her mouth to object but then closed it and nodded as she stood.

"I'm sorry," she said quietly.

Before she could move away, she heard Stacey speak again.

"It won't be easy, accepting you, but if you love my son and he loves you, I will try. When this is all over, we'll try."

Daisy smiled sadly and walked away. It was a nice sentiment anyway, even if it didn't ever become reality.

CHAPTER 21

Mark Leadbetter listened to his daughter tell him her thoughts and opinions about what had happened the night of the gala. With every word that came from her mouth, he felt his gut get heavier and heavier. Sasha believed Rex had been a gunman and had been shot and killed by the cops. The sadness in Mark over that wasn't the thought that it might have happened, but that if it did, he wasn't even the slightest bit surprised by it.

Hearing about Sasha's belief that David was likely the supermarket shooter, though - that was another level of blow to the guts again. Stacey wouldn't believe it could be true. Not David. He was the good one of the family. He'd hardly ever been in trouble with the law at all. No, Stacey wouldn't accept that. And they hadn't had any notification of Rex's death, so he couldn't be dead either. Somewhere someone had gotten details mixed up in some kind of Chinese Whispers thing. Her kids were all safe and sound.

As Mark watched Stacey's face, he could see that she was choosing to not believe. He wasn't going to try and convince her everything wasn't alright. They had no facts yet. For all he knew, she could be right, and he could be wrong in believing something had happened. No-one had heard from either of their sons. Sasha had only seen David briefly. Everything could all be mixed up. Until they came face to face with the cops, there was no way to know.

Stacey moved close to her daughter and put her arm around her shoulders. Daring to draw her close, Stacey was again surprised. Something had been changing in Sasha since her stabbing. Stacey had been watching that, but it felt like something had changed again, in a more significant way. It had happened in just the last few days. Stacey put it down to the gala job going wrong. Of course that would change someone. It didn't even occur to her that somewhere in the mix of craziness that was happening around her family, a guy might have entered her daughter's life.

CHAPTER 22

For a long while, James sat where he had been when Sasha had left. Everything felt screwed up. It had been a crazy existence for quite some time. Since the moment those bullets had flown through the supermarket window, and Max had been in hospital in a coma, everything in life felt like it had started to change. His baby sister getting married and now having a kid. His brother being shot and now apparently being involved with some girl even though he'd always loved all women, just like James. And now, finding out that the girl who'd been catching his eye all over town for months was actually the sister of the guy who had somehow been involved with the shooting.

Regardless of the crazy shit surrounding them, he liked Sasha. She had some weird views of the world and the people in it, but she was refreshingly different from girls he'd dated and shagged. He could still remember her standing naked. The vision of a naked woman would normally inspire his body to jump to life in arousal. He hadn't felt that. All he'd felt was a need to care for her and not let her do that to herself. For a while, he'd noticed her changing when he'd run into her. Now he wondered if she was, in fact, changing *him* somehow through those random meets.

For a moment, he pulled out his phone. One way to forget her would be to shag another woman. That would be easy. He started to look through his long list of play friends. Then he turned the phone off. It was no use. That was no cure. For once, he just didn't feel like having sex. What he actually felt like was being around family.

He stood, readied himself, and left. He was going

to talk to his father. If there was anyone he could trust to talk about something completely, no matter what, it was him.

~~~~~

"Dad?" James called out as he entered the large Stonewarden family home. "Dad!"

Mitchell heard his son's voice and moved quickly. It was a rare thing when James wanted anything from him other than the free food in the kitchen.

"What?" he asked when he reached the foyer. "What's wrong?"

James looked at his father. He looked panicked.

"Sorry. I didn't mean to freak you out."

"It's okay. What's up?" Mitchell asked, walking up to his son.

"I … I just … can we talk?"

Mitchell was surprised but pleasantly so. He'd been feeling real unwanted in recent times. Having any of his kids need him for something was a welcome thing to hear.

"Yeah," he replied as he moved into the living room. They sat together on one of the large old sofas. "What's going on with you that has you coming all this way over here?"

"I want," James started to say. It had seemed like a good idea, talking to his father about the situations surrounding him. Now it felt weird. He took a breath and continued, determined to do as he'd wanted to do. "Okay, so I have a few things that have been happening that are overlapping in a weird way. Trying to think about them alone is useless - I can't think. I want your perspective."

Mitchell nodded. "Okay."

"For a while now, I've been running into this girl all over the place, and we got talking. No big deal. It was just talking now and then."

"Right…" said Mitchell, nodding.
~~~~~

"Then the night of the gala, she was there, and I could tell she was talking to someone through comms. When you gave me the signal to leave, I took her with me..."

"This is the girl you brought to the hospital..."

"Yes! Yeah ... Sasha. Anyway, I've just found out that ... that her last name is Leadbetter..."

Mitchell was surprised. He didn't know a lot about that family, but he'd heard the name a bit on the news.

"Dad, her brother is the one who stole Max's car."

James watched his father's face. Almost instantly, he could see things turning over in his father's thoughts.

"Her brother shot at Max and Charlie?" he asked, his face deadly white.

"No," said James. "Well, Sasha doesn't think so, and the cops didn't think so. But Dad ... when I took her to her house ... the car that Charlie described from the day of the shooting was *there*."

"But you said it wasn't her brother."

"Not her brother Rex who was charged with stealing the car..."

Mitchell could feel his heart racing. Ever since that moment when he'd learned Max had been shot, he had wanted to find out who was behind the shooting. He wanted revenge. Whoever had pulled that trigger had to pay.

James watched his father stand up sharply and start pacing. Immediately he wondered if telling his father had, in fact, been a good thing to do.

"Are you telling me you *know* who used the gun that day?"

James hesitated. Was voicing his thoughts the right thing to do? He'd wanted vengeance too, but now he knew Sasha...

"I'm saying I *think* I know," he finally replied. "Of course, I can't be sure. The cops investigated at the time, and they didn't find any evidence to point to that family…"

"That means nothing and you know it," said Mitchell. "How many things have *we* gotten away with?"

James felt his heartbeat getting stronger and faster by the minute. He was angry at himself for bringing the matter to his father. He'd wanted someone to listen. He hadn't considered his father might want to act and do something if he knew who'd used the gun that day.

"Dad, you can't do…"

"Don't tell me what I can and can't do…" James heard his father say in a deathly tone.

Just then, the front door opened and Max walked in. It wasn't difficult for him to sense the tension in the room.

"What's … going … on?" he asked slowly, looking from his brother to his father and back again.

"James thinks he might know who shot you."

Max looked at his brother in disbelief. Even if James knew, why would he have told their *father?!*

"Dad," he said, moving up to Mitchell. "You have to forget whatever James just told you."

"Someone has to pay…"

"No!" Max screamed at him.

Mitchell was stunned by his usually happy son talking to him in such a manner.

"*I* was the one who was shot," Max continued. "*I* was the one who was in that coma. You don't know what it was like for me, lying there and not being able to move or speak. If you go and do anything, this is going to turn into a blood feud. Please don't do anything. Please, Dad…"

Mitchell heard the depth of the plea. He saw tears come to his son's face as he spoke. It was enough to calm him, at least for the moment. He moved to Max and pulled him into a hug.

"Alright, but this isn't good," Mitchell said.

"James, what else do you know ?"

James looked at his father and then at Max. The latter was giving him a look that blatantly said, 'please don't say anymore'. James wanted to be honest with his father and say exactly who the suspected gunman was. As he took a moment to remember how it had felt seeing his brother in the coma all those weeks, he knew he had to do as Max wished.

"Nothing," he said. "I don't know anything else, and I don't even know if what I told you is fact. I didn't mean to wind you up. I just wanted to talk about this girl…"

Mitchell forced himself to expel a fake chuckle.

"What about her?"

"You got a girl, big brother?" Max asked as he pulled away from his father. There was an opening to change the subject. He was going to seize it. "Is my wayward brother falling in *lurrrve*?"

"Hell, no. But she's part of a family who … forget it. I shouldn't have come here. I'm sor…"

His words were cut off as his father stepped forward and pulled him into a tight hug.

"James, we do things that aren't lawful. We always have. You can't judge her by her family any more than she can judge you by yours."

James pulled away from the embrace.

"But Dad, it's not quite the same…"

"I *know*," said Mitchell. "I know, but if you don't think she was the one who did any of those things, there's a chance she didn't even know about it…"

"I don't think she did. Her reaction seemed real."

"Then tread carefully and take your time. Really assess the situation before you turn away. Just … just be sure she can be trusted before you tell her anything."

"I've never shared anything about us with anyone…"

"I know, but it's different when you meet

someone special, James. Trust me in that."

James thought his father was crazy. It had been weird enough that Ash knew all about the Stonewardens. James had no intention of sharing that kind of information with anyone, no matter *who* they were, and he sure as hell wasn't sharing anything with Sassy Girl - if he ever saw her again, that was.

Max left them and went upstairs. He was stressed that his father might do something stupid. It was a word that he'd never have used in regard to his father, but if some kind of war was going to break out, that was how he'd describe his father over that decision. Stupid.

Downstairs, James lowered his voice.

"Dad, the cops are on the tail of the one with the gun. Please do nothing. If he's the one, I don't think it's gonna be long before he's held to pay. Please promise me you'll let the cops handle this. It would kill Max…"

"I know," Mitchell said quietly. "You're right. The cops will do their thing. Hopefully, they'll catch the bastard. What does that mean for you and this girl, though?"

James shrugged his shoulders.

"There wasn't anything going on anyway."

Mitchell raised his eyebrow at his son. "If she didn't mean anything to you, I doubt you'd have come all this way to talk to me about her."

"I came to talk about … yeah, maybe."

"It's been a long time coming that some woman stood out from all the rest," Mitchell said quietly. The fact that the girl was a Leadbetter did not sit well with him. The flip side of that was that he did want his sons to find the same happiness he'd had with Caroline all the years they'd spent together. Ash had accepted Charlie despite what the Stonewarden family did. Could the Stonewardens accept a Leadbetter regardless of what *their* family did? It wasn't the same degree. Of course it wasn't. Stonewardens robbed. Leadbetters shot and killed.

Hearing arguments in his head, Mitchell knew he'd be thinking about Caroline as soon as he was alone. He needed her at times like that. He needed her calming effect and her sound logic. He needed her arms around him and her lips on his to distract him from the harshness of reality. He needed *her*…

"Dad?" James asked when he saw his father's eyes begin to well up in tears.

"Yeah, I'm fine," Mitchell replied as he wiped his eyes. "Sometimes, I miss your mother so much. Don't waste time, James. Every day you get to spend with someone is special, and those days *are* limited. No matter who the woman is who turns your head and reaches your heart, seize her and hold her. Don't waste a moment. Once those moments are gone, there's no getting them back."

James watched as his father spoke. It wasn't hard to see that his dad was emotional. James felt guilty. If he hadn't gone to the house and said things he'd said…

"Don't worry," Mitchell said. "I promise you I'm not going to do anything and I'm not going to repeat what you've told me. Like you said, the cops will catch up with whoever pulled the trigger that day. And I do know Max doesn't want to keep being reminded of it. It's all okay."

The two men faced one another for a long while.

"Okay," said James.

"But your real question…"

"It doesn't matter."

Mitchell stood straighter and took on the voice of authority again.

"It *does* matter. What has you wound up about this girl? Do you like her that much, or is it just what her family's done that's making her sit in the forefront of your mind?"

James considered that question and shrugged his

shoulders.

"I don't know."

"Well, what I can tell you is that your mother had a lot to adjust to when she married me, just as Ash had a lot to adjust to when he married your sister. In a perfect world, everyone we fall in love with would be good and perfect. It isn't always like that. Sometimes we fall in love with people we don't want to. Then the choice is whether to be happy with them or be unhappy without them. That isn't an easy choice to make. Whatever you choose, only you and I know who she is…"

"Dad, I couldn't hide that," said James. "Her family's always on the news…"

"I know. It wouldn't be easy, but that's a long way off. If she has a brother who's on the run right now, she probably needs space with her family anyway. They'll be torn up by it, I'm sure. Does she have parents?"

"Yeah, I think she's got both still," James said.

"Give her space then. Let this flow through to wherever it's going to with their family and the cops. Stay away. Please. I don't want you caught up in it. Not forever - just for the moment until something comes through the news."

"I wasn't going to go chasing her anyway," James said, nodding.

Mitchell hugged his son again. He was lucky to have his kids. He knew that. They were a great bunch of people, despite what they as a family did. He was proud of them. If only Caroline could see how they all turned out…

"I'm going to have a shower," he said in an effort to get away before tears began again. "Unless you have anything else to talk about?"

"No, I'm good. Thanks, Dad."

Mitchell smiled at his son and made his way to the bathroom. There he turned on the shower and finally let the tears come.

~~~~~

James left his family home just as confused and frustrated as he had been before he went there. He shouldn't have spoken to his father. The look on Max's face had told him that as soon as Max had heard what they were talking about. It was yet another pointless thing James had done recently.

He'd been sidetracked in recent times by the planning and the aftermath of the intended theft. His part-time job had been ignored, and he hadn't even been with a woman. He needed to get himself back on track. He needed to start feeling like his normal self again.

Automatically he found himself driving down to the beach. It was something he needed to realign his thinking and get himself back on the road to normal life once more.

As he parked his car, he thought back to the last time he'd been at that particular beach. On that day, he'd seen Sassy Girl, and she'd eventually sat with him on the sand. They hadn't talked that day, but having her close to him had felt nice. For a fleeting moment, he wondered if there was any chance she was at the beach again at that moment. Looking down toward the sand, he saw no-one.

It wasn't the most tropical day, but he was warm enough as he wrapped up in his warm jacket. With the tide coming in, he had a smaller slice of sand to enjoy than normal. He didn't care about that either. He sat down on the sand and closed his eyes. As if in meditation, he absorbed the sound of the waves and the feeling of the slight breeze on his face.

At first, he forced his head to move into planning and motivational mode. He needed to get on with regular life. That meant he should go and see his boss and pick up some shifts. Working was always one great way to tune his mind out to other things. The other great way was to have a damn good shag. With that thought, he pulled out his phone and glanced through his contacts.
~~~~~

Each of the women in there was someone he enjoyed stress-free time with. They had an understanding. If the mood suited both, they both indulged. He had the same friendship with each and every name in his phone contact list. No-one ever got nasty. No-one ever got jealous. At different times his list had been longer, but a few play friends had found themselves in relationships and delivered him the same old 'we can't be friends anymore' speech. He'd never been upset by that. He'd only been happy they were happy.

Despite trying to maintain a focus on planning and refocusing, his mind wandered back to Sassy Girl. Sasha Leadbetter. He now knew her full name. It was a name he hadn't anticipated learning, following those occasions they'd run into each other.

Despite a part of him not wanting to, James kept finding himself wondering if she was alright. What was happening in her family right at that very moment? She might have one brother wanted by the law. She might have another brother who could have been shot and maybe even killed. James took a moment to imagine that situation with his own family. If there was a chance something weird happened like Regan was on the run and Max was dead, how would he be coping with that right now?

James felt a shiver run down his spine. He could still clearly remember Max lying in the hospital bed in the coma after he *had* been shot the year before. Imagining him dead was a little close to the reality of what everyone had been feeling at the time.

No matter who her family was, James was still thoughtful of Sasha. She was a girl who hardly knew how it felt to smile, let alone enjoy the pleasures of the body. She was completely different from James, and yet knowing she was from a family involved in crime somehow pulled in some kind of similarity between them. Not that she knew *his* family was in crime, of course. He hadn't mentioned anything about that, and she hadn't asked. It was a different type of crime anyway, James had to admit. The Leadbetters seemed to have been on the news an awful lot for violence or stealing. The Stonewardens were subtle and discreet. For hundreds of years, no-one had suspected them of anything they'd done. They were more than criminals. They were also *illusionists*.

Noticing the water creeping closer, James stood and flicked the sand off his jeans. He closed his eyes to the fading sun and took one final deep breath of sea air. The first thing he needed to do was get on with some regular work again. Women could wait - *all* women. It wasn't a normal thought for James Stonewarden. As a general rule, women were always on his mind and in his bed. Even he could see and feel that something was changing inside of him. He couldn't be sure, but he suspected that establishing the rapport with Sassy Girl that he had so far *definitely* had something to do with that. But what was there to do? It might be that her brother was the one who delivered the bullet into *his* brother. Had she really not known that, if it were the case?

He walked briskly along the sand and up to his car. Once inside, he turned on the heater and again sat still, watching and listening to the waves. There was nothing that could be done about *anything*, he knew. He couldn't see Sasha and ask her if she was alright. He couldn't chase the brother that he suspected had pulled the trigger that day. He wouldn't wish for her younger brother to have been shot.

All he could do was wait and let fate do its thing - whatever it was that fate actually intended.

CHAPTER 23

Stacey Leadbetter sat still for a long time in the café she was at with her husband, Mark, and her daughter, Sasha. She'd heard all that Sasha had told them about the night of the gala. She'd also heard Sasha's version of events regarding seeing David at the house and how he'd seemed at that time. To anyone passing by, they might have thought Stacey Leadbetter was calm. On the inside, however, she was shaking with an overload of emotions. Her hand was being held firmly by Mark. When she looked into his eyes, she saw pain in them that she suspected was an exact reflection of her own. Where were their two sons?

"If they were accused of anything, the cops would be here right now," Mark said in an attempt to lessen his wife's concern. "They know where we are. They know how to find us. Why would they sit and wait if they were after David?"

"We haven't been back to the house. We don't know they're not there..." Stacey said quietly. Sitting out on the edge of a public street like they were made her feel exposed and vulnerable. She didn't like it, but Mark wanted them to not be seen as hiding or looking for their sons. He wanted them to seem as if nothing were out of the ordinary.

"We aren't going back," he said. "Not yet."

"Then how are we to know when we can go home?" Stacey almost yelled at him, forgetting in the moment to be calm and discreet.

"Daisy could go," Sasha offered as a suggestion. When both of her parents looked at her, she continued. "She's not one of us. She could just do a drive-by and not go into the house. No-one knows about her and Phillip.

No-one would be looking out for her or her car."

"I think she's done enough…" Stacey began to say and then stopped herself. That was yet another piece of information that had played with her emotions.

"Ma, I only met her for a few minutes, but I saw her and Phillip together," Sasha said. "And she told us what she heard. If she didn't care about him, she would have kept quiet. When Rex was found guilty of only stealing that car, you were happy. Why would you be mad now that he wasn't put in prison?"

Mark looked at his daughter. He thought that was the longest speech he'd ever heard come out of her mouth. Not only was it long, but it was eloquent and well structured. He was curious at how much his usually-angry daughter was changing so quickly.

"Have you seen Nicky over the last couple of days?" he asked. It was completely out of context to the conversation, but he found himself quite dumbstruck by Sasha. It was almost as if she was someone he hadn't met before.

Sasha looked at her father and shook her head.

"Nah, I'm not going near her and Susan with all this going on," she said. "If they call, I'll make some excuse. I don't want to lie to them, but they deserve better than to get caught up in our crap."

Stacey blinked and looked at her daughter. She, too, was beginning to wonder what was going on with her daughter. It had been strange enough that Sasha had hugged her when she'd arrived at the café. Now she was even *sounding* like a different person.

For a moment, the boys were forgotten. For only a sliver of time, Stacey found herself distracted, and it was welcome. Then the force of not knowing where her boys were came crashing down on her again.

"Call her," she said, for the moment confusing Mark and Sasha. "Call and get Phillip's flower to do a drive-by of the house. She knows where it is. She picked him up that day they went away together," she continued and saw Mark nod in confirmation.

Sasha pulled out her phone and just sent a text to Phillip.

'Can Daisy drive past the house?' she wrote with intended conciseness.

In Daisy's apartment, Phillip read the text and immediately understood what was wanted. He turned to Daisy.

"What is it?" she asked him. He had that look on his face where he wanted to say or ask something but wasn't sure he should. "Phillip, just tell me."

"Could you drive past my family's home?"

Daisy considered for a moment. "To see who's there?"

"Not to get out and go inside. Just to drive past and casually see if anything's happening there - and maybe to see if David's black Valiant is there," Phillip said, looking distinctly uncomfortable. "Sorry, I shouldn't have…"

"Of course I will," Daisy said, cutting him off. She moved to him and kissed him. "I can do that for you and your family."

Phillip watched as she picked up her car keys and purse and then moved to him once more. He wrapped his arms around her and kissed her passionately. He felt uneasy about whether she should go anywhere near anything Leadbetter at such a time, especially the house. The unknowing about his brothers pushed him to ignore that uneasiness.

"Don't stop," he said. "Don't even slow down. Please don't bring any attention to yourself. If you think someone sees you and starts tailing you, lead them to the mall or something. This is your home and your safe place. Don't risk bringing them near here."

Daisy nodded and kissed him again softly.

"Don't worry," she said. "I'm only going for a

drive. I'll be back soon."

Phillip remained still as she walked out. He hated that she was being dragged into his family's drama so deeply and so often. He couldn't wait to marry her and get rid of the Leadbetter name forever. There was no way he wanted kids that inherited his last name.

No. Fucking. Way.

~~~~~

Daisy sat in her car. When she'd learned about Phillip's family, she'd expected things could get hairy at times. Being involved in a shooting at a charity event was still way out of the range of what she'd expected. She was in it now, though. She loved Phillip, and she wanted a family with him. Part of that had to be doing what she had to with whatever the Leadbetters did. It made her nervous, but it didn't push her to want to walk away from him. That thought did make her question her own sanity. Who in their right mind would stay involved with a man when his family was doing all that crap?

She started the engine and smiled to herself.

She would.

~~~~~

As she drove into the neighborhood where the large Leadbetter home stood, Daisy took a deep breath. Part of her wanted to stop the car and not go any closer, but she had to. Even with all that she'd known about Phillip's brother, Rex, she too wanted to know what had happened to him. Yes, he'd cornered her that night in the carpark with three friends and the intention of harming her. Yes, he'd been accused of the shooting in the supermarket. Yes, he'd been charged with stealing that car. Regardless, he was still Phillip's brother, and he was just a kid. Imagining being in Stacey's shoes and worrying about where her child was drove Daisy on to keep the car moving as normally as she could.

Once in the street she needed to be at, she could immediately see a police presence close to the

Leadbetter house.

"Holy fuck," she whispered out loud. She'd been to enough crime scenes in her work to know *that* wasn't good. As she drove past the front of the house, she could see that the front door was closed. That was good, she supposed. She expected there might be plenty in that house to have everyone charged. She couldn't be sure of that. It was only a guess. She hoped she was wrong. The thought of Phillip being charged over something in his room scared her.

Before driving fully past, she took note of the cars on the street. There were definitely a number of plainclothes cops sitting in wait. She also saw that the black Valiant Phillip had asked her to look out for wasn't there.

Without any hesitation, she continued driving. She'd found out a lot in those few seconds. There was no paranoia on anyone's part. The cops were there, and they were lying in wait for *someone* to come home.

~~~~~

Phillip waited patiently on Daisy's sofa with his head pounding in emotion overload. He was angry at *all* Leadbetters for the stupid lifestyle they believed they had to live, generation after generation. He was still in disbelief over David owning a gun, let alone going and firing it into a supermarket in the middle of the day. Rex was his impulsive, idiotic little brother, but the thought that he might be hurt or worse scared Phillip most of all. There was definitely a difference between expecting someone to die young and then realizing that it could be a reality.

On top of all that, Daisy had now been pulled into the dramas of his family. She was only on the outside, but she was now associated with his father, his mother, and his sister. He wished he'd handled so many things differently so that the present moment in time just wasn't happening.
~~~~~

Hearing her key in the apartment door, Phillip jumped up and rushed to her as she walked in. He pulled her into his arms and held her tightly.

Daisy let him. When she was honest with herself, she knew that she felt sorry for him. He was a part of a criminal family, but she still believed that inside his heart, he wasn't a criminal. He was a good man, and he was a man who did know how to feel and express his feelings.

Phillip pulled away and kissed her softly.

"Are you alright?" he asked.

"Yeah, I'm fine, but there are cops at your house," Daisy replied, nodding. "They're waiting for you guys."

"And the car?"

"It's not there," she answered. "He must have left between Sasha seeing him and the cops arriving."

Phillip turned away from her and sat on the sofa again.

"Thanks for doing that," he said quietly, regretting that he'd had to ask her to do *anything* to do with her family.

Daisy watched him and then moved to sit beside him.

"Phillip, I am going to be a part of your family…"

"No, Daisy," he said, looking at her deeply. "*I* am going to become a part of *yours*. This life isn't for you. It isn't even for me. I want to be away from it."

"You don't mean you'd walk away from your mother and father…"

"If it comes down to it and this shit doesn't stop, then yes, I really do mean it." He paused and placed his hands on either side of her face. Doing so, he remembered how green her eyes were. She had such beautiful eyes. "I want us to have a family. They won't be a part of this criminal crap."

Daisy nodded and smiled sadly. Inside she loved hearing him talk like that. Having been a lawyer even for the short time she had, she'd seen some extreme crime families … and what they did to people who tried to walk away. The thought made her shudder. She was thankful when she felt Phillip engage her lips again.

"I need to message Sasha," he said when he pulled away. He could have kept kissing her … at any other time on any other day.

~~~~~

"I don't like just sitting here out in the open like this, Mark," Stacey said to her husband.

Mark nodded.

"I know. As soon as we hear something…"

Each of them heard Sasha's phone vibrate.

"They're there," Sasha said to her father. She said nothing more. Everywhere there were ears. Her father would know she was saying that the cops were at their house. His nod confirmed his understanding.

"We can't just never go home," Stacey said quietly. "Isn't it better we go home and engage them? Distract them?"

Mark looked at his wife. She'd seen so many things through their life together, but she still sometimes amazed him at her simplistic view of things. Her answer wasn't easy, but he didn't think it really mattered where they did or didn't go. He may as well make things easier for her. He nodded.

"We can go home."

"No!" Sasha said with strength. "Why don't we go and visit Dais…"

"No," Mark said forcefully in response.

Stacey looked at her daughter.

"I'm not going to lie," she said. "It will take me a while to get used to what that girl does for a living and the fact that she was on Rex's case. But if she loves Phillip, we aren't going to drag ourselves full-on into her life. Your brother is long overdue for finding happiness. I appreciate her help in what she just did, but we aren't
~~~~~

going to ask anything else of her."

Sasha started to object but decided to keep quiet. She looked down at her hands. Her becoming deflated was visible to both of her parents.

"Where have you been staying?" Mark asked her, the question only appearing in his mind at that moment.

Sasha looked up and wondered how much she should divulge about the pretty boy she'd stayed with. She'd told her parents that she'd gone home and seen David there that very morning. She'd told them what had happened in the gala building and that she'd left when she heard gunshots. The entire section of time in between, she'd left out of the conversation.

"Answer my question, Sasha," she heard her father say.

"I left … I left the gala with a guy I'd met a while ago," she said. "He let me crash at his place."

"Can you go back there and stay tonight?"

Sasha felt tears come on. She *was* supposed to be staying there that night. That was *until* she'd learned who his brother was, and he'd found out what *her* brother might have done.

"No."

"Did he hurt you?" Stacey asked, nervous. The equation of Sasha + boy hadn't even crossed her mind as any kind of likelihood. As she thought about how much she'd been watching her daughter change, she found herself wondering about who he was to have been able to affect Sasha like he appeared to have done.

Sasha shook her head. "No."

"Is there more that you haven't told us?" Mark asked. He felt dread inside. He didn't particularly want to hear what was coming but felt he had to.

Sasha took a deep breath.

"I didn't know until today, but he is the brother of the guy who was shot in the supermarket months ago."

Mark and Stacey exchanged looks of confusion.

"Let me see if I have this right," Mark continued. "You *know* the family of the boy who was shot that day?"

"No," Sasha replied, shaking her head. "I saw this guy around town a few times. We didn't talk about things like that. We just said hi now and then."

"Well, how do you know he's that guy's brother?" Stacey asked.

"He … today we saw the news. He knew straight away that I was a Leadbetter. He recognized the name from Rex being charged and put two and two together. That's all."

Mark rested his head on his hand and rubbed his eyes. Everything was just so fucking *messy*. When he raised his head again, he looked at his daughter and saw her eyes watering. After so many years of only seeing her angry, he found himself wanting to seize the moment of her looking so vulnerable. He would have preferred that she go elsewhere when he and Stacey went home and faced whatever was waiting there but what was the point of that? Eventually, everything they'd ever done was going to catch up to them.

He stood and held out his hand to his daughter. Looking up at him, Sasha realized she'd never actually hugged her father. She was in her twenties, but she could not remember one time she'd walked into his arms. Hell, apart from pretty boy, she'd never really walked into *anyone's* arms.

Mark watched as Sasha stood and walked to him. Tentatively but surely, she allowed him to wrap his arms around her. It was something that should have been natural for a parent to feel by the time his kids were adults. The lack of having had any contact like it with Sasha throughout her whole life made Mark even more emotional. He pulled her close and held her tight. No matter what happened to any of them after that moment, he was going to be remembering the moment his always-angry daughter finally let him hug her, for the rest of his life.

He pulled away reluctantly but looked at his wife.

"Let's go home," he said quietly.

Stacey looked at him, smiled sadly and stood, nodding. No matter what was about to happen, it was probably long overdue.

~~~~~

Approaching their home, Mark was wary but saw no crowds of cops at all. As the three of them ventured up their path toward the front door, he finally heard a voice.

"Mr and Mrs Leadbetter. We need to talk."

Mark and Stacey turned around and focused on the face behind the voice. It was the same detective who had hauled Mark into the station a short time earlier. He looked like he expected opposition to his request. Mark only nodded and continued to put the key in the door.

"Sasha, go to your room, please," Stacey said to her daughter. She was grateful when Sasha only nodded and walked away without any argument.

"Come into my office," Mark said, guiding his wife and the detective further down the hallway.

"I have come to deliver news of your son," the detective said. Neither Mark nor Stacey said anything. They didn't know which son news was coming about, but they expected the worst. "Rex..." he started to say.

Stacey was surprised to see a sliver of emotion in the man's eyes. She wondered if he was a parent, imagining being told what he was going to tell her.

"Your son Rex was shot at the gala event. He didn't survive."

Stacey heard the words but felt her head go blank. Then the fog started to clear.

"You killed my son? You killed my baby boy?"

The detective looked at her.

"When he pulled out a gun and fired into the
~~~~~

crowd, he was instantly ... taken down."

Mark looked with a blend of surprise and no surprise. In his heart, he'd suspected Rex was the other shooter.

"Rex didn't own a gun, Detective," he said.

"He had with him a gun that he used that night, and ballistics has shown that it's the same gun that shot a young man in the supermarket shooting last year."

Mark thought quickly. He and Stacey had just lost one son. They knew - suspected - that Rex wasn't the one who had used the gun in the supermarket at all, but the cops - they didn't seem to know that at all. To Mark's eyes, it wasn't even occurring to them.

"What happens now?" he asked. He knew he should be showing grief for losing his son. That would come later. For the moment, he had another son out in the world somewhere, and from Sasha's words, David might not be in sound mind. Finding him had to also be a priority for Mark.

"We will need you to come to the morgue to complete a formal identification of ... your son," the detective said.

Stacey finally broke down, crumbling to the floor. Her baby boy was dead. They'd thought that might be the case, but now it had been confirmed. He'd been a ratbag of a kid all his life, but he was still one of her babies. He'd only done what he'd been raised to do. It was her fault. She should have stood up to Mark. She should have stood up to everything about being a part of the 'great' Leadbetter clan.

Mark moved down and put his arms around her. He knew it wasn't yet really sinking in, what had happened to Rex and the fact that he'd never see him again. At that moment, it was seeing Stacey in so much pain that drove on tears of his own.

"I don't understand any of this," Mark said through his tears. "Why would he shoot at people? How do we know you're telling the truth in that?"

The detective maintained calm as he spoke.

"There's security camera footage that shows him pulling out the gun and firing it first, but there will be an official inquiry into his death."

At the word, a further loud sob came from Stacey.

"He shouldn't *be* dead! You could have arrested him if he did what you say he did. You could have put him in jail. You could have done anything else. Why did you kill my baby?"

The detective stood. He'd met Rex Leadbetter in previous times and knew he was just a kid. Although 21, he had a less mature outlook and nature. He was always going to be a kid that got in trouble with the law, but even the detective had one question on his mind - had Rex Leadbetter really deserved to be killed that night?

"Please come to the morgue when you are ready," the detective said and then quietly left the room and left the house.

Mark remained kneeling on the floor beside his wife, holding her as she sobbed. He had released some tears, but the rest would have to come later. There were things to be done. The other kids would have to be told. A funeral would have to be arranged. The body would have to be identified. At that, Mark let out a sob. That was what his youngest son was now - just a body, lying in a morgue, waiting for someone to confirm he was who they thought he was.

Stacey didn't move for a long time. She'd always expected Rex could leave them at any time due to his boisterous and impatient nature but being told the news was still too much to bear. She felt paralyzed at the knowledge. Then the guilt began. She was the one who had told Mark to step down from being head of the Leadbetter family. She was the one who had forced a violent and unfeeling man like Pete Leadbetter to the head and into the place of planning that stupid robbery.

She could have prevented all of it from happening if only she'd supported Mark and not questioned how he would handle the job. It was all on her. Her son was dead because of her. Every day for the rest of her life, she would live with the knowledge that she had effectively killed her own son.

Mark could tell that Stacey's head was running away on her, and not in a good way - not that there *could* be a good way with the news they'd just received.

"What's happened?" they both heard Sasha ask from the doorway.

Seeing her mother in a heap on the floor and her father holding her as best he could, Sasha knew in her heart what news had just been delivered. She rushed forward and put her arms around both of her parents, not taking even a moment to consider the action. She'd never done it before, but she felt she had to do it. For that moment, their grief was more important than hers.

She discretely looked at her father and moved her lips in question.

"Rex?" she asked and saw him nod at her. "Dead?" She saw him nod again.

Sasha held her mother more tightly. It had been weird hearing that Pete had been killed. He had been a member of her family, but she'd hardly known him. But Rex? Her little brother? How was that even possible? She'd never see him again? They'd never been close, but still, she felt tears come to her eyes. She'd suspected he might have been one of the gunmen that night. As she realized she hadn't truly believed it, there was no denying what had happened. Now there was proof. Rex had gone in there with a gun.

"We have to find David," Mark said. It felt like the wrong time to be thinking about anyone other than Rex, but he didn't want David feeling alone, and he sure as hell didn't want him doing anything that could result in the same fate as his brother.

Sasha nodded and pulled away.

"How?" she asked. "He's probably hidden the car by now, right? He wouldn't drive it when the cops know that's his car…"

Stacey heard the conversation happening over the top of her head and pulled herself together. One son was dead. She couldn't let the other be caught or killed too.

"His girlfriend. Do you know where she lives?" Stacey asked Sasha.

Sasha shook her head.

"No. I don't know anything about her. He's never introduced her to us, but, Ma, he wouldn't go there surely. He'd be afraid of leading cops to her door."

The three of them slowly stood up.

"I need Greg and Rhett," Mark said, pulling out his phone.

"They've gone away," Sasha said, remembering the last phone call she'd received from Greg.

"What?"

"Greg told me to tell you he's headed away somewhere, and he'll be in touch."

Mark heard the words, but it took him a few minutes to comprehend them.

"FUCK!!" he yelled. He couldn't believe it. Right when he needed his cousin and his closest friend, both had disappeared.

Stacey realigned her thinking in her head. She couldn't focus on Rex right at that moment. She had to do what she could for her other son.

"Is he on the run, do you think?" she asked. "If he knows Rex was shot then the gun will be with the cops. It might not lead back to him at all."

"I don't think he knows, Ma," Sasha said. "When I saw him, he was looking for the gun here in the house. If he saw Rex use a gun, he must have been uncertain if it was his."

Stacey shook her head.

"None of this makes any sense," she said. "Why did he use a gun? Why did *any* of them even *have* guns? Was that the plan all along? To go in there and just shoot at people?"

Mark had been wondering the same thing. If Pete Leadbetter hadn't already been killed, Mark believed that he might have gone to kill him himself. The guy had always been psycho and murderous. Mark knew he should never have stood aside and let his cousin Pete step up and be in charge.

"Should I tell Phillip to come home?" Sasha asked quietly. "And Anya?"

Stacey let out a long, deep sigh. Since returning to town, she hadn't even given her youngest child one single thought.

"Yes, please," she said wearily as she walked into the kitchen and sat at the large dining table.

Sasha pulled out her phone and sent a message to Phillip. She moved toward her mother and sat beside her, putting her arm around her shoulder in an attempt of support.

"I've told Phillip to come, and to pick Anya up on the way."

"Good," Stacey said, nodding. "He's the best support for her right now."

~~~~~

Stacey and Mark later stood and looked at the three children who were at the table.

"Your brother..." Mark started to say before beginning to break down. He held his chin up and started again. "Your brother - Rex - was ... shot ... at the gallery shooting the other night."

Phillip hung his head low. He had so much wanted that to not be the case.

"Is he...?"

"Yes, Rex is dead," Stacey pushed out of her mouth. Her sight was settled on Anya as she said it. Rex
~~~~~

and Anya hadn't been close - none of her kids were particularly close except for her oldest and youngest - but Anya was the one who had yet to live through any pain.

Anya heard the news, stood, and went to pull her mother into a hug. Although only 15, Anya was savvy enough to know what was going on at any time with any person in her home. She watched people, and she understood them. The news wasn't a surprise, but it was sad. It was all the sadder with how she knew it was going to affect their mother.

"A cop was here when we came home. Someone has to go and identify the b… *him*," Mark said, not wanting Stacey to have to do it.

"I'll go," Phillip said. He'd never seen a dead body before, but he sure as hell didn't want his mother going and seeing Rex like that. "I can go now…" he said, standing.

When he looked at his mother, he saw her nod and begin to cry. The sight caused his own eyes to water.

"What about David? Where's he?" he asked before he walked out.

"We don't know. Do you know where he'd go?" Mark asked him.

"Not off the top of my head, but I'll drive around and see if I can see him anywhere he used to hang out."

Phillip turned and went to his family one more time before leaving. He held his mother and father tightly and then kissed Anya on the top of her head before finally walking out of his family home.

~~~~~

Phillip drove around in a blur. He had to pull over to find where the morgue was. Once he had that direction, he moved forward with going to see his dead brother. He didn't particularly want to do it, but it had to be done, and his mother shouldn't have to see Rex in that state.
~~~~~

Weaving his way through corridors according to the signs and directions by staff, he finally stood before a body that lay with a sheet over it. He hated being in the room. The coldness of it made him feel like he was in the middle of a horror movie where evil spirits were going to appear before him.

The procedure was followed. The sheet was pulled back. When it was, Phillip had to look for a long time. The face of the person lying before him was definitely *like* Rex, and yet ... wasn't. What lay before him was like a soulless husk of the brother who'd constantly been in trouble since he was a young kid. Phillip looked and looked at him but found himself emotionless. He felt numb. Surely that wasn't the way he *should* feel - but he did.

"Could I have some time with him alone?" he asked the morgue attendant, who nodded and moved into the office next door.

Phillip changed where he stood, looking from one angle and then another. He thought back to the day he'd gone with Rex to the storage unit. Surely there must have been some way he could have handled anything differently that would have had a flow-on effect and stopped his brother from now being as he was. In his heart, he knew it was pointless to go over anything from the past. Rex was dead. Phillip was looking at undeniable proof of that. There was no way to go back and change anything in the hope that the outcome would be different.

He wondered briefly how his mother really would feel, seeing Rex like that. In some ways, he looked more at peace than he ever had. For a long while, Phillip just looked and looked. It was Rex, but in many ways, it wasn't.

Once the attendant returned, Phillip signed the documentation and slowly left. Looking back into the room, he saw the sheet raised over Rex's face once more.

That would be the very last time he saw his brother.

Finally, as he walked away with that thought in his mind, the tears came.

CHAPTER 24

After what seemed like an endless day, Sasha finally lay her head on her pillow as she climbed into the warmth of her bed. Her mind was all over the place but what hit her hardest was that her wayward younger brother would never walk into their home again. She'd never again see his face with its perpetual sneer. She'd never again hear of his antics that were at least one step too far in the eyes of their parents. She'd never again see … him.

Turning to one side and pulling her knees up toward her chest, she let tears come. An entire clump of time had resulted in her feeling the heaviness that was her life now. Everything had been looking so good with Nicky having come into her life and making her feel not only accepted but even a little liked and important. Then things had turned.

She took a moment to think back over the entire weekend. Her role at the gala event had been minimal, and even that had gone to crap. She knew she was lucky to have been on the outskirts of whatever had gone down. She knew she was fortunate to have been able to get out of there without being caught up in anything.

She also knew who was to thank for that - that guy - James. He had helped her when she had needed it. He had provided her with a sanctuary and a place of safety when she didn't know where else to turn. He had let her cry and not once told her to harden up. And when she'd presented her body to him, he had honorably dressed her and not taken advantage.

She tried to remember what she could about the guy who had been shot - James's brother. Nothing came to mind. The supermarket shooting was something her family had been accused of but then dismissed from. She hadn't taken any notice of who had been injured because it wasn't of any importance to her. Now she wished she'd actually listened to a news broadcast. Suddenly she found herself wanting to know more about that guy who'd been in the wrong place at the wrong time. She couldn't remember the names of the brothers who had been at the hospital she'd gone to with James. Even if she could, she didn't know which one was the one who'd been shot. Suddenly she wanted to know more about him because it might have been her own brother who had pulled the trigger.

She also wanted to know about him because he was the brother of the guy who'd been chipping away at her heart and earning her trust. That was something that very few people in her life ever had been able to.

~~~~~

Across town, James Stonewarden tossed and turned. Since returning to his apartment after visiting his father and then taking some time to do serious thinking on the beach, he had fallen into a daze. He'd cleared his mind long enough to call his boss and secure some shifts in the weeks ahead, but other than that, the entire day was just one long blur.

Of all that had happened throughout the day, the thing that most wanted to occupy his mind was the conversation he'd had with Sassy Girl on the beach when they'd had lunch. She was afraid of sex. That intrigued him and made him angry on her behalf. Because some asshole had treated her badly, she was now under the impression that sex was just some horrific thing that was done to women. James had never met any woman who felt that way. It still gnawed at him.

He really wanted to be angry with her and her family. The anger toward her brother would still be there if he was indeed the one who pulled the trigger. Whether it had been intentional or not to hurt anyone, using a gun and shooting into a supermarket in the middle of the day
~~~~~

was just insane. In reality, how could he have *not* intended to shoot people?

But then there was Sasha. Should she be ostracized because of what her brother did? James couldn't help but feel sorry for her. She'd been so angry the first few times he'd seen her. Now he'd learned how badly she'd been treated by some asshole. It was hard to maintain the level of hatred James had felt when he'd first seen the news and realized she was part of that same family.

The more he thought about her, the more he became concerned for her. Was she alright? Was she safe? Had she made it somewhere that she could feel secure? Had she had *anyone* who she could lean on for support?

His questions and thoughts plagued him long into the night. He willed his mind to turn off, but it didn't - not for a very long time.

CHAPTER 25

Despite the utter craziness that was happening in the Leadbetter home, Sasha stuck to her promise of spending time with little Nicky. She was just a kid. She didn't deserve to be caught up in anything going on with Sasha's family. She also didn't deserve or need to feel like someone special to her had abandoned her. Sasha knew exactly how that felt. She wouldn't do it to Nicky.

"What are we doing today?" the ten-year-old asked as the two of them began to walk.

Sasha looked at Nicky and smiled as best she could.

"I don't know, Nicky-kid," she said. "What do you feel like doing? We could … go get ice cream at the mall … or … go to the beach … or go see a movie…"

"Movie! And then beach?"

Sasha laughed and nodded.

"Movie and then beach it is then."

The two of them walked a distance in silence.

"Are you okay, Sasha?" Nicky asked, sensing a difference in her new friend.

"Yeah, I'm good," Sasha replied. "I have some grown-up stuff going on, but I'm not going to think about that today. Today is *our* day, right?!"

Nicky nodded and smiled but knew something was off. Grown-ups never said what they meant, but Sasha was usually upfront. Nicky could overlook the aura of sadness coming off Sasha if that was what Sasha seemed to need.

<p style="text-align:center">~~~~~</p>

Seeing a movie had been a great choice. For over an hour, Sasha found her mind tuned out to everything real as she indulged in laughing like the child beside her.

It felt like stress was released, and everything was realigned again. It wasn't. Life was still crap, but for a short while, it felt like she'd been allowed to just take a little holiday in her thoughts.

"Did you like that?" she asked Nicky as they left the cinema.

"Yes, it was funny. You laughed *heaps*," Nicky said, smiling up at Sasha, who smiled in return.

"I sure did. That was a great idea, Nicky-kid. Now, do you still want to go to the beach for a while before your mum picks you up?"

The nod and smile she received said it all.

~~~~~

James Stonewarden had been thinking about Sasha Leadbetter for too long. He needed to find her and talk to her. Each day he'd gone to the same spot near the beach in case she'd been there, but so far, he hadn't been lucky to see her.

On the news, he'd heard of her brother's death. Despite that in some way being associated with what had happened with Max, James's heart was heavy with a longing to make sure Sasha was alright. She'd made an impact on him. He couldn't walk away completely without at least checking how she was.

Resigned that she wasn't going to turn up anywhere he might happen to be, he drew in a deep breath and pulled up outside her family home. The action made him nervous, but hearing she was okay would outweigh any discomfort.

On the front porch, he could see a man and a woman sitting on a seat swing. Even from the distance he was at, he could feel their misery. He almost restarted the engine to drive away. Instead, he climbed out and began to walk up the path.

With two sets of eyes on him, he gulped. Although he and his family were criminals in a way, he knew he was at the home of a completely different type
~~~~~

of criminal. He felt justified in being just a little fearful of approaching the people he could see.

"Is Sasha here?" he forced himself to ask as he neared the porch.

Mark and Stacey both assessed the guy in front of them. He was clean cut with an almost austere look about him. Perfectly dressed and groomed, both were surprised to the point of almost being speechless.

"Who wants to know?" Mark asked, curious about such a clean pretty-boy wanting to see his angry daughter.

"Well, *I* do," James said, knowing it was a bit cheeky but not stopping the quip before it escaped his mouth.

Mark couldn't help but smile. He'd felt overwhelmed with grief for a week. It didn't feel bad to smile at the smart-mouthed young man before him. Then he considered Sasha's version of events from the gala weekend.

"You were at the gala and took her away."

"I did," James replied, nodding.

"You know we lost our son that night," Mark continued.

James stood still and nodded again.

"Yes," he said. "I am very sorry for your loss."

Mark was pretty sure the guy in front of him was the one who had reached out and helped Sasha. To clarify, he dared to ask the question he most wanted answered.

"Your brother was the one who was shot in the supermarket?"

"Yes," James replied quietly. "Please, is Sasha here? I just want to see how she is."

Stacey listened to the entire conversation and was surprised. Before her was the brother of the guy that one of her own sons might have shot. That was still uncertain, but even to her, it looked likely. How could the young guy before her come to their house, knowing that?

"Please don't hurt my daughter," she said out loud unintentionally. Immediately she saw the young man focus on her with a serious look on his face.

"I have no intention of hurting her," James said. "Look, can you tell me where to find her? I've been hoping to talk to her all week."

"She's with a young girl she spends time with…"

James nodded. "Nicky."

"Yes. They usually head down to the beach playground or the mall."

"Thanks," James said and turned to leave. Before he reached the sidewalk, he turned to them again. "Your daughter is more vulnerable than she lets on, but I think she's much stronger than you might give her credit for."

With that, he jumped in his car and drove toward the beach. It hadn't been the easiest interaction, but he didn't care. He just hoped he could find Sasha.

~~~~~

"I don't even know what to say about that," Mark said to Stacey after the car was out of sight. "He isn't at all what I'd pictured when she said he'd helped her."

Stacey felt a little dumbstruck.

"I've always worried that Sasha would never have anyone outside of family who could care for her," she said. "I've been wrong in that, haven't I?"

"I think we both have," Mark said as he pulled his wife closer and kissed her. They were in a dark place, but something about the knowledge that their daughter might have a young man on her tail provided a sliver of sunlight for both of them.

~~~~~

As soon as Sasha and Nicky arrived at the beach, Nicky ran straight to the playground.

"Will you push me on the swing, Sasha?" she asked and immediately received a smile and nod.

"Sure thing. Hop on and let me help you reach for the sky, Nicky-kid."

The two of them got into the swing fun. Hearing Nicky giggling was always good for making Sasha smile. For a while, she forgot everything else and let herself just indulge in the freedom and joy that came from being with her young friend. Then she heard Nicky speak.

"He's coming."

"Who?" Sasha asked.

"You know. *That* guy."

Sasha heard the description and knew exactly who Nicky meant. Instantly she felt a panic flow over her. She didn't want any confrontation in front of Nicky. She didn't want Nicky to know about anything that had been happening in her family. She resumed her pushing of Nicky on the swing and breathed deeply, hoping James wouldn't see them and, instead, would walk right past, down to the sand.

~~~~~

James noticed the two of them and halted in his steps. He didn't have to say hello. Maybe he *shouldn't* say hello. They didn't look like they'd seen him. He could just turn and get back in his car....

No, he didn't want to do that. He wanted to talk to her, but ... 'Fuck!' he screamed in his head. He didn't want to turn away from her. He'd been thinking about her all week, especially after hearing weird things on the news about her family.

He turned away. Then he turned back. He could see the kid with her, so they wouldn't be able to really talk anyway, and he had no desire to stress her out any more than she likely was. He also didn't want her to feel like he no longer wanted to know her. She obviously already had enough crap in her life, and he'd suspected by things she'd said to him that she sometimes felt abandoned by people around her. He didn't want to
~~~~~

contribute to that.

He began to walk toward the playground.

~~~~~

Through the corner of her eye, Sasha could see him moving toward her. She cursed inside her head and resolved to take whatever was coming. What she wished for most of all was that he didn't abuse her in front of Nicky. That was more than Sasha thought she could take. Hurt her, yes, but not in front of the kid.

When he was close, she could feel his hesitation. His walking speed slowed the nearer he got. As the gap closed to only a few feet, he stopped. Sasha turned and looked at him without stopping pushing Nicky on the swing.

James could see uncertainty in Sasha's eyes, along with a healthy mix of fear. He hated seeing that. It seemed like he'd gained a little bit of trust until that last moment he'd seen her, and had since lost all of it again.

He took the final step forward.

"Hey, you know her name yet?" he and Sasha both heard Nicky yell out. It was enough for both adults to realign focus and put on a smile.

"Hey, Nicky. Yeah, I finally do know Sasparilla's name," James said, forcing a grin onto his face. Instantly he heard a small giggle come from the kid. It helped relax him before he turned to face Sasha. Her hands were actively pushing the swing each time it came back to her, but other than that she appeared frozen. "Can we talk?" he asked her. Immediately he saw her look at Nicky's back with a look of frustration. "Not now. I mean later." He watched her face, but she said nothing. "Okay, just tell me you're okay, please."

Sasha was surprised by the desperation in his voice. She forced herself to nod and reply.

"I'm okay," she said quietly.

James lowered his voice and leaned in closer to her.
~~~~~

"Are you safe?"

In response, he saw another nod. That was enough. He wanted to talk to her, but knowing she was safe and okay was a start. If that was as much as she was willing to give him, that was acceptable.

"Okay," he said quietly and prepared to walk away. "Don't go hitting and breaking the sun, Nicky!" he called out, purposely putting himself in her view and smiling at her. His words were received with another little giggle.

"James," he heard Sasha say loudly. When he turned, she was still pushing the swing, but she was watching him intensely. "Please don't leave."

He walked up to her and looked into her eyes. He'd never liked women needing too much from him, but the need in her eyes he wanted to confront and take care of.

"I'll go and do some thinking down on the sand. I'm within reach," he said quietly and saw her nod in understanding and relief.

Sasha watched him walk away and felt a calm come over her. She didn't know what he wanted from her. Hell, she didn't even know what she wanted from *him*. But once again, when she felt she needed someone, he was there. Despite the hurt her family might have delivered to his, he still wanted to see her and talk to her. She wasn't going to just walk away from that.

~~~~~

Down on the sand, James felt his nervousness heighten. The anger he'd felt at Sasha and her family had dissipated and then disappeared. As it had worn away, what had remained was only concern for her. He'd gone to the beach every afternoon for the past week in the hope that he'd see her. He hoped she would come down and talk to him, but he accepted there was a chance she wouldn't. She hadn't said what was happening with Nicky. Perhaps there wasn't going to be any alone time
~~~~~

today anyway. He resolved to just wait and see what happened.

~~~~~

"Hey," Sasha heard Nicky's mother, Susan, call out as she approached. Sasha was sitting on a seat, watching Nicky on the climbing frame and slide. "How are you going?"

Sasha saw Susan sit beside her and smiled.

"I'm doing okay. How are you?"

"I'm good. Thanks for still spending this time with her, Sasha. I know your family is grieving right now."

Sasha felt tears threaten but gulped them down.

"Yeah, but other things are important too," she said. "Nicky's real important. She shouldn't suffer because of our sadness."

Susan looked at the young woman. Really, Sasha Leadbetter was extraordinary in so many ways. It was sad that it had taken so many years for her to be noticed by people for the goodness inside of her.

"You're a good person," Susan said. "I feel fortunate to have had you cross our paths that night."

"Me? Good? Thank you, but there's no good in me."

"I think you're wrong in that," Susan replied softly but didn't receive any reply.

Nicky came running over and greeted her mother with a large smile and hug. Once again, Sasha wondered why she'd never received anything like that as a child. Her mother had never been mean, but why hadn't she ever hugged them as kids? The two of them were sharing hugs now, with all that had been happening lately. It was nice. Why hadn't Sasha and her siblings been *raised* with those hugs?

"Are you coming to have dinner with us?" Nicky asked her, breaking her out of her thoughts. Immediately Sasha felt like she was going to have to let Nicky down. She wanted to talk to James. She didn't want to hurt
~~~~~

Nicky in the process.

"Not today, Nicky," Susan interrupted, to Sasha's relief. "You and I have to go to Grandma's place for dinner. She needs some company right now."

Nicky looked sad, but Sasha smiled at her.

"Next week?" she suggested and instantly received a great grin.

"Yes! Pizza!" Nicky said, making Sasha laugh and nod.

"Pizza for dinner next week. That sounds awesome."

Sasha watched as the two of them stood and walked off. She waited till their car had driven away before she looked down the beach. She could see James sitting as he had before, looking out over the ocean. She still didn't know what she wanted there but she was at least sure that she did like having him around.

~~~~~

James heard and felt her approach and sit down noticeably closer to him than she had done previously. When he turned to look at her, he could see the seriousness on her face.

"How are you holding up with all that's happening?" he asked her gently. He was still afraid of saying or asking the wrong thing and her bolting or pulling out that beloved knife on him.

"I'm doing okay," Sasha replied quietly.

"I saw the news. I'm sorry about your brother," he said. Instantly he saw tears begin in her eyes. He extended his arm out in invitation. He was glad when she moved closer and huddled against him, letting his arm rest around her and hold her. "How's your family doing?"

"It's hard. I think my mother's taking it hardest. Rex wasn't … I dunno … he was reckless and always in trouble, but he was still my brother." She paused and assembled words in her head before speaking further. "I
~~~~~

guess you felt the same when your brother was shot."

"For a while, it was uncertain if Max would survive, but he did pull through, and he's fine now, so it's not anywhere near what you must be feeling. The only person who I've known who's died was my mum. I don't think even that would be the same as losing one of my brothers."

"I hate the thought of losing my mother. We've never been close, but I know she's there. I don't know what I'd do if..." James heard her words tail off. He pulled her closer. "Did you come here to talk to me?" she asked, pulling away and looking at him.

"Yeah," James said, nodding. "I've been coming here each day this week, hoping to see you."

"Why? My brother hurt yours."

"Maybe he did, and I *was* angry at your family about that. All I've been thinking about lately, though, is you. I needed to know you were alright and I didn't know how to contact you other than turn up at your house. I've just come from there."

"You went to my house?" Sasha asked in disbelief. "Why would you *do* that?"

"Because, like I just said, I was worried about you, and I wanted to make sure you're okay."

"Why?"

James looked at her with a mixture of sadness and fear. He was sad for her living the life that she had. He was fearful of saying the wrong thing and losing her completely.

"Because I care about you," he said softly as he watched her face. As soon as he saw her lips form to ask the same question again, he smiled and cut her off. "And before you ask *why*, I don't know. You've crept up on me somehow and knocked me over. All I know is that trying to be angry at you for whatever your family might or might not have done just hasn't been working. I've been far more worried about you than feeling angry about anything else."

Sasha closed her eyes as she rested her head on his shoulder. Feeling his arm around her was nice. She liked it. She didn't want to fight that.

For a long time, they sat in silence.

"I still don't want to have sex," she said quietly, making him laugh out loud.

"Sassy Girl, sex has not been on my mind for a long while! You're safe with me in that regard, as you well know with that towel-drop trick you pulled. Don't you worry about me in that regard."

"You don't want to change how I feel about sex?" she dared to ask.

James looked at her and moved so that she had to look at him.

"I do, actually, but not for me - for *you*. Thinking about you being so closed off to something so nice fucks me off no end," he said. "I hope that someday you change your mind and give someone a chance to show you it can be different."

"You mean you?"

"No, I mean *someone*. Whether it's someone soon or someone later on … just be open to the idea that it isn't always bad and horrible. That's the least that I hope for, for you."

Sasha pondered. It was nice having such a conversation with him. He opened her eyes up to other ways of seeing things.

"What do you like about it so much?" she asked and could see his face turn thoughtful.

"Hmm, that is a very good question," James said. "Well, I suppose it's connecting with someone in a way that you are … fully engulfed in them? I dunno. There's the physical pleasure of touch, but it's also like being encased in a tight bubble with one person, and neither of you have any other distractions. For the duration, it feels like that person wants to be nowhere else and doing nothing else except just being with you. And while you're feeling that way, you know that they are too, so yeah, it's pretty good. I think so, anyway."

"Touch doesn't feel good, though," Sasha said quietly.

James pulled right away from her and turned so that he was sitting cross-legged, facing her full-on.

"I was just touching you when I had my arm around your shoulder."

"That's different…" Sasha began to argue.

"Is it? How?"

"Because…" she started to say. "Because there's clothing between your arm and my shoulder."

"Alright," James said, holding out one hand with his palm up. "You've held my hand before."

Sasha nodded. When she sensed he meant for her to place her hand in his again, she did so. She watched as his fingers moved lightly over her palm and the back of her hand. Neither said anything.

As she watched their hands move across each other, James watched her face. She was such an intriguing person in herself. After a long while, he saw her raise her eyes to his.

"Is it painful?" he asked her.

She shook her head. "No."

"Is it unpleasant?" he asked and received the same response. "Is it *pleasant*?"

Sasha moved her fingers over his skin. They were light and gentle with each other. She liked the firmness of his hand. She knew she'd liked holding it and the strength it had given her when they'd been in the hospital with his sister.

"Yes," she acknowledged.

James was pleased with her response but didn't react. He said nothing, and he did nothing. He would hold his hand out for as long as she wanted. The look on her face as she kept exploring the simple touch of her hand against his was incredible.

"It's my brother's funeral tomorrow," she said, alarming James with her change of subject. "Would you … could you…" she started to ask but then found she couldn't.

"Do you want me to come?" he asked quietly. When he looked into her eyes, he saw tears forming as she nodded. "I can do that."

"I know he stole your brother's car and…" she started to say as sobbing began.

James moved closer to her and put his arms around her.

"I'll be there for you." He held her for a long time as she wept. When she stopped and pulled away, he looked into her eyes. "What time and where?"

Sasha shrugged. She didn't even know.

"I'll have to ask. Sorry, I don't even…"

"How about I drive you home, and you can get me the details then," he suggested.

Although not sure she wanted him to come home with her, Sasha nodded. He'd already met her parents apparently, according to what he'd said earlier. There was no-one else that lived at home now with Rex gone and David's whereabouts unknown. From now on, it would only be her, her parents, and Anya.

After the two of them stood, James held out his arms to her. Once again, she walked into them but didn't hug him back. He was okay with that. It was enough that she let him touch her even though she still believed she hated touch.

"Did my parents give you a hard time when you went there?" she asked, trying to lighten the mood as they walked toward the car park.

"No," James replied. "Your dad asked me specific questions, which I answered honestly."

"What questions?"

"Sasha, your mum and dad know it was my

brother that was shot. Did you tell them that?"

"Yeah. I was trying to not talk about you, but my father asked *me* specific questions too."

James laughed softly.

"Yeah, parents are annoying like that."

~~~~~

When they arrived at the Leadbetter house, James jumped out of the car and opened the door for her. Mark and Stacey were still sitting on the swing seat with their arms around each other. They looked unhappy but comfortable. They reminded James of his sister, Charlie, and her husband, Ash. He still wasn't sure about the whole rest-of-your-life thing as far as love went, but when he saw couples like that, he did question what he was really afraid of.

James let Sasha set the scene. He was surprised when she reached out to invite him to put his hand in hers, but he happily obliged. Together they approached her parents.

"I take it you've already met James," she said quietly.

Although surprised ... no, *stunned* ... at the sight of their daughter holding hands with a man, Stacey quickly got herself together.

"Well, we haven't been introduced, Sasha, but he sure did want to find you earlier."

Sasha felt her face blush. The sight made Mark smile on the inside. He'd been thinking Nicky was the sole reason his daughter was changing. Now he wondered if that was the case at all.

"I'd like James to come to Rex's funeral with me tomorrow," Sasha said quietly, looking from one parent to the other. Their faces showed nothing. They said nothing. "Please."

Mark looked over James again. It was something else, wanting to be close to the Leadbetter family when they had caused grief in his own family. He hoped like
~~~~~

hell the kid in front of him wasn't looking to use and hurt Sasha. Mark truly believed that if any of his remaining kids were hurt in any way, he really wouldn't be able to take it.

"Of course it's okay, Sasha," he heard Stacey say as she squeezed his hand. It was her silent signal to either be supportive or shut the hell up. "James, you are welcome."

Sasha breathed out a sigh of relief that was heard by all. James asked for and was granted the information he needed and then said his goodbyes. Before he climbed into his car, Sasha came to him one more time and nudged against him, encouraging him to put his arms around her.

"I'll see you tomorrow," he said quietly as she pulled away from him and returned to the footpath.

~~~~~

From where they sat, Mark and Stacey both watched the entire interaction. Their daughter allowed the guy to put his arms around her. More than that, she looked like she really *wanted* him to. Of all the surprising and unexpected things that had happened in their family in recent months, *that* might have been the most surprising of all.

"I know it's weird, but he's been there for me when I've needed someone," Sasha said when she returned to the porch.

Stacey stood and moved to hug her daughter.

"Then don't be afraid to lean on him however you need to."

They pulled apart, and Sasha moved into the house, leaving Mark and Stacey alone on the porch again. Inside both of them was extreme sorrow and guilt about so many things. They had to keep going, though. They still had two daughters living in the house with them. That was something to latch onto and hold as a reason to just keep going.
~~~~~

CHAPTER 26

On the morning of the funeral, Phillip Leadbetter woke with Daisy wrapped tightly around him. Despite everything that had happened, he still smiled when he was with her. The death of his baby brother had been devastating, but for the most part, he worried mostly about his mother. She seemed to be moving forward and doing whatever needed to be done. She'd cried each time he'd seen her, but Phillip sensed that there was grief much deeper than what she showed. He worried about what extent that grief might come out in the future.

Today he had a funeral to go to. They were going to say a final farewell to Rex. Phillip felt the guilt of not having handled anything well, right from the moment he'd found out that Rex had stolen that car from the supermarket car park. He kept running situations through his mind, wondering if at any point after that, he could have done something differently that would have prevented his brother's death. It was a pointless exercise. It was natural, but he tried and tried to stop his mind from thinking about it. He had to focus on more happy things. He wanted the woman beside him to be his wife. He wanted to take her last name and never be a Leadbetter again. He wanted the kids that she'd been so eagerly asking him for. More than ever, he believed his mother could appreciate and feel needed by grandchildren. They would be as much for her as they would be for Daisy.

The body beside him moved, huddling even closer. Phillip chuckled quietly. He was glad she was in his life. He still didn't know what she saw in him, a simple grease monkey who came from a family of crime. He'd had to stop wondering about that. There was never any real answer to the question.

"Hey," he heard a sleepy voice say. When he turned his head, he could see Daisy's eyes were trying to open, rather unsuccessfully. He smiled and kissed her lips softly. "More," she said, making him grin more and kiss her again. "Much more."

Phillip laughed and rolled her onto her back. As he settled down between her legs, she finally opened her eyes fully and smiled at him.

Daisy suspected it was going to be another difficult day for him. She hated that he had so much misery in his life. She wanted to pull him away and only make him happy, but that wasn't real. His brother had died, and today he had to show support for his family. They'd discussed if she would go or not. She wanted to. He wasn't sure his family would like it, and it was a day he didn't want to be disrespectful to his parents. The decision was yet unresolved.

Daisy pulled him down to her and kissed him passionately. Nothing was said for a long while as he slid into her slowly and lovingly, grinding his hips down on hers in a way that resulted in her climaxing just from that. When he'd reached the same place, he relaxed down on her and indulged in the feeling of safety that came from her arms holding him tightly.

"What time do you need to go?" she asked him as a way to let him know she didn't expect to go.

Phillip raised his head and looked at her.

"I'll leave here at eleven," he replied and kissed her softly. "I want you to come with me, Daisy."

"I thought you didn't think your parents would li..."

"I know, but I need you there with me. You are going to be my wife and the mother of my children. My parents have to accept you sometime."

"I agree, but today, Phillip? At your brother's funeral? Is it really the time to upset anyone?" she asked as she gently ran her fingers through his hair. "I don't mind missing it. I understand…"

"I know, but if you want to come, I want you to come."

"Okay."

~~~~~~

Across town, Mark held Stacey tightly in their bed as she wept. She'd been doing a lot of crying since the news had come, as had he. Mark didn't know if she was yet at the pinnacle of her grief, but all they could do was get through every single day and then sleep before getting through the next.

They hadn't been intimate since receiving the news about Rex. With the exception of the last weeks of each of her pregnancies, it was the first entire week they hadn't indulged in sexual pleasures. It had been the last thing on their minds, but as Stacey's tears dried and she kissed Mark, both knew it was needed. On that particular day, hours before they would bury their son, they needed to love one another.

Stacey kissed him deeply. As soon as she indulged in it, she found herself hungry for it. She quickly discarded the t-shirt she'd slept in, lay back, and guided his mouth downward. She needed her mind to escape everything real for just a little while. When she felt her husband's tongue hit its target, she moaned and focused on that one little thing.

Mark worked her slowly to make it last a long time. He wanted her to be mindless to the task ahead later in the morning. He wanted to spread the pleasure out and show her how much he loved her.

After she exploded in deep climax, Stacey guided him upwards and reached down to encourage him to move into her. She felt him move with unwavering control and grace as he slipped into her over and over.

Kissing his wife passionately while feeling himself wrapped in her wetness was a deliciousness
~~~~~~

Mark hadn't even realized he'd missed. Indulging in it, he found it almost overwhelming.

"Don't hold back," he heard her whisper. "Please."

At her request, he started thrusting faster and harder until he was moving with power and speed. The faster and harder he pushed into her, the more she moaned. Seeing and hearing her like that only pushed him on more. Finally, he exploded, the orgasm rocking his entire body.

"Thank you," Stacey said after a long time of silence. "I've missed this."

Mark kissed her.

"I love you so much," he said as tears began.

"I know," Stacey replied before kissing him. "I love you too. Today's going to be so hard," she said, feeling sobbing coming on again. "How do we keep living without him?"

Mark held her close and tried to soothe her while he fought back his own tears.

"We keep moving forward in honor of him, Stace," he said. "We got to enjoy 21 years with him. It wasn't long enough, but we were blessed in having him for that long."

Stacey nodded and wiped her tears.

"I know."

For a moment, she gave thought to the child she'd had that hadn't survived. They would have been an adult too if they'd lived past those moments of birth. They had lost her as well, and they had survived. It wasn't the same as losing Rex, but they'd get through it and survive.

"Phillip's bringing his woman with him," Mark said after reading a forewarning text from his son.

Stacey wasn't surprised. Her oldest son must have felt torn in the situation he'd been in with the woman he loved.

"Well, I think that's only right, Mark. He kept her away from us for so long, worried how we would react at her having been on Rex's case. He shouldn't have to keep her from us. We need to accept her as his partner."

"I know," Mark agreed. "And she was good to share with us the information she did. I don't think we should dwell on Rex's court case either."

"Our children are really growing up. Phillip has his Daisy. Sasha has James..."

"You don't think they're *together*, do you?" Mark asked, stupefied by the thought of his usually-angry daughter letting *anyone* into her life in that capacity.

Stacey laughed softly and enjoyed the feeling of being able to in what would be a horrific day ahead.

"I think it might take time for him to break through her barrier entirely, but from what we saw yesterday, I think he's well on his way there. I've never seen her seem so *close* to anyone as she did when she was with him. It's nice to see."

"But what kind of man is he? How does anyone look past what he has to?"

"I don't know. I don't know if *I* could in his situation, if someone in his family had hurt one of us. Maybe that says something about his character, though - and about how much he cares for her."

"Maybe."

~~~~~

Arriving at the funeral parlor, Stacey, Mark, Sasha, and Anya could see masses of people assembled already. The strength of the Leadbetter clan was on full display. Many of them would hardly have ever met Rex, but he was one of their own, so they turned up to honor his life. For a fleeting moment, Stacey wondered how any of them truly felt, given what had happened to Pete that same night. There was presently no official Leadbetter leader as such. She hoped no-one came knocking on her door in an attempt to lure Mark to that position again. She hoped that some Leadbetter far, far away would do whatever they wanted and just leave her
~~~~~

and her husband and kids alone. She'd put up with the Leadbetter way of life for more than thirty years. It had taken one of her babies. Now she wanted nothing to do with it anymore.

They stood and lightly spoke to the faces they knew. At the front of the room was the coffin. Inside of it was her baby boy. She couldn't look at it. If she did, she wouldn't make it through the day. She needed to just remember him when he was alive. She didn't want to think of his lifeless body and the husk that it now was without his soul attached to it.

"Ma," Stacey heard Phillip's voice call out. When she turned, she saw him approaching with Daisy beside him.

Daisy looked on as Phillip enveloped his mother in his arms. From all that she'd read about the Leadbetter family as a whole, she never would have pictured them to be affectionate at all. As she was deep in that thought, she saw Phillip's mother approach her with a hand extended.

"You make my son happy," Stacey said. "It's time to forget the court case of before and just look to the future."

Daisy felt tears come to her eyes at the speech that had been presented to her. She went to reach out to shake Stacey's hand. At the last moment, she found herself pulled close against Stacey in a full-on hug. Daisy had no hesitation in hugging Phillip's mother right back. After everything that Phillip had worried about, perhaps they'd worried about nothing after all. Perhaps everything would be alright, and his family could accept her after all.

Phillip smiled and then moved to hug both of them, making them both laugh softly, although he could see they both had tears in their eyes. From his side, he saw his father approach.

"Welcome, Daisy," Mark said to the woman in

front of him.

Daisy reciprocated by shaking his hand.

"Thank you."

Phillip beamed. It wasn't the right time to be happy, but he felt glorious inside at seeing both of his parents react to Daisy so well. Anything could happen at any time, but it was a good start.

"It's about time I met your flower," they all heard Anya's young voice add in. Phillip couldn't help but laugh. "Hi, I'm Anya," she said to Daisy as she pulled her hand into a handshake. "I'd like to say he's told us all about you, but he hasn't. You're his best-kept secret."

Daisy looked at the young woman and laughed softly. Phillip had told her Anya was 'like a ray of sunshine'. Daisy could see he hadn't been exaggerating.

"I am very pleased to meet you, Anya," she said, smiling broadly and receiving the same in return.

~~~~~~

James Stonewarden looked in the mirror. He was going to the first funeral he'd been to in eleven years. The last had been that of his mother. He hadn't known the guy who this funeral was for but thinking about him being of similar age to Max made it real easy to think about how hard it must be for Sasha and her parents.

Looking at his watch, he finally moved. He'd said he'd be there, and he was determined to not let her down. He had no idea how funerals worked or what the correct etiquette would be, but regardless, he would be there for her.

Once at the funeral parlor, he could see masses of people. It alarmed him slightly. He had imagined it would be a small family affair with maybe a dozen people at most. He wasn't prepared for the hoards that seemed to fill the inside of the building and flow out toward the street.

He walked around in an attempt to see Sasha or her parents. Finally, he saw them making their way to
~~~~~~

the front of the large room of seats. Quickly he moved forward.

"Sasha," he said as loudly as he dared. He saw her turn and look at him before moving back towards him. He gladly opened his arms and wrapped them around her as she walked into them.

"It's about to begin," Sasha said. "I need to sit with my parents."

"I know. I'll be at the back. I won't leave," he said, daring to reach up and touch her cheek. It was a bold move of intimacy, but he just needed to touch her. He was glad she didn't flinch or move away.

Sasha nodded and pulled away. She hadn't minded the feeling of him touching her face. In truth, it had felt kind of nice. She put that thought away and returned to her family. Although she couldn't sit with him, she was glad to know that he'd turned up and he was going to stay.

~~~~~

The funeral seemed to be over quickly. Despite his wayward lifestyle and incredible ability to find himself in trouble, Rex Leadbetter's death had hit a great many people. Throughout the service, Mark held Stacey tightly and willed his strength to spill over onto her. They shouldn't have lost their son. Guilt lay deep inside of Mark for handing the reins over to his cousin Pete. Guilt lay even deeper inside of Stacey for nudging Mark to hand the reins over. Both would feel that guilt for a long time to come, but they had to get through that day, and the next, and the one after that. They still had one child who was only a teenager. They would work harder to keep her safe.

When everyone filed out of the service, Stacey saw James slowly and gently approach Sasha again. Stacey watched their interaction. She watched what he did and how he did it. She could see that he had sussed out something about Sasha that perhaps no-one else had.
~~~~~

The way that he made sure she could see he was there, without rushing toward her in any way that could have caused stress in Sasha, told Stacey that he wasn't just intending to use Sasha or hurt her. He was already in tune with exactly what she needed and how she needed to be treated. The thought made Stacey smile. Someone had come into her daughter's life who would guide her softly and slowly, enabling her to blossom at her own pace. Somehow the thought of that helped to make such a miserable day seem just that little bit brighter.

"Who's that?" Stacey heard Phillip ask as he appeared beside her.

Stacey chuckled softly.

"I think your sister has an admirer."

"But who *is* he?" Phillip pushed.

"He's someone who I think has been helping her in many ways. Look at her. I've never seen her like that."

Phillip watched. He suspected the guy was the one Sasha had told him about - the one who had ensured her safety the night of the gala event, *and* the brother of the guy who'd been shot in the supermarket. Phillip secured the image of James into his memory. If he laid one unwelcome finger on Sasha...

"Phillip," he heard Sasha say, not even realizing she'd walked right up to him while he was thinking about her. "Phillip, this is James," Sasha continued.

Phillip watched as the guy in front of him held out his hand for a handshake. Doing a quick appraisal, Phillip was surprised. His sister was a tough looking girl with all of her tattoos and her raw approach to everything, including personal presentation. The guy being presented was immaculate in grooming. In some ways, he oozed money while at the same time kind of not doing so.

"Hello, James," Phillip finally said as he shook the guy's hand. Looking at Sasha, Phillip resolved to not be the protective big brother. If there was any woman on the planet who could look after herself, it was Sasha. Even in her vulnerable moments, she had a strength that was there, even though she didn't always see it herself.

Introductions were made between Daisy, Anya, and James before Sasha led him away from her family.

"Thank you for coming," she said to him as they stood off to the side in a quiet corner of the grounds. "I know it must be hard for you to be here."

James smiled sadly. It should have felt *incredibly* difficult for him to be there … but it didn't.

"I want to be here for you. Whenever. Wherever."

Sasha felt tears threaten. She rubbed her eyes in an attempt to not let them flow. As she did, James reached up and gently coaxed her hands away.

"You don't have to hide being sad," he said, remembering a similar conversation they'd had on a different day, in a different place.

Sasha nodded.

"I know," she said as the dam broke. She was partly crying for the sadness of the situation. She was partly crying because she was actually starting to feel kind of happy. Unable to even try to look strong, she moved close to James in the way he was now getting used to. He wrapped his arms around her and held her quietly, letting her cry as much as she needed to. It was a comfort he was beginning to enjoy a lot.

When he felt her arms come around and embrace him in return, he felt something in his heart he'd never felt before. A hug would normally mean nothing much. Receiving a hug from Sasha Leadbetter felt like the most amazing thing to him.

From a distance, Sasha's brother, mother and father, all discretely watched the interaction. The day wasn't about Sasha but seeing her look almost happy was so new that it was almost hypnotic watching her. Seeing her allow a man to hug her, *and* her hug him back, was enough to stun all three of them.

~~~~~

Sasha held onto him tightly as her tears flowed. He said nothing. He did nothing. She appreciated how much he gave her strength to lean on him and just let her cry herself out without having to feel ashamed about it. It felt strange to hug him back, but at the same time, it felt right. She hadn't forgotten that his brother had been shot, possibly by someone in her family. He probably needed someone to lean on too.

As the tears dried up, she pulled away slightly so she could look at his face. He was still a pretty boy, but that was nothing to her. Looking into his eyes, she found herself studying them. She'd never really liked people looking at her too much. In that, she was changing, too.

"Do you want to kiss me?" she asked quietly. Instantly she saw surprise on his face before he grinned at her.

"I don't know if this is the time or place for that," he said.

"I know. That doesn't tell me if you *want* to though."

James laughed.

"Stop being a sassy girl," he said, making her laugh and relax.

Sasha pulled away from him. She felt happy, but she also felt that today she probably shouldn't.

"I should get back to my family."

James nodded. "I know."

"I..." she started to say, suddenly feeling sad again. "I really do appreciate you being here."

James stepped toward her again and gave her one more hug.

"I *want* to be here for you."

"I still don't want sex," she said, half in jest to make him smile.

James couldn't help but laugh out loud.

"Okay," he said, nodding, not able to think of any
~~~~~

other reply.

"Please don't just disappear," she said with an incredible sadness in the tone of her voice.

James looked into her eyes.

"Why would you say that?"

"I just…" Sasha started to reply. The thought of the last guy she trusted doing what he had still made her angry and sure that all guys hurt women.

"Sasha, I'm right here," James reassured her. "I'm here for you…"

"I *know*. I know you are. But will I see you again?"

"Are you kidding me? You turn up *everywhere* I'm going," he said, lightening the mood and making her smile. "Have you got your phone? Do you want me to put my number in it?" he asked softly.

Sasha pulled her phone from her pocket and presented it to him. She'd never called a guy. She didn't know if she ever would. It would be quite nice to know how to contact him if she needed to, though.

James entered his number and handed the phone back to her.

"I'm here for you. All you have to do is call or message me."

"Okay," she said, nodding. "I need to get back to my parents."

"Okay."

James watched as she turned away slowly and began walking toward her family. He saw her look back at him once … twice … and then she was immersed in people. He walked back to his car and drove away, his head full … but not quite as full as his heart was.

For the first time in his life, James Stonewarden was actually feeling his heart.

It was pounding. It was aching. It felt heavy with emotion.

And it felt great.

~~~~~

Mark Leadbetter held his wife, Stacey, well into the night in the private retreat of their bedroom. The day had been long and emotional. Their youngest son was gone forever. There was no doubt about that. They would never again see him, hear him, or learn of the crazy stuff he'd done. Whether they would ever see their next oldest son was unknown. So far, David hadn't shown himself except to Sasha that day. He and his car had disappeared from sight and sound.

In the quiet of his heart and head, Mark had hoped that David would resurface at least for his brother's funeral. If anyone had seen him there, no-one had let on, but Mark suspected he was long gone.

David. The quiet one. The one who crossed paths with the law hardly ever. That he could be the one who fired upon innocent people in a supermarket in broad daylight was still unfathomable to everyone in the family. But there was one upside. At least he could be *alive*. That was more than could be said for Rex.

On the run wasn't an ideal existence. Mark had known enough people through his life that had done it, and it was a hard way to live. He wasn't even sure that David needed to be on the run. From what police had indicated by announcements, they believed Rex had been the shooter *both* times. But did David know that? It was a subject not worth pondering. David had acted and then reacted. Now it was solely up to him to figure out what he was going to do and when. He would have to do it without any input from his parents.

Hearing Stacey's sobs as her body convulsed in emotion helped Mark to keep his concerns at bay. What he wanted most of all was to scoop his remaining family up, carry them away, and store them somewhere safe. Somewhere that the Leadbetter name wasn't known. Somewhere that they could all start over.

Thinking back over the day, he let himself
~~~~~

consider two happy things that were happening. Phillip had his Daisy. For all that Mark should have not wanted to know her, knowing she'd helped on the prosecution side of Rex's trial, he couldn't feel that way. Finally seeing Phillip so happy, and seeing Daisy look at him exactly the same way, Mark had to be happy for his oldest son. Phillip was a good man with a good heart. Both of his parents had known that for a long time. He'd always followed instruction and carried out the crime jobs assigned to him, but deep in his heart, he was *good*.

The other thing to smile about was Sasha. Mark only had to cast his mind back a few months to remember how angry she'd always been. When he'd seen her with a guy - even if they were only friends - Mark thought of a rose opening up into bloom after being closed tight for all of its life to that point.

"I can feel you smiling," he heard Stacey say from her huddle in his arms.

"I was thinking about Phillip and Sasha," he replied as Stacey sat up enough to be able to look into his eyes. "They both looked happy today, despite everything."

Stacey wiped her eyes and nodded, a smile also gracing her face.

"I know," she said. "Who would have thought? Maybe there's hope for them after all. Maybe we *will* get to become grandparents!"

Mark chuckled. It felt wrong to smile and laugh on the day they'd buried their youngest son. At the same time, it felt good. It felt good to have something so happy to smile about when things had seemed serious for so long.

"Maybe."

After a few minutes of silence, he heard Stacey whisper, "Love me, Mark."

When he looked at her face, he saw tears beginning again. It was no effort at all to pull her closer and kiss her with all the passion she needed at that moment.

CHAPTER 27

"Hey, Sassy!" Sasha and Nicky heard that voice call out. With two weeks having passed since Rex's funeral, Sasha was treating Nicky to an afternoon out at the local mall.

"I think he *likes* you," Nicky said, smiling up at Sasha.

Sasha laughed softly and winked at the young girl beside her. The previous couple of weeks hadn't been easy, but slowly everyone in the Leadbetter household was loosening up … those that were left, that was. The dynamics of the household had changed. Now Sasha had opened up to more people, she was finally finding the patience to interact with her sister. She'd never had time for Anya before, but that was changing too. They were too different to be close, but the communication line was opening up. Finally.

"Hey, wait up!" the girls heard again.

Turning around, Sasha saw James slowing from a mild jog. When he looked right at her, he smiled before turning to Nicky.

"Hey, Nicky," he said. "How's things with Saspodimus today?"

Nicky shook her head and rolled her eyes, but the smile on her face was unmissable.

"You know her name!" she said to him. She didn't know him, but he was likable too. As far as adults went, Sasha and James were okay.

James chuckled.

"Yeah, I do. But don't you think she *suits* Saspodimus for a name?" he asked, making Nicky laugh.

"No!"

He realigned his focus on Sasha.

"What are you guys up to?"

Sasha smiled at him. She was liking the smiling thing. She now particularly found it easy when around *him*.

"We're going to get some ice cream, and then we're going to see a movie. Nicky's mum is picking her up at four from out front."

"Ahh."

"Are you coming too?" Nicky asked, looking from one adult to the other and back again.

"Well, if Sasha will ask me, I might," he said, winking at her in reply.

Sasha laughed softly.

"Wanna have ice cream with us and then come see a movie?" she asked him.

James stepped closer to her and looked into her eyes as he ever so lightly touched her bare arm.

"I'd really like that."

Two hours later, the three of them walked from the cinema to the front entrance of the mall.

"Mummy!"

Sasha and James watched as Susan showed her usual open arms and then picked Nicky up in a spinning hug. Always when she saw that, Sasha wished her mother had been so close to her when she was little. Always when James saw anything like that, he was reminded of his own mother and how loving she'd been.

"We have to get going. Grandma's coming to see us tonight," Susan said to Nicky before turning to Sasha. "Thanks, Sasha," she said quietly as she seemed to shyly look at James.

"Oh, Susan, sorry. This is James. James, this is Nicky's mother, Susan," Sasha said when she remembered they hadn't been introduced.

"I am pleased to meet you, Susan," James said.

"You also seem to have made an impact on this little one," Susan said, smiling at him. "So I'll thank you too. Both of you are ... well, you're amazing." She paused and looked at the smile on Nicky's face. "Next week?"

"Absolutely. I'll catch you then, Nicky-kid," Sasha said, sharing a personalized handshake with Nicky.

After mother and daughter were out of view, James turned to the woman beside him. He didn't want to push her into anything, but he was pleased when she turned and moved slowly toward him and into his arms. He was even more pleased when once again her arms wrapped around him.

"You didn't call," James teased her gently, making her smile.

"Yeah. I'm not much of a phone chatter."

James nodded. "Okay."

"What are you doing now?" Sasha asked as she pulled away from him. "Were you on your way somewhere when you saw us?"

"Nope. I have to work tonight from eight, but I've got a few hours free till then."

"You work?" she asked. The idea hadn't even crossed her mind since he seemed to appear at any time of day or night.

"Yeah," James replied, laughing softly. "Not much, but I do work in a bar downtown."

"Are you a stripper?" Sasha asked, imagining him ... hmm, where did *that* thought come from?

James threw his head back as a roar of laughter escaped him.

"You're in a mighty fine sassy mood today, Sasha Leadbetter. *No!* I'm a bartender. Just casual, though. I had a heap of time off recently, but I'm back on regular roster now."

"Okay, well, do you wanna hang out from now till then, or do you have to sleep or something?"

James shook his head.

"I don't nap before work. What do you want to do?"

"I want..." Sasha started to say before feeling her face go red. She closed up, and James saw it.

"You want … what?" he asked softly as he moved right up to her once more.

"I want … I want you to *touch* me."

"Like this?" He lightly ran fingertips of both hands up and down her forearms slowly.

"Yes … but..."

"But … what?"

Sasha looked him in the eye.

"Can we go to your place?"

James gulped.

"Sasha, I'm not going to have sex with you, if this is another attempt at..."

"No, I don't want that either. I just want … I just want to explore simple touch. Just like you're doing now."

James studied her face. It was so relaxed compared to when he'd met her. If he hadn't seen with his own eyes how angry she'd been those first few times they'd run into each other, he would hardly believe now that she could have such a level of anger in her at all. In her eyes, he could see how much she wished he'd help her get past a huge obstacle in her nature.

Slowly he raised one hand and caressed her cheek. As his fingertips lightly moved to the line of her jaw and then up into her hair, he continued to watch her eyes.

"James Stonewarden," both heard a female voice say from behind them. When they turned, James saw one of his semi-regular play friends, Jessica. "It's been a while. When are you going to come and see me again?"

James openly cringed. He was surprised at seeing her. He was further surprised at the fact that even though he always got turned on when he saw her, suddenly he didn't seem to have any such feeling inside of him at all. Looking at her at that moment, he felt … nothing. No attraction. No sexual tension. All the physical feelings he'd felt for his play friend in the past were just gone. It was a surprising revelation, but a welcome one.

"Jessica … ah, hi," he mumbled.

Sasha watched the interaction and felt a rush of emotions flowing right through her. The one that she hated to feel, though, was anger. It was like a tidal wave rising and thumping down on her. She fought to breathe deeply to control it. She talked to herself in her head as she distanced herself from the conversation that was happening in front of her. She kept talking to herself, telling herself there was nothing to be angry about. James was becoming a friend to her - a non-sexual friend. He'd admitted he had friends he had sex with. He hadn't hidden that. There was no reason to be angry or upset or anything else she might be feeling.

Over and over, she chanted inside her head while she remained silent on the outside.

"Jessica, I'm involved with someone," she heard him say. The words made her groan and have to hold back the anger further still. He was involved with someone? Holy fuck! She hadn't even asked him if he had a girlfriend. Not once in all the times they'd seen each other had she asked him that. What a fucking idiot she was. *And* she'd dropped her towel and stood naked in front of him … *fuck!*

"No worries," she heard the woman say. "We've had some fun. You know where to find me if you want to play again."

James watched as Jessica said her final words and simply walked away. The ease of it relieved him - until he turned and saw the look on Sasha's face.

"What?" he asked her, surprised by the tenseness he could clearly see.

Sasha looked at him but said nothing. She had no

idea what she was supposed to say or even *could* say.

"Sasha, why are you looking like that? I told you I had friends like that…"

"You didn't say you had a *girlfriend*!"

Sasha watched as a grin broke out on his face. The sight infuriated her.

"No, I guess I didn't. And you know why? Because I don't."

"But you just said…"

James stepped up to her.

"I just said what I had to, to get her to not want to see me again."

"Why would you do that?" Sasha asked, confused. "You *like* having friends you fu…"

"I *did* like that."

There was silence for a long while. James could almost see her trying to formulate words and thoughts in her head before she spoke.

"You don't like having friends like that now?"

James shrugged his shoulders.

"I'm kind of liking a *different* kind of friend right now," he said.

"Really?"

James grinned broadly and nodded. "Really."

"What kind of friend is that?"

"The kind who sits with me in silence sometimes without needing conversation. The kind who doesn't want to use me for sex but not spend time with me in any other way. The kind who seems to *really* like my hugs."

Sasha smiled shyly. "Me?"

"Yep, definitely you," he replied, laughing softly.

"Even though I don't want sex?"

"Even then."

"I might not *ever* want it."

James nodded. "I know. I hope you will, but I'm not going to push you into that. Our boundaries are set. I won't be trying to push over them."

"But if I do … sometime … want to cross the boundary?"

"Then I hope that whoever you do that with, they treat you like you deserve to be treated."

"And if I want to cross it with you?"

James stepped forward and cupped her face in his hands.

"Then you have my promise that I won't hurt you," he reassured her.

Sasha studied his face. He wasn't lying. He wasn't being some asshole, trying to seduce her by making her believe he *wasn't* seducing her. She trusted his words, wholly and securely. She was safe with him. There was no doubt in that.

And that was something completely and utterly new for Sasha Leadbetter.

~~~~~

Walking into his apartment, Sasha found herself remembering back to the night of the gala event. She still hardly knew him, but she'd known him even less then. He could have done anything to her that night, but he hadn't. Instead, he'd welcomed her into his apartment, just as he was now.

Thinking back to that weekend, she focused only on her time with him. If she didn't, she knew she'd be thinking about all that had gone wrong, including the death of one brother and the flow-on disappearance of another. She was getting used to living normal life again, but only if she didn't stop and think about those things too much.

"I need to eat before I go to work. Do you like steak? Salad?"

"Oh, you don't have to feed…"

"Sasha," he said, grinning. "I'm making dinner. Do you like steak?" he asked again and saw her nod meekly. "And salad?"

Sasha nodded again as she grinned at him. At that
~~~~~

moment, she truly believed she understood what other people were talking about when they said they'd found happiness. She suspected it could get even better, but right where she stood felt pretty darned good.

~~~~~

Sitting down beside one another on the small couch, eating their simple meal, neither spoke for a long while. It felt relaxing enough to just sit and eat and enjoy the feeling of having someone to sit next to. Nothing more was needed.

After finishing, Sasha stood up and grabbed his plate.

"What are you doing?" James asked, amused.

"Dishes."

"Sasha, I can do the dishes tomorrow…"

"No!" she said with more force than she meant. "No, I don't want to keep putting things off till tomorrow. Sorry, I know it seems silly, but I have to get on and do things today, James. Sometimes there just isn't any tomorrow to come…" she said as he saw tears begin in her eyes.

Instantly he jumped up, took the plates from her, and then pulled her into his arms.

"Come on then," he said when he felt her body relax again. "Let's get these done. You're right. I'm just being a lazy bum, and dishes don't get any more enjoyable if you wait. You only end up with *more* dishes to wash!"

Sasha nodded and let him lead the way.

~~~~~

"I only have another hour before I'll have to jump in the shower and get ready for work," James said when they returned to the sofa.

"Oh, do you want me to leav…?"

"No! I want you to stay right here. I'm just keeping an eye on the time," he said as he relaxed back against the sofa back.

Sasha watched his body movement and mirrored it. They sat close, facing one another but not touching.

"I like being around you," she said softly. "When I'm with you, I feel normal, like I'm just an average girl."

James smiled and reached out slowly, touching his fingertips to the back of her hand as it sat on her lap.

"There's nothing average about you."

"I *want* to be average," she said.

"Why?"

"Because all my life I've been different from … *everyone*. I don't want to be that girl who stands out all the time. I want to just be unnoticeable."

As James watched her face, he felt their hands moving. She was changing things so that she was now lightly touching the back of his hand. He remained still, letting her explore as much as she wanted to.

"I don't think you could ever be unnoticeable, Sasha. You're an incredible person…"

"No, I'm not…"

"Yes, you *are!*" James said with passion in his voice. "You can see just as well as I can how much you've changed in only these past few months. *You* are doing that, no-one else."

Sasha looked up into his eyes, then studied his lips. She felt the pull - she just didn't know what to do with it. She'd never longed to kiss anyone before. What she felt was natural and happening without her driving it. She didn't know it could be like that.

"Can I kiss you?" she asked him softly.

James remained still. He felt it too, but there was no way in hell he was going to move quickly and scare her. He only nodded, saying nothing, doing nothing else.

Sasha took a deep breath and slowly moved closer. She looked into his eyes again, but that felt too raw. She felt too vulnerable like that. She lowered her eyes to focus just on his lips. That removed some of the anxiety. Not looking into his eyes, she could pretend she was doing something alone, like she was detached from him.

The gap closed as she lightly pressed her lips to his. James remained still, unmoving, letting her move her lips as she wanted to. It had been a long while since he'd been with a woman. Generally, he didn't let too much time pass between seeing one and seeing another. The craziness of the previous couple of months had shifted women to the wayside in his life. That had been his excuse for not being his usual attentive self to the women of his acquaintance.

As he felt her lips moving against his, he found himself experiencing a different kind of kiss. With the aspect of sex having already been firmly removed from any possibility, he found himself able to focus just on the feeling of her lips on his. There was no need to rush to grope. There was no need to rush to undress. All of that simply didn't exist in the moment. Because of that, his awareness of their lips was heightened. It had been so many years since he'd kissed a woman but not then had sex with her that it felt like it was his first kiss all over again.

He held his hands and body back. The only thing connecting them was their lips. He wanted to pull her into his arms and engage her tongue with his. Knowing he could do that, but not daring to do it in case she freaked out, made him acknowledge just how important she really had become to him. She'd been hurt in the past. There was no way in hell he was going to contribute to her hurting again.

Sasha explored. Moving her lips this way and that, she tentatively moved a little closer to him. They both had one knee up on the sofa. As she moved closer to him, their knees touched. It was like a barrier, signaling a proximity alert to her. She pulled away from him.

"Will you touch me now?" she asked quietly.

James took a deep breath.

"Touch me first," he said.

Immediately he saw surprise on her face. That expression was quickly replaced by curiosity. She raised one hand and moved toward touching his cheek. When her fingers were only an inch away from his skin, she stopped and looked into his eyes one more time.

"Don't stop, Sasha. If you want to touch … touch."

Sasha closed her fingers over the distance. She'd touched his hands, and now she'd touched his lips. Letting her fingertips lightly dance over the line of his jaw, she felt a faint roughness, like he hadn't shaved that morning. She ran her fingers along the length of it from one ear, down around his chin, and up to his other ear. He didn't have any visible beard, but she didn't mind finding that sliver of stubble. It made him seem less perfect and more real.

As her eyes drifted back to his lips again, Sasha felt the pull to kiss him once more. Instead, she dropped her sight to his hand and took it in hers.

James watched as she lifted his hand and moved it against her cheek. He gently took control and began to touch her jawline just as she'd just done to him. In front of him, he saw her close her eyes as if indulging in the touch. It was such a strong focus in its entirety that he was mesmerized. With him, sex had always been rushed and passionate. He was only touching her face, but it felt infinitely more intimate than the sex he had with any of his numerous play friends. It seemed like a long while that they sat like that with Sasha enjoying the feeling of his skin against hers and James enjoying watching her enjoyment.

Sasha opened her eyes and looked into his. The way he was watching her should have made her uncomfortable with the intensity of his eyes. It didn't.

James was hesitant to break the mood, but it had

crept up on him that time was passing.

"Sasha," he said as he gently stroked her cheek again. "I need to have a shower and get ready for work."

Sasha pulled away, suddenly feel stupid and confused.

Sensing her change in mood, James leaned in to kiss her gently.

"I won't be long," he said, regretful that he had to rush.

Sasha watched him as he stood and walked into his room, then moved into the bathroom. As she heard the water start, she sat back on the sofa and closed her eyes. Gently she touched her lips. She could still feel his kiss. It was so surprising, his gentleness. She had for so long expected no such thing possible that she felt slightly stunned.

Her thoughts were interrupted by the sound of something resembling singing emanating from the bathroom. She couldn't help but smile and then laugh softly. He was a pretty boy, but *that* aspect of him sure wasn't pretty!

He would be going to work. When Sasha thought about that, she pondered why her parents had always wanted their kids at home. Sure, they survived on theft, but the rest of the world went out and did normal jobs to earn their money. She wondered if she was employable. As she considered doing a real job, she shook her head. She wasn't ready for that. She needed to work on her people skills more before she could go into a workplace. She was changing - no doubt about that - but there was still a long way to go. That had to be her priority for the moment - that and helping a little 10-year-old girl to gain more confidence and realize how amazing she was.

~~~~~

"Do you want me to drop you home?" James asked as he readied himself to leave. After checks of wallet, keys and phone, he finally stopped still and
~~~~~

looked at Sasha. She looked like she'd sat as still as a statue the whole time he'd been running around getting ready. "Are you all good?" he asked as he smiled and walked to sit beside her.

Sasha looked at him and smiled sadly. She felt like she might have made an idiot of herself over a guy - the one thing she'd sworn she'd never do again.

"Yeah."

James slowly and gently eased in and kissed her softly. It was such a different kind of kiss from what he was used to, but that only made it feel more sensual. As he pulled away, he saw her smile shyly. The sight was so relieving that he let out a deep breath as he grinned.

"Right. Come on, Sassy Girl," he said as he stood and held out his hands to help her up. "I'll take you home, unless you want to go somewhere el…"

"No, I'll be going home. Thanks," Sasha replied as she edged her way forwards into his arms. She was glad when his arms wrapped around her. It was a comfort she was finding she needed more and more.

In the car, Sasha felt a wave of sadness roll over her. She'd let a guy kiss her. Was she stupid in that? Had she given him the green light that he could now do to her whatever he wanted? As she questioned that, she turned and looked at him. Was he just like all other guys, doing whatever it would take to get into a woman's pants? She knew he already had friends that he had sex with. Why would he bother with her if that was what he wanted? He could just go and be with any of them.

James felt her eyes on him and glimpsed at her briefly. He didn't ask what she was thinking about. Whatever it was, it was consuming her. He was cool with that. They had their times when they just thought inside of their heads. It bothered him not at all.

As he pulled up in front of the Leadbetter home, he turned to her.

"This has been a great afternoon, Sasha. Thanks for letting me join you and Nicky."

Sasha smiled sadly. His words felt like a huge rejection to her - like the kisses hadn't even happened. Regardless, she nodded.

"I enjoyed it too," she said as she turned away from him.

She thought that would be it until her door magically opened and he was already standing there, guiding her out. The feeling of him tentatively pulling her into his arms helped release a little of the stress that had been creeping up on her.

"Are you feeling comfortable with me kissing you?" James asked her quietly. He wanted to kiss her and keep kissing her. He didn't want to freak her out.

Sasha smiled slightly and nodded, looking at his face. She liked his face. She guessed *everyone* would like his face, but she realized then that she saw in it much more than the pretty perfection of it. She saw honesty and strength. She didn't pull away at all when he leaned down and kissed her gently. Instead, she tightened her arms around him and let herself give a little bit more effort to kissing him back.

James eased away, smiling.

"It's hard for me to pull away from you, but I can't be late for work," he said.

"I know," she replied, nodding. "Go! I'll see you … around."

James laughed as he opened the driver side door.

"I don't have your number. Text me, and I'll call you tomorrow after I get up."

Sasha nodded, smiled, and waved before finally beginning her wander up the path to her home. As she heard the engine start and the car to pull out, she glanced back and saw him grinning and waving at her. It was such a small gesture but made her giggle slightly inside. Her mind fought to take her to a negative place. It tried to tell her that he was using her … that he only wanted one thing. The words in her head were destined to make her want to find her blade and caress it, believing it was her only friend. Her heart argued, insisting that he was a good guy. He *wasn't* using her, and he *wasn't* only after sex.

As she walked in the front door of her home, she was well aware of the conflict going on between her head and her heart.

She decided to listen to - and believe in - her *heart*.

CHAPTER 28

Mark and Stacey Leadbetter were finally allowing themselves to move forward. It was hard, knowing one son was gone forever and not knowing where another one was. Each day they loved each other and pushed themselves. Each day it got a tiny bit easier and more natural to wake and get on with the day without pondering too much about the sadness in their lives.

"It's good to have you here," Stacey said to Daisy quietly. In an effort to bring her into the fold, the Leadbetter household was having the first sit down dinner together. It hadn't taken much for Phillip to hear the insistence in his mother's voice that he bring Daisy too.

"Thank you," Daisy replied.

Sitting among the family, she felt slightly intimidated. She'd read almost all there was to read about every single person sitting at the table. The only one not on record so far was the youngest - Anya. But out of all of them, the one who most intrigued Daisy was surely Sasha. The lengthy words she'd read about the young woman's long violent history had etched everything about Sasha into Daisy's mind. As she sat near her at the large family dining table, she found it difficult to align who those words were about and who was actually right in front of her.

"It's nice that Phillip has a flower," Anya piped up with a large grin on her face.

Phillip smiled. Day to day, he still officially lived in Greg's house but stayed over at Daisy's mostly.

"No sign of Greg yet?" Mark asked, pulling a cloud back down over everyone.

The smile on Phillip's face drifted away as he

shook his head.

"No," he said. "I'm not there much, though. It *is* possible he comes and goes, and he's just not there when I am."

"No, he said he was going away and wouldn't be reachable," Sasha added into the conversation. Her speaking and contributing to conversations was still something everyone was adjusting to. "Reckoned he needed time out, or something like that."

Mark sighed and nodded. He missed his cousin. He missed his friend, Rhett, too. Nothing had been heard from either of them. All he could hope was that they were safe.

Rhett. Greg. David. All gone without a trace. For a moment, he let himself believe that perhaps they were all together, safe and protecting one another from whatever it was that they were all running from.

"Are there going to be baby flowers?" Anya asked in an attempt to lift spirits again.

Daisy burst out laughing and looked at Phillip. Stacey watched with a sliver of glee as her oldest son turned and looked at the woman beside him. Besotted. That was the word she would use to describe that look. The thought made her very happy indeed.

"Well, actually, first we have something else to do," Phillip said as he took Daisy's hand in his and looked around at everyone. "Daisy has agreed to become my wife. We are getting married."

Mark looked on as Phillip raised Daisy's hand to his lips, smiling at her the whole time. For that moment, he considered that what his oldest son was experiencing, was something his youngest son never would. As far as Mark knew, Rex had never had a proper girlfriend. Now the opportunity for him to do so had passed forever. Mark gulped back a sob that threatened at the thought. It wasn't a moment to be sad. It was a moment to rejoice.

"Congratulations to you both," he said, smiling

sadly. "It's really nice having you with us, Daisy. You will be a welcome addition to our family."

"Actually," Phillip said, swallowing heavily in uncertainty about how his father would react. "I'm joining her family, not the other way around."

Stacey looked at her son, confused. "What?"

"I … am…" he started to say. "I've decided that instead of Daisy taking the Leadbetter name, I am going to take her family name instead."

Mark looked at Phillip. So many emotions crossed his mind. Disappointment, disbelief … but then understanding. He nodded.

"Given how things are with our family, that may not be such a bad idea. So," he continued, looking straight at his son. "What will your last name be?"

"Leefton," Phillip replied quietly, looking around all of the Leadbetter faces sitting with him.

Mark nodded again.

"Well, no matter your last names, Daisy, you are still welcome as part of our family."

Daisy grinned in relief. Any parent could take their child wanting to change their surname in any way. Both of Phillip's parents had handled the news remarkably well. She wondered if either of them had ever wished they weren't a part of the Leadbetter name.

~~~~~

"It wasn't so bad, telling your parents about the name change," Daisy whispered to Phillip that night as they lay in bed.

Phillip pulled her close.

"No. To be honest, I think they've had too many scares lately. I think they both know what it would mean to have a different surname." He turned enough to be able to kiss her. "So, future wife, when would you like to get married?"

Daisy pushed him back and straddled him, grinning.
~~~~~

"As soon as you want to."

"Hmm. Do you want or need a big wedding?"

"Nope," Daisy replied, shaking her head from side to side. "Your family, my family, and a couple of handfuls of friends between us would be perfect."

Phillip sighed in relief inwardly. He wasn't an attention seeker. He wasn't a performer. He just wanted to marry her. He'd happily have done it quietly on the beach with only two witnesses if she'd wanted that.

"Well, I know my parents and sisters are flexible, so you talk to your family and friends, and we'll arrange a date to suit everyone," Phillip said.

He was rewarded by Daisy smiling, leaning down, and kissing him passionately before taking both of them to the heights of intimacy yet again.

CHAPTER 29

Mark Leadbetter lay back and watched his wife, Stacey, slowly moving up and down on him with incredible control. No matter how much they each aged and their bodies changed, she remained the only woman in the world that he had ever wanted to touch and be intimate with. She was everything to him. If anything happened to her, he didn't think he'd survive.

Stacey watched her husband's face as he reached up with his hands to guide her down. Their lips connecting while she continued to move on him made the circuit complete. They were made for one another. Despite the roughness of the family he'd been born in, she couldn't imagine ever being with another man.

The combined joy of her lips and torso moving resulted in an orgasm growing quickly. The heat of pleasure flowed through Mark's entire body. As it did, he moved his arms around her and held her tightly.

After a long while, she eased up slightly and looked down into his eyes.

"We're gonna be okay, aren't we?" she asked him as she felt her emotions heighten and a tear begin.

Mark pulled her down to kiss her deeply.

"We are."

As he held her closely, he gave thought to the three people missing from his life now.

David. Rhett. Greg. He didn't want to keep pondering the same question over and over, but he did. He couldn't go very long at all without the same question voicing itself in the forefront of his mind.

Where were they?

~~~~~

The End
~~~~~

FURTHER BOOKS
IN THE
FORBIDDEN CONFLICTS
SERIES

Forbidden Conflicts
Book 4
Sapphire
of Prejudice
ANN M PRATLEY

SAPPHIRE OF PREJUDICE
(FORBIDDEN CONFLICTS SERIES - BOOK #4)

Greg and Rhett. They've grown up together since they were teenagers. They've fought together. They've stolen together. They've even loved women together. But something deeper has existed in one of them for years. He's hidden it well. Being part of the great Leadbetter gang and family, the prejudice of certain situations has always been loudly expressed by many of its members - too many, and certainly enough to make anyone fearful of what would happen if feelings were revealed and brought out into the open.

A night has passed when finally, in a moment of wondering if he'd survive till morning, Rhett's taken the chance and kissed the person of his desire. Given their circumstances, what can they do, and where can they go?

Meanwhile, as Phillip Leadbetter continues on his path of happiness with his Daisy, someone from her past has grown obsessed with her and wants her back. To what degree will he put into effect a plan to get her back, and get Phillip out of her life forever?

~~ NOTE: This book does contain adult sexual content and LOTS of swear words.

Forbidden Conflicts
Book 5
Emerald
of Wisdom
ATLEY

EMERALD OF WISDOM
(FORBIDDEN CONFLICTS SERIES - BOOK #5)

When Mitchell Stonewarden lost his wife to cancer more than a decade ago, he vowed to never give his heart to anyone else. With all of his children now adults, and a new generation of Stonewardens having already begun, he's finally started to wonder - does he really want to be alone for the rest of his life? The handover of the family business to his oldest son, Vic, has seemed to be free of difficulty or issues - but has it? Mitchell knows little of his oldest son's private life away from the family. He is surprised by what is brought to his attention that he had no idea about.

While Mitchell finally starts to move on into a new chapter of his life, another of his sons - Max - is on his own path of discovery in life and in love. Previously well-known as 'Romeo' to his family and peers, he begins to wonder if Christy - a surprising addition to his life - has grown to become more important to him than any other young woman he's ever met. When her work at a homeless shelter tests the boundaries of her safety, Max's commitment to her is also tested, making him wonder if he will, indeed, end up hurting her.

Meanwhile, on the other side of town, the Leadbetter family is shattered by an unexpected turn of events that leaves Stacey wondering if she is going to lose the man she's loved for more than three decades...

OTHER BOOKS
BY
ANN M PRATLEY

POWER MOORE INVESTIGATION TALES
~~ Crime Solving ~ Action ~ Adventure ~~

A POWER MOORE INVESTIGATION TALE
RESOLUTION of HAPPINESS
ANN M PRATLEY

RESOLUTION OF HAPPINESS

Fiona Thompson - better known as Flo to everyone who knew her - took a plunge and stepped out of her comfort zone and into the world of online dating. With persistence, she found her prince. He ticked all the boxes. He was handsome. He was financially secure. He loved her. He married her.

She was warned by friends and family that there was something off about him. She didn't listen.

Then she woke up cold, inside the darkness of a wooden box.

Join Special Agents Ashley Power and Tim Moore as they investigate the disappearance of Flo, going on a surprising journey that nobody in Flo's world could possibly anticipate.

HOME BY THE SEA

ANN M PRATLEY

HOME BY THE SEA

A decade ago, homeless people began disappearing from four neighboring towns. Day to day, the commuters making their way to and from work never took notice of the less fortunate they passed. They didn't notice as the number of homeless reduced. They didn't even notice when entire groups of homeless people vanished.

A young woman, eager to find out where her grandfather disappeared to, began trying to find him. When four police departments dismissed her, telling her that her grandfather would no doubt turn up when he wanted to, she was too young to realize she should pursue the matter further.

Now, ten years on, she's stepped up and pushed harder for something to be done to find not only her grandfather but also the countless other people who seemed to have disappeared around the same time.

Called in to investigate the disappearances, Special Agents Ashley Power and Tim Moore find themselves searching for - and finding - so much more than they thought they would.

TIGER IN OUR HOUSE

ANN M PRATLEY

TIGER IN OUR HOUSE

When Alana Templeton goes to do the simple task of hanging her laundry outdoors, she becomes aware that something is not as it should be in her yard. The sound she hears is one that many people might not recognize at first. For Alana, it is, surprisingly, a
sound she's heard before.

Being in the yard, with her toddler in the doorway of their home, she knows the right thing to do is whatever she can to save him. The previous time, she succeeded, but will she this time?

A woman and her infant being put in danger of being attacked by the large animal that has escaped the local wildlife park, not once but twice, prompts an investigation into whether there might be more than just bad luck behind the two events. It seems unlikely that someone could have used such a beast for an attempt on someone's life. Then again, it seems unlikely that the animal would escape its confine and end up at the same location two times in a row.

Sent to figure out what might be behind the strange occurrences, Special Agents Ashley Power and Tim Moore begin to delve into an elaborate and rather unconventional scheme to hurt someone through
an act of revenge.

A POWER MOORE INVESTIGATION TALE
CATCH A CATFISH KILLER
IAIN M. PRATLEY

CATCH A CATFISH KILLER

After a suspicious gas explosion wakes a usually peaceful community, what is left of the home reveals the charred remains of Bob Masters, a hospital orderly who has a solid reputation as someone good-hearted and caring. When fire scene investigators confirm their findings that the explosion was intended, so begins a murder investigation. The one question that's on everyone's mind is why? Why would anyone intentionally try to hurt such a kind and hard working man?

Called in to work out what could have gone wrong in what appears to be a simple, quiet life, and who could be behind such a horrific act, Special Agents Ashley Power and Tim Moore start to realize how much more to someone's life there can be other than what people see on the outside.

Embark on a murder mystery involving crime solving of the digital kind. Initially, through studying online actions and conversations, it becomes evident that catfishing - an unfortunate and sad aspect of modern day dating - seems to be at the root of what begins to be a pattern. Even knowing this, the journey of discovery the agents are subjected to still surprises them.

Catfishing: a deceptive activity in which a person creates a fictional persona or fake identity on a social networking service, usually targeting a specific victim. With it being such an easy way to take advantage of people in the modern age, it may take quite some detective work to solve the mystery of who is ever behind any screen, at any time.

A POWER MOORE INVESTIGATION TALE

DJ OF
INCAPACITY

ANN M PRATLEY

DJ OF INCAPACITY

High numbers of shootings in one small town after another begin to put people across the country into a panic, wondering what could have inspired such horrific occurrences to happen. Called in to work as part of a large taskforce to try and figure out not only why the shootings are happening, but also how, are Special Agents Ashley Power and Tim Moore. Neither have before seen death on such a large scale in their law enforcement careers, and what they have to see during their lengthy investigation isn't for the faint-hearted.

~ Author's Note: DJ of Incapacity is not a whodunnit. You'll figure out, rather early on in this book, who is doing what, so be prepared to be taken into the darkness of the suspect's mind…

~ The books of the Power Moore Investigation Tales series are standalone stories and can be read in any order.

A POWER MOORE INVESTIGATION TALE
HOONIGAN
ANN M PRATLEY

HOONIGAN

Tristan Clarkson has woken up, over and over, bound to a chair, and unable to see. He has no idea where he is, or why he is in the situation he's woken to. His memory is vague, protecting him from recent events that will eventually haunt him for the rest of his life. He wants to remember, but at the same time, his mind acts as though he really, really doesn't. Initially, he's confused. With each waking, his memory clears that little bit more, as do his senses. He soon becomes aware that the very person who has abducted him, is in the room with him, determined to make Tristan pay for something he can't even remember.

Meanwhile, in a hospital nearby a patient has been taken. With the help of Special Agents Ashley Power and Tim Moore, an investigation begins into where the man has been taken, and who would have reason to remove him. With the patient having already been weak from time in a coma, time is of the essence in finding him alive.

Hoonigan is a blend of crime and suspense, intermingled with the strength of friendship, and the awakening of one father's realization of just how much his son really means to him.

ANN M PRATLEY
Alessandra
Chisholm Manor
Book 1

ALESSANDRA

After receiving news from her parents of a possible
betrothal, Alessandra, an 18 year old with an ingrained
belief that no-one would ever wish to marry her, finds
herself in a love so great that at times she cannot breathe.
Married to someone as inexperienced as herself, she
finds herself on a sexual journey of learning
and exploration.

The combination of their mutual inexperience
contributes to Alessandra discovering a degree of
emotional and physical love that she has
never before realized could exist.

That love will be tested by someone from her past with
sinister intentions. Jealous of the physical love
Alessandra shares with her husband,
he is set on doing whatever it takes
to have the woman he desires,
no matter the cost.

ANN M PRATLEY

Elizabeth

Chisholm Manor

Book 1

ELIZABETH

When innocence and scoundrel collide…
When Elizabeth Chisholm visits Venice with her family, she is unexpectedly drawn to Lord Byron - a man eleven years her senior. What she sees him present to her is grace, gentlemanlike behaviour, and an enthusiasm to pursue her. What she doesn't see is how much of a scoundrel he is - something he can easily hide from a mind and a heart as pure as hers.

Having grown up watching the deep and intense love of her parents - Alessandra and Edward - Elizabeth does all that is asked of her day to day but, now the age of eighteen, deeply yearns for someone to love her. The attention she receives from the handsome lord nicely fits into her desires, but where does she fit into his?

As Elizabeth is lured into the ongoing uncertainty of Lord Byron's attention, a young Scotsman wants to overcome his intense shyness. The love of art is something that he shares with Elizabeth, but he knows he can't compete with the confidence and handsomeness of the English lord.

At the request of Elizabeth's brother, Charles, the young Scotsman proves his worth by attempting to draw Elizabeth away as more things are learned about Lord Byron's actions across Europe, but is it too late? Is the reputation of Elizabeth Chisholm already sealed and irreparable, just through being associated with the scandalous English gentleman?

FREEDOM OF FLIGHT SERIES
~~ Shifter ~ Young Adult ~~

FREEDOM OF FLIGHT
CHRISTIAN
ANN M PRATLEY
1

CHRISTIAN
(FREEDOM OF FLIGHT SERIES - BOOK #1)

Twenty four year old Christian Shaw has a good life. He's had a rocky ride with being charged for a crime he didn't commit, but he's come out on the other side, older and wiser. He has good friends who've stood by him. He has a family who loves him. However, there's something about Christian that he's never understood. There's something about him that sets him apart. It has made him not want to get close to anyone.

Now someone's appeared unexpectedly. To his surprise, she's just like him. Even more importantly, she has the knowledge to help him understand more about the strange existence he lives. But is she as nice as she appears, or could she have a darker reason for seeking him out and devoting time to him?

Providing an insight into one man's strange journey of coming to grips with who he really is, 'Christian' tells a story of courage, friendship, and crime solving intrigue.

FREEDOM OF FLIGHT
BRANDON
ANN M PRATLEY
2

BRANDON
(FREEDOM OF FLIGHT SERIES - BOOK #2)

For fifteen years, Brandon McStevens has held himself away from everyone he knew prior to the day he turned fourteen. That day changed his life forever. Something happened to him that he can't explain to anyone. He feels ashamed and embarrassed. The only way he's ever been able to move past that and live has been to find somewhere else to reside.

Since leaving his family home, he has continued to live in a small cave. Nestled high above a small coastal community, he has come to spend most of his time enjoying the ocean … oh, and up in the sky. He doesn't know how it happened. He doesn't know *why* it happened. All he knows is that despite understanding how much hurt he must have caused when he left home all those years ago, he now lives the only existence he can imagine.

He's never met anyone like him. He's never *seen* anyone like him. Until that day when that woman and her dog saw him change, no-one had ever seen or heard of him doing that. To this day he regrets having shown himself like he did. But time passed and it has all been forgotten … or has it?

Certain he's the only one like himself, he's surprised when two people come looking for him … and have much to tell him. Finally, the time will come when he no longer has to feel like a freak of nature … or so alone.

FREEDOM OF FLIGHT
TRINITY
ANN M PRATLEY
3

TRINITY
(FREEDOM OF FLIGHT SERIES - BOOK #3)

A strange series of events have been happening in cities around the southwest of the country. When one bank is robbed on a small scale, it makes the banking professionals and law enforcement curious. When a second, then a third, then a fourth are also robbed without anyone knowing how it's been done, agencies combine resources to begin the search to find out who has been doing it and how.

Trinity Love is a twenty-five-year-old woman who's been surviving week to week, doing what she can to find money for her next meal and a roof over her head. In a unique way, she needs neither. She has a level of survival instinct built into her that should enable her to live a good life on the straight and narrow. That kind of life is one that she's never wanted or sought.

Seeing the latest news broadcast about the bank thefts, Brandon McStevens notices something about it that catches his attention. Talking to his new friends, Kelly and Christian, they decide it might be worth investigating.

1
THE
Golden
DESIRES
ANN M PRATLEY

THE GOLDEN DESIRES
(THE GOLDEN DESIRES SERIES - BOOK #1)

He wanted to escape. They needed to survive.

When Isabella starts to dream of a stranger, she's awakened inside with feelings she has never felt before. She knows he's not someone she's ever seen before, and he is not of her village. He is a stranger, and she's desperate to determine if he is real or he is a part of her imagination.

Far away, a businessman desperate to escape the noise and stress of the city embarks on a journey to find peace and the solitude he increasingly needs and desires. But at his destination, he will find much, much more.

2
THE
Golden
SUPREMACY
ANN M PRATLEY

THE GOLDEN SUPREMACY
(THE GOLDEN DESIRES SERIES - BOOK #2)

What is lying in wait, eager to destroy them?

Living in an ancient village after having passed from present time to hundreds of years into the past, Trent Solace has been monitoring the health of Isabella following the battle they fought in 'The Golden Desires'. Both feel the entity they thought they'd eliminated might not be gone at all, but instead just hiding.

The unknown entity has proven it knows how to manipulate people, making them think things that they wouldn't have otherwise. It controls the minds and bodies of whoever it invades, leaving the host unaware of what they've said, thought, or done over weeks, months, or even years.

Over distance and time, Trent and Isabella met and fell in love, choosing to live together in the ancient village of peace and harmony. Now they must prepare for a second strike from the hidden enemy.

What is it? What is its end game?
And who is its puppet now?

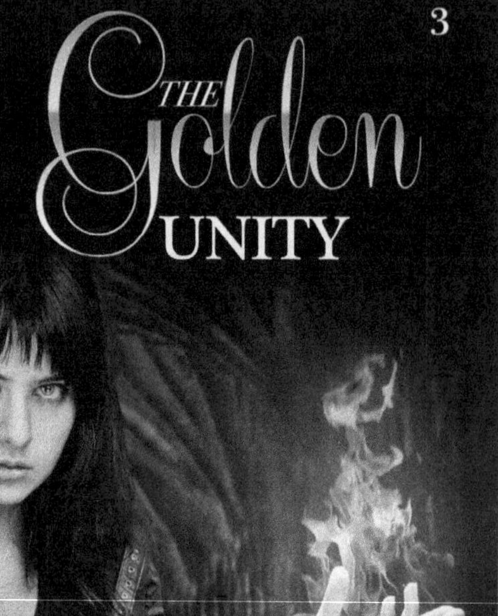
3
THE
Golden
UNITY
ANN M PRATLEY

THE GOLDEN UNITY
(THE GOLDEN DESIRES SERIES - BOOK #3)

Cesare is the golden child of the village. With brilliant
yellow hair that's unlike the color of anyone else's,
he's a cheerful child who, in the eyes of
some, can do no wrong.

Esmeralda is the product of two biological parents who
have buried deep within them, something that makes
them easy to manipulate by the being that has not given
up on wanting to destroy the ancient village. The young
lass with the blue-black hair captures attention and
intrigues the villagers. When they look at her, they feel
confused. It's impossible to determine why but there's
just something *different* about Esmeralda.

Despite them being opposites in nature and appearance,
the two have grown up together as best friends, just as
their parents did before them. The goodness of Cesare
showers a level of kindness and friendship on Esmeralda
that she cannot turn away from. Esmeralda's uniqueness
has always held Cesare's attention. Between them, they
have found a balance that keeps them together as friends.

But what will happen as they move into their time as
young adults? They are unknowing that they are meant
to be paired, but at the same time, they are meant
to be adversaries.

What does the puppet master have planned now? And
how will these two gifted youth react to someone trying
to manipulate them against their will?

A third strike from the puppet master. Will it win in its
plan of attack this time?

TOTAL FREEDOM SERIES

TOTAL
FREEDOM
ANN M. PRATLEY

TOTAL FREEDOM

For Debbie King, life began feeling like it was all too difficult. At fourteen, she continuously felt like she would never achieve, she would never have friends, and she would simply never fit in. When she meets Craig - someone new who seems just like her, also with low self-esteem and no belief in himself and what he has to offer - Debbie finds the strength to focus more on him and less on herself. They are both unpractised in making friends, but they find it in each other. When they discover their musical talents, their lives entwine further.

Living unhealthily, the time comes when Debbie knows she must extract herself and rebuild who she is as a person. When she returns, life seems better. She reconnects with Craig, but what should she do when another man starts to vie for her attention?

Steven is the complete opposite of Craig. There's little he has in common with Debbie, but she is drawn toward him as his attention increases. Slowly, she moves closer to him and further away from Craig.

Enjoy a love triangle story that begins in the mid-teens and matures and grows into young adulthood. Romance, stresses, passions and some hard decisions are what Debbie finds herself working through as she embarks on adulthood and the mature situations that come with it.

TOTAL NEW
BEGINNINGS
ANN M. PRATLEY

TOTAL NEW BEGINNINGS

In her early adulthood Debbie made a choice. She had two men who loved her. She chose one. She lost the friendship of the other. Twenty years on, tragedy strikes. Mother to three grown children, she has to find the strength to be there for them, while pushing her own grief aside. Dealing with the loss of the man who's been by her side for two decades pushes her into depression. As every day seems harder than the last, the feeling of loss is heightened by finding her husband's journals. Hesitant at first to look inside them, she eventually does. Almost instantly she regrets that decision. In her husband's writing she reads things that lead her to question whether she ever really knew him at all, or if they had actually been strangers for two decades.

The combination of the loss of her husband and the uncertainty about who he really was pushes her to retire into a dark room with no desire to leave. She wants to shut out the world and not believe what she knows in her heart is reality. With her youngest daughter, Poppy, still living at home, Debbie is eventually pulled from the darkness by her daughter's pleas. As the dark days start to fade, Debbie can start to see the sun shining once more. Finally she can find the strength to keep going and start to move into a period of recovery and growth. Finally she can accept that it's okay to accept help and lean on others.

As she starts rediscovering her ability to embrace life again, her daughter's determination to help her mother brings someone from Debbie's past back into her life. A friendship is re-established. It's time to let go of the past and begin a new future. It's time for total new beginnings.

Did you ever hear the words in your head … 'what if'? What if you chose one path earlier in life but later had the chance to walk down the path previously unchosen? Would you?

ANN M PRATLEY
Finding
Himself
Again

FINDING HIMSELF AGAIN

In a small seaside area of Sydney, Australia, 28-year-old Tom Santini has recently returned to the outside world after ten long years in jail following an error of judgment in his youth. Readjustment hasn't been easy but luck has taken a turn for him. The woman that his brother, Graham, has been seeing is a woman with connections. Through her, Tom has finally found an employer who will give an ex-criminal a chance to start over. It hasn't been an easy six months since his release, but Tom is learning to face his situation with reality and step up to take responsibility for his decisions.

Settled in his job at Toby's Stop'n'Dine, Tom's attention is captured by a young woman who enters. She's beautiful and alluring but, seeing and talking to her, he can deeply sense her being on the run from something … or someone.

Cat is smart, sexy and a woman who will make him wonder if he does, in fact, have a chance at being happy in love, despite his past. But why does she spook so easily? What - or who - is she on the run from? Tom knows that whatever happens, he has to think before he acts. He is determined to do things differently when it comes to dealing with difficult situations. He's already missed out on so much. He cannot go back to prison.

What can he do to calm and keep safe the woman who he so recently met but already has made a difference in his life? How can he save the woman with a deep-seated passion that drives him crazy…

The woman who understands just how important and difficult it is to find oneself again …

PAINFUL DELIVERANCE SERIES
~~ Obsession ~ Romance ~ Psychological Trauma ~~

1
PAINFUL
DELIVERANCE
ANN M PRATLEY

PAINFUL DELIVERANCE
(PAINFUL DELIVERANCE SERIES - BOOK #1)

She just wasn't made for inflicting pain.

She knows it's nothing abnormal. She knows others enjoy it. But with every new level of pain he directs her to deliver to him, Alexis feels another piece of her soul die. He has wealth and he has power, and she knows he won't easily let her go.

But she has to leave. Escape. Move on. Forget. She has reached her limit of what she can do. The plans are in place to get away. She just has to hope that wherever she goes - whoever she meets - she won't find herself in exactly the same situation again.

DARKNESS OF HEART

ANN M PRATLEY

DARKNESS OF HEART
(PAINFUL DELIVERANCE SERIES - BOOK #2)

She thought he'd stopped looking. He hadn't.

She got away from him to start a new life. She moved on. But in his mind, he still loves her and needs her. He still believes that she loves him. That she is meant to be his. That he is meant to be hers.

He will not give up searching for her. He will not give up *fighting* for her. He will pursue her and stop at nothing to get her back. But it will come at a cost … a sacrifice much greater than he will see coming. A sacrifice that will finally wake him up and bring him back to stark reality.

REVIEWERS SAY:

"... author did a great job of making brief references from the first book. Lincoln, Lexi and Alexis are back, though perhaps the most complex character is Diana ... very easy for me to recommend this book with 5 of 5 stars."

"This story continued the journey of Alexis, Anthony and Lincoln while giving us a new perspective into the repercussions of Lincoln and Alexis's relationship: from the POV of Lincoln's wife Diana! I loved her addition to the story ... kept the tension of the story just right, balancing the calm new life Alexis has been building and keeping the reader engaged."

"It is a book of courage, the courage to leave everything you know behind, the courage to change, the courage to face your fears, and the courage to face the unknown."

FRIENDSHIP OF DESIRE

ANN M PRATLEY

FRIENDSHIP OF DESIRE
(PAINFUL DELIVERANCE SERIES - BOOK #3)

Tom and Samantha. Feisty friends from childhood who feel like they know each other inside out until the day comes when one of them suggests they go to a BDSM club together, and become formal play partners. Pushing the limits of what each of them can individually stand in their lifelong friendship, they attract and repel like magnets, until the time comes when they must choose how they will relate to one another - and what kind of relationship they will go on to have in the future.

While on this journey of discovery, the two of them meet and make a new friend - Alexis. A young woman with a hidden and secretive past, and a mystery surrounding the relationship she has - or has had - with a renowned business entrepreneur who begins to integrate himself into Samantha's life, unknown to any of them whether he has done it for him, or for her … or for Alexis, being the mysterious link from his past.

REVIEWERS SAY:
"While this book is billed as the third in a series, I would classify it more as a spin-off ... I enjoyed this book. Samantha and Tom's relationship was sweet. Their exploration and experimentation, and how it stressed the boundaries of their (frustratingly) platonic friendship was fun to read about. Fans of Ms. Pratley's first books in the Painful Deliverance series will surely enjoy this more intimate peek into Samantha and Tom's relationship."

ANN M PRATLEY

Blade
of
Envy

A FOUR SWORDS NOVEL - BOOK 1

BLADE OF ENVY
(FOUR SWORDS SERIES - BOOK #1)

They expected quite a different kind of destruction...

In the realm of the House of Mordasini, the three royal offspring of King Maynard and Queen Azura are beginning their journeys into adulthood. As the eldest, Prince Aldin, starts to obsess about his future role as the next king, so also begins an obsession about his younger brother. Torn between wanting to be the one who rules over everyone else, but also wanting the life that is being set up for his brother, Aldin begins a journey of envy that grows darker as time passes.

Meanwhile, as one brother ruminates about the life of the other, their younger sister, Princess Semera, appears to grow ill. In the quiet of her deep slumber, something surprising begins to happen as, from a distance, she unknowingly becomes someone else's focus.

ANN M PRATLEY

Blade
of
Love

A FOUR SWORDS NOVEL - BOOK 2

BLADE OF LOVE
(FOUR SWORDS SERIES - BOOK #2)

In the kingdom of the House of Mordasini, a future king is waiting for the day to come when his father will die. While there's nothing to suggest that King Maynard will be leaving this world anytime soon, his oldest son, Aldin, increasingly desires to be the one on the throne.

With the darkness that has been residing in his soul since he was a child, ideas begin to flow inside of Aldin's mind. All around him, there are things happening that go against his idea of how the realm should be run. In particular, the realization that his father has granted permission to his brother, Prince Iztal, to wed is something that adds to Aldin's hatred for his brother - a hatred that has grown into an intense obsession.

While brothers continue to share their volatile relationship, their sister continues to experience signs that a beast will soon arrive in the realm, eager to cause destruction. Everyone thinks they are ready for the beast's return, but are they?

THANK YOU!

Thank you so much for reading my book, 'Diamond of War' (Book #3 in the Forbidden Conflicts Series)'. I greatly enjoyed writing this story and I appreciate your enthusiasm for reading it.

~~~~~

If you would like to make contact with me, please:
Visit My Website
http://authorannmpratley.wixsite.com/writingisbliss

Visit my Goodreads Author Page
goodreads.com/author/show/14777236.Ann_M_Pratley

Thank you,
Ann M Pratley
~~~~~